ALSO BY MATTHEW KIRBY

The Clockwork Three
Icefall
The Lost Kingdom
The Quantum League
A Taste for Monsters
Star Splitter

THE DARK GRAVITY SEQUENCE

The Arctic Code
Island of the Sun
The Rogue World

Assassin's Creed: Last Descendants—Last Descendants
Assassin's Creed: Last Descendants—Tomb of the Khan
Assassin's Creed: Last Descendants—Fate of the Gods
Assassin's Creed: Valhalla—Geirmun's Saga

Diablo: Book of Lorath
Diablo: Book of Prava

THE LOST HORADRIM

THE LOST HORADRIM

MATTHEW J. KIRBY

RANDOM HOUSE WORLDS
NEW YORK

Random House Worlds
An imprint of Random House
A division of Penguin Random House LLC
1745 Broadway, New York, NY 10019
randomhousebooks.com
penguinrandomhouse.com

ISBN 978-0-425-28489-6
Ebook ISBN 978-0-399-59407-6

Printed in the United States of America

1st Printing

First Edition

BOOK TEAM: Production editor: Jocelyn Kiker • Managing editor: Susan Seeman • Production manager: Erich Schoeneweiss • Copy editor: Laura Dragonette • Proofreaders: Debbie Anderson, Emily Cutler, Julia Henderson

Book design by Alexis Flynn

Title-page art: Joseph Lacroix

The authorized representative in the EU for product safety and compliance is Penguin Random House Ireland, Morrison Chambers, 32 Nassau Street, Dublin D02 YH68, Ireland. https://eu-contact.penguin.ie

For Josh and Tyler,
with whom I have spent many hours slaying demons.

THE LOST HORADRIM

CHAPTER ONE

Lorath felt the rage within him stir—a beast awakening in its lair. They had come too late, and the village before them stood empty. No voices answered their calls. No smoke rose from cookfires. The foul air of the surrounding marshland smelled of rot and the tang of rust, and the moss-draped trees trembled with the distant shrieks of vile things. The settlers had built their huts up on a low hump of grassy earth in the midst of ancient stone ruins, perhaps hoping the fallen walls and broken arches of a dead city would offer some meager protection.

"Looks abandoned," said Donan. The young man smacked a biting fly from his cheek as he peered ahead.

"No," said Lorath. "Not abandoned. Not by choice, at least. Something happened here."

"Perhaps," said Tyrael. The former angel's armor glinted in the wetland gloom, and a slick of sweat covered his dark brow. "Let us find out."

The three men pressed forward, familiar with the dangers of the terrain through which they had trekked for the past several days.

The Blood Marsh, which lay beyond the forests outside the city of Westmarch, was a treacherous expanse of bog and fen through which too few of the ancient roads remained above water. Monstrous creatures slithered, swam, and prowled through its twisted trees and fetid pools. In elder days, the great city of Corvus had towered there, but the marsh had torn it down with time and patience. It was now an inhospitable place, keeping out all but the most daring, desperate, or foolish. Lorath and his companions had come here following a trail of blood and rumors, hunting evil. According to the terrorized people living at the edge of the wetlands, a vicious new cult had established an enclave somewhere deep in the marshes. Lorath had hoped to learn more from the residents of this now-empty village.

They climbed the grassy rise, then halted as they approached the settlement's boundary, watching and listening from behind a crumbling wall covered in lichen and threaded with vines. The muggy air moved a little at that height, and somewhere in the village, it set a scrap of dangling metal ringing against a wall. From somewhere else, hollow wooden chimes rattled like bones. Otherwise, Lorath heard nothing. Saw nothing.

"Let us separate and learn what we can," Tyrael said. "Stay vigilant. Call for aid if you encounter trouble."

He climbed over the wall and pushed straight ahead, directly into the heart of the village. Donan looked at Lorath and tipped his head to the left, and Lorath nodded. The younger man crept away in that direction, armed with his staff. Lorath proceeded to the right, polearm at the ready, toward a section of the village more heavily encroached upon by bramble and trees.

The settlers had built their humble huts out of rough-hewn wooden beams and marsh reeds daubed with red clay. Lorath poked his head through the open door of the first one he came to and found disorder within. The furniture had all been overturned and broken. Flies buzzed over dried bloodstains on the packed-dirt floor, but he saw no other remains. He found the same in the next hut, and the one after—indications of struggle and violence, but no dead.

Then he heard voices. They spoke no intelligible words but grunted and chattered like animals.

Lorath raised the blade of his polearm, quietly making his way toward the sounds. He soon discovered their source in a muddy paddock near the edge of the village, where a pack of bogans picked over the corpse of a mule. Most of the beasts—half a dozen or more—were smaller, hunched and simian, with knuckles that touched the ground, but there was a brute among them, twice the size and three times as aggressive. Tusks the length of scythes jutted from its slavering maw, and it bristled with crude armor fashioned from antlers, fur, and bone. Bogans were feeble-minded and debased creatures but not necessarily evil by nature. Whatever had happened to the village, they had not caused it, though they were dangerous all the same, and a threat to any that might return there. Lorath adjusted his stance to attack, but then one of the beasts grunted an alarm, snout raised to the wind. They had caught his scent. He had to act quickly.

He leapt out from his hiding place and advanced. The boggit chattering ceased in momentary surprise, then turned to shrill howls as they leapt into a frenzy, thrashing and pounding their fists into the mud. The brute turned its thick shoulders to face Lorath and let out a spittle-flecked roar. Then it charged him with such thunderous speed and ferocity it nearly caught him off guard. He raised his polearm in time to make a thrust, which the bogan easily shoved aside using the bracer and hide of one forearm, even as it swung the other fist. The blow caught Lorath in the chest and sent him flying, gasping for breath.

The bogan roared and charged again. Lorath hadn't yet gained his footing and could only roll out of the way. Then he sprang to his feet and slashed low—not a killing stroke, but he managed to clip the beast's thigh.

The boggits had now surrounded him, and he risked being overwhelmed by their number. He swung his polearm around in a wide arc to keep them at bay, and he succeeded for a few moments. But the brute suddenly snatched up a startled boggit and hurled the screaming creature at Lorath like a living missile. The beast ended up impaled and wriggling on Lorath's polearm before he tossed it aside in disgust.

Seeing this, the other boggits now scrambled away from the brute as desperately as they did from Lorath's weapon, but they did not yet flee the fight.

The brute pounded its chest and slammed its fists into the ground, preparing to leap at him. Lorath checked his footing and braced his weapon, but before he had cause to use it, a gleaming streak severed the brute's head from its shoulders, and its body collapsed in a fountain of its own blood. At that, the remaining boggits finally lost all morale and scattered, shrieking through the trees in retreat.

Tyrael stood over the fallen brute holding El'druin and used his cloak to wipe the angelic sword clean. "I told you to call for aid," he said.

Lorath leaned on his polearm. "I needed no aid—"

"That is not the point!"

For a fleeting moment, Lorath thought he glimpsed a shadow of the frightening power the former angel had given up when he renounced his divine nature; at such times, Lorath found the man's towering presence unnerving.

Tyrael inhaled, eyes closed, then sighed. "We are Horadrim, Lorath. *You* are Horadrim. You are sworn to a greater purpose than fighting skirmishes for the sake of your pride. We are still too few in number for you to take such needless risks." He glanced around the paddock and the village. "We should end this hunt and move on to more important labors."

"More important?" Lorath said. "Have you not looked inside these dwellings? Some evil has happened here."

"That may be," said Tyrael, "and normally, of course I would help anyone who needed it. But we have no reason to believe they need it, and we are on a more important mission."

"Then you might want to come with me," Donan said, having arrived from elsewhere in the village. He stood outside the paddock, raised an eyebrow at the corpses of the two bogans, then added, "I found something interesting," before marching away.

After glancing at each other, Lorath and Tyrael followed. They traversed the village, passing under the ancient ruins and through a silent plaza where spiky grasses grew between the paving stones. They reached the far side of the settlement and came to a circular colonnade, which the settlers had apparently been using as a place of worship. Lorath noticed a large altar flanked by two braziers, each containing the ashen remains of offerings. Sigils and symbols had been chiseled into the columns, recent enough that they had not been weathered by time.

Donan pointed at the markings and said, "Pagan symbols . . . not unlike those seen in old Sharval."

Tyrael glanced around. "I still see no sign of demonic activity here."

"Look behind the altar," Donan said.

Lorath and Tyrael did as he suggested and found a grisly display at odds with all that they had seen thus far. Someone had used blood to draw a ritual circle on the ground, and in its center rested what appeared at first to be a small bowl. Then Lorath realized it was the top of a human skull.

"Blood magic," he said. "That *could* be demonic."

Tyrael frowned but said nothing.

"There's more." Donan held up a small leather-bound book. "I also found this journal in one of the hovels nearby. The home of their priest, I think." He opened the book. "Listen to this: *We have found the blood-drinkers. Savian located their encampment on a bog island a dozen leagues to the north and west. He proposes that we attack them now, but their position is well fortified. Lannard and some of the others worry our losses would be too great. They would rather bolster our defenses here and trust in our number as a sufficient deterrent. I fear that hope is misguided. The blood-drinkers have shown no such caution in their attacks elsewhere. Some power emboldens them. I only pray we are strong enough to stand against it.*" Donan closed the journal. "That is the final entry."

"Blood-drinkers?" said Lorath. "Vampires?"

"Unlikely," said Tyrael. "The priest writes as if the people here did not fully understand their enemy."

"Where *are* the people?" asked Donan. "I've seen no bodies—"

"They've been carried off," said Lorath, rage stirring again. "While many of them were alive, no doubt. Some may still live, if we move quickly." He turned to Tyrael. "Or do you still wish to call off this hunt?"

Tyrael bent and picked up the skull cup from the blood circle on the ground. He turned it over, studying it, then set it upon the altar. "We do not know who the attackers are. However, whether they are vampires or demonspawn, I agree that it is our duty as Horadrim to intercede." He glanced at Lorath.

They departed from the settlement and marched northwest, deeper into the wetlands. With each passing league, they found the terrain more forbidding, a labyrinth of sluggish streams and stagnant pools where paths that appeared firm would give way suddenly to quagmires of sucking mud. The trees and brush around them closed in with fiendish thorns. The air thickened with the noxious fumes of decay, and the biting insects grew more voracious. A chilling fog seeped into their clothing like the grasping fingers of the dead that haunted the scattered ruins.

"Why would anyone choose to live out here?" Donan asked, soaked to his waist, his boots caked with muck.

For all that the younger man had been through, he still looked with naivety at the broken world the Horadrim labored to repair. Lorath answered him with some bitterness: "Perhaps they prefer the dangers here to those in the city."

The younger man lowered his voice. "Is it . . . difficult? For you to return here, I mean?"

Lorath clenched his jaw. "What's past is past."

A moment went by. "Is it true you went down below the marsh, into Corvus with Tyrael?"

"I did." Lorath had no desire to see those sunken halls and roads ever again.

"A city of the Firstborn . . ." Donan shook his head in wonder. "What—what was it like?"

Lorath knew he meant no harm. Donan was eager, and very clever—no doubt a valuable recruit to their order—but his curiosity often led him down paths best left undisturbed. "It was empty," Lorath answered, in a way that ended the conversation.

Night fell halfway through their journey, and they had no choice but to make camp on the driest patch of earth they could find. They lit no fire, to avoid attracting unwanted attention, and ate from their dried stores. The crescent moon peered down at them through drifts of pallid, sickly clouds, offering little light. In the darkness, the marsh came alive with the drone of insects, the grunts and croaks of amphibians, and the lonely call of a distant owl.

Tyrael took the first watch, and Donan fell asleep quickly. Eventually, Lorath drifted off as well, but familiar nightmares assailed him. He had been free of those dark dreams for some time, but his return to the Blood Marsh had awakened old memories, and he soon found himself in Corvus, within an underground tomb, watching helplessly as Malthael, the Angel of Death, cut down his fellow Horadrim; and then he was in Westmarch, the city of his birth, as Malthael's army of reapers swept through its streets, slaughtering all in their path. He saw a small child with red hair who stood paralyzed before a ghostly shadow looming over her, and he rushed into battle to defend her. He swung his polearm slowly, as though against a mighty current, but he managed to defeat the wailing reaper. Then he took the child's hand, and she looked up at him. She was not a child he knew. She was every child in Westmarch, and Lut Gholein, and all the other ravaged cities where the innocent died by the thousands.

"Come with me," he told her. "I will keep you safe."

In the next moment, an arrow struck her in the chest, almost passing through her small body. Lorath watched in shock and horror as blood bloomed across her dress. She died in his arms, eyes wide in terror and filled with tears of pain. Lorath howled in powerless rage, then awoke with a start. He came to in his bedroll in the Blood Marsh, worried that he might have cried aloud in his sleep.

Donan snored next to him, undisturbed, but Tyrael was watching him, a shadowy silhouette against the marsh, his eyes two sparks of light like dim stars.

"The deepest wounds take the longest to heal," he said.

Lorath sat up feeling embarrassed and defensive. "What would you know about injury?"

Tyrael spoke with patience, despite Lorath's effrontery. "I am now as susceptible to harm as you."

Lorath shook his head. "I know. Forgive me. It's just that . . . you don't need to worry about me. I'd rather we focus on healing Sanctuary."

"What makes you think the two are different?" Tyrael asked.

Lorath made no answer to that and rose to his feet. "I'm awake now. You might as well get some rest."

The former angel nodded and moments later had settled himself against a tree, eyes closed, though Lorath wasn't ever sure how much the man actually slept. Tyrael may have become mortal, but he wasn't exactly human—or, at least, he wasn't the same kind of human as Lorath, Donan, or the settlers they hoped to save.

The rest of that night passed without incident, and after spending another day slogging through marshland, they came upon the blood-drinker encampment in the gloom and mist of an evening drizzle. A palisade of tall, sharpened wooden stakes hid the interior from view, but that was not its only defense. The enemy enclosure occupied a small hillock in the middle of a stagnant mere. The water there smelled rank, with a different kind of foulness than was found elsewhere. As Lorath drew closer, he realized the odor emanated from human remains. The blood-drinkers had filled their natural moat with the bones of their victims. Hundreds and hundreds of victims. Lorath glimpsed a rib so slender it could only have come from a child, and deep within himself, a roar shook the lair of his rage.

"Why—why would they do this?" Donan's hands hung at his sides, his shoulders slumped in horrified disbelief.

"Depravity," Tyrael answered. "And cruelty, to make the crossing that much harder for those who would come here seeking justice for the slain."

Lorath picked up a long stick and prodded the water, down to the soft mud and silt of the lake bed. "No one can cross this without a boat. You'd be mired up to your waist." He left the long stick where he had lodged it and peered at the fort. "There must be a bridge or path somewhere."

He crept along the shore, keeping to the tree line, and the other two followed behind. Lorath listened for any sounds coming from inside the encampment but heard none. Were it not for the woodsmoke in the air, he might have believed it stood empty.

The rain eased as they made their way around the mere, and the mist thickened to a low-hanging fog over the water. On the far side of the island, they discovered a wooden causeway laid on uneven pilings. It stretched across the moat, some fifty paces from the shoreline to the fort's main gate, in full view of a squat tower where a single shadowy guard stood watch.

"So it isn't *entirely* empty," Lorath whispered.

"But it's so quiet." Donan crouched down next to him. "Their main force must be elsewhere. Perhaps away on a raid?"

"It would appear so," Tyrael said.

"Fortune is with us." Lorath pointed at the gate. "If we can get inside, we can take the whole encampment. Then we lie in wait for the rest of the blood-drinkers to return."

"How do we get inside?" asked Donan.

Lorath grinned. "Through the front door."

CHAPTER TWO

They lit a campfire in a clearing in the woods surrounded by cypress and swamp oak, near enough to the shoreline for the guard to see it clearly, even through the fog. Moments later, a cry of alarm went up inside the fort.

"Do you think they'll take the bait?" Donan asked.

Lorath nodded. "Right now, I'd wager they're trying to decide which of them will come out here to investigate."

"How do you know?"

"The priest answered that in the journal you found," Lorath said. "These blood-drinkers are emboldened. Overly confident. They feel strong behind their wall and their moat. They can't imagine a foe who would dare oppose them."

"And we must avoid making the same mistake," Tyrael said, "until we know what power emboldens them. Now, ready yourselves." He sat on a log near the fire and pulled his cloak around himself to cover his armor, having insisted on being the one left exposed, while Lorath and Donan hid among the nearby trees.

Before long, the gate opened, and a solitary warrior left the safety of the fort. Lorath readied his polearm as the fiend trotted along the causeway through the fog, heavy boots drumming on the rough planks. The thudding stopped when the enemy reached the shore, and Lorath heard the ring of a drawn blade. The blood-drinker made no effort to approach the campfire quietly, stomping and snapping twigs, and when he stepped into the light, Lorath saw he matched Tyrael in height and the breadth of his shoulders. For armor, he wore the gnarled hides of swamp creatures beneath a dirty cloak. He wielded a broadsword, and he carried a wooden buckler with a battered metal boss. Human skulls with the tops of their craniums removed hung from his belt, and crimson sigils covered his face and his skin, drawn in what Lorath assumed to be blood.

"You chose the wrong place to rest, traveler," the warrior said as he passed the tree Lorath hid behind.

Tyrael sat like a statue as the blood-drinker approached. "Who do you serve?" he asked.

The warrior halted. "What?"

"Which foul being do you serve?" Tyrael asked. "Name your master."

The warrior chuckled. "Those are your last words? Odd choice."

Lorath sensed the man would attack with his next breath, so he leapt from behind the tree and charged. The blood-drinker had only enough time to spin around before Lorath drove the point of his polearm deep into his chest, delivering what should have been a killing blow. But instead of collapsing, the warrior merely grunted, then used his buckler to backhand Lorath with shocking strength, throwing him across the clearing, where he landed hard, stunned, gasping, struggling to remain conscious as he rolled onto all fours.

Tyrael had drawn El'druin, and Donan now stood in the firelight with his staff. Both men looked on in surprise as the blood-drinker dropped his buckler, gripped the haft of the polearm still stuck in his chest, and pulled the blade free. Then the warrior hurled the weapon at Lorath like a spear, which he barely dodged. The polearm struck a tree instead, its point embedded deep in the wood.

Tyrael and Donan attacked as one, their actions coordinated, practiced, fluid. But the blood-drinker moved with incredible speed, and he seemed unaffected by the few blows the two Horadrim managed to land.

Lorath wrenched his polearm from the tree and rushed to join his comrades. He didn't know what infernal power strengthened their foe, but he assumed the blood-drinker needed his head attached to stay in the fight. He seized an opening in the melee, leapt high, and swung his blade wide, a strike that would leave him vulnerable to counterattack if it failed.

The warrior tried to duck, but Lorath's polearm found his neck and sliced halfway through the meat of it, a wound that seemed to stagger the blood-drinker at last. The enemy swayed on his feet, spraying blood, and the tip of his sword dropped, though still he refused to fall.

Then Donan rushed in, head down, and drove his shoulder hard into the warrior's stomach, shoving him backward toward the campfire. The blood-drinker stumbled and toppled into the flames, and in the next moment, his cloak went up in a blaze. That was when he finally showed the first signs of pain, thrashing and howling through his savaged throat.

"Silence him!" Lorath hissed.

Tyrael brought El'druin down and finished the decapitation Lorath had started. The clearing fell silent as oily smoke rose from the burning corpse.

"We needed his cloak," Tyrael said.

"In the fog, yours will do well enough," Lorath replied.

"You attacked too soon," Tyrael said. "We learned nothing."

"He was about to attack *you.*" Lorath wiped the blade of his polearm clean on a patch of velvet moss. "And we learned all he would have told us. The real answers are inside that gate."

"Are either of you injured?" Donan asked.

Lorath had sustained wounds in battle without realizing it before, but this time, he had emerged unscathed. The other two Horadrim had likewise avoided any serious damage.

Donan crouched and leaned closer to the burning body, squinting through the smoke and the flames. "He wasn't a vampire. But his power seems to have come from blood magic. I wish I could have studied the symbols on his skin before the fire got to them."

"No time for that, anyway," Lorath said. "They'll be expecting him back. Let's move."

They arranged themselves as they had previously planned and moved toward the causeway. Donan and Lorath went first, posing as captives driven forward by Tyrael, while he marched behind, cloaked and hooded, impersonating the blood-drinker. The fog did much to obscure them, just as Lorath had hoped it would, and they made it almost to the gate before the guard on the watchtower called out to them.

"What have you brought back, Garack?" he asked.

Tyrael said nothing. The gate remained shut.

"Oy, Garack!" the guard shouted.

"Now," Lorath whispered. Then he and Donan spun around and charged toward Tyrael, shouting and feigning an attack. Tyrael allowed them to bring him down so they scuffled in the fog, trusting that it would get the guards' attention.

The tower guard bellowed a cry of alarm and an order to those below. Then the gate opened, and three warriors barreled out onto the causeway, two men and a woman. None of them looked as imposing as their emissary to the campfire had been, but their size would matter less than their power if they were all practiced in blood magic.

"Remember," Tyrael whispered, "take off their heads as quickly as you can."

The three blood-drinkers had little time to react as the Horadrim suddenly turned and launched their assault. Lorath's polearm cleaved the head from the first to come within reach, one of the men. The other two skidded to a halt, and then El'druin flashed. Another head wheeled through the air and splashed into the mere, and the third blood-drinker turned to run. Donan pounced on him, caving in his skull with repeated blows of his staff while Lorath raced toward the open gate.

He found one more warrior inside the fort, and he dispatched him quickly with an upward thrust of his polearm through the man's throat and into his head. That left only the guard on the watchtower, who by then had taken aim at him with a bow. Lorath threw himself against the base of the tower as an arrow whistled past him. Then he heard a gasp from above, and the guard slammed into the muddy earth at Lorath's feet with Donan's dagger in his back. Some of the blood-drinker's bones had snapped when he hit the ground, and yet he still tried to rise, gurgling on his own blood. Lorath put an end to him just as the other Horadrim raced through the gate.

"Is that all of them?" Donan asked.

"For now, I think," Lorath said, turning to survey the encampment.

It was a squalid place, littered with bones and refuse. At its center lay an enormous communal hearth and a ritual altar caked with so many layers of dried blood, it almost resembled wax. Wretched hovels surrounded the fire, constructed more poorly than even bogan dwellings. Lorath had no idea how many slept in each, but he assumed some several dozen occupied the fort.

Behind him, Tyrael shut and barred the gate. "We have no idea when the rest of these blood-drinkers will return. Donan, you will stand the first watch on the tower. Lorath and I will investigate the encampment."

"Yes, Tyrael," Donan said with a slight bow of his head. As he climbed the rickety ladder up the tower to take his post, Lorath shook his head, somewhat bemused by the younger man's continued deference.

"I will begin with that altar," Tyrael said. "See what you can discover in their huts."

"Will do," Lorath said.

In the hovels, he found soiled and flea-ridden bedding, rudimentary furniture, skull cups like the one left behind in the village, and human bones that showed signs of gnawing. In one, he located the fort's cache of plundered goods, including barrels of ale and bottled spirits, jewelry, spices, honey, and oil. In another, he found a stash of weapons, mostly crude blades and a few crossbows. A smell of decay pervaded the encampment, and flies filled the heavy air with incessant buzzing. Lorath had seen all he needed to pass a sentence of death on the blood-drinking cultists, but he continued his search with diligence, following Tyrael's command, until he came upon something unusual.

In a corner of the enclosure, a low wooden platform covered an area ten paces across, and when Lorath stepped up onto it, his footsteps sounded hollow, as if there were a deep opening in the ground beneath the wooden beams. He soon found a trapdoor secured with a padlock that broke under a few blows from the metal foot of his weapon. He kicked the shattered lock away, then bent to lift the door.

The smell that erupted from the opening drove him back. He buried his nose and mouth in his sleeve at the elbow and realized the odor was different from the stink of death that surrounded him: it was the smell of living human waste. He approached the opening again, and peering down into the hold, he discovered the blood-drinkers' food stores.

It was difficult to see in the darkness, but in the column of pale moonlight that fell through the opening, human prisoners lay in a stupor of despair, weltered in their own piss and shit. Lorath dropped to his knees and called down to them, "Hello! Can you hear me?"

One of them looked up, raising her head slowly, as if she were too weakened even for that movement. Through the filth that covered her face, she appeared to be Lorath's age, with dark hair, or hair made dark by mud and blood.

"Hello?" Lorath called to her.

"Wh—what?" she replied with a weak, hoarse voice.

"Don't be afraid," Lorath said. "We're here to free you. Rouse the others, if you can. I will return."

He then raced back toward the central campfire and altar, where he enlisted Tyrael's help, and together they worked to lift all the survivors out of their subterranean prison. Tyrael even volunteered to go down into the pit when necessary to aid those too weakened by their ordeal to climb out on their own. The Horadrim shared what food they had, and Tyrael led them to a miserable little spring he had located that fed the fort's supply of potable water. As the survivors revived, they recounted how they had come to be in that place, and all told a similar tale of attack and capture by warriors who could not be slain.

"They can be slain," Lorath said, sitting next to the woman he had seen down in the pit.

"You may have killed six of them," she said, "but can you kill fifty? Because they number at least that many."

"We will find a way," Lorath said. "This horror will soon be ended. For now, rest."

He left her and went to relieve Donan on the watchtower. The younger scholar then went down to consult with Tyrael, and Lorath turned to face the causeway and the marshland beyond. The fog had begun to break apart into wisps, while off in the trees, the flames of the burning corpse had diminished to a smoldering flicker. He saw no signs of the returning blood-drinkers, and some time later, as the first ruddy flush of dawn appeared on the horizon, Tyrael climbed the tower and stood next to him.

"We have searched the encampment," he said. "This place contains only the evil that humanity is capable of inflicting on itself."

Lorath nodded, unsurprised, already feeling defensive and wary of what he knew would come next.

"It is as I tried to tell you," Tyrael went on. "This was not our hunt."

"Then whose hunt is it? What good are the Horadrim if not to stop this kind of evil?"

"Do you suppose it is easy for me to witness the suffering of others?" Tyrael gripped the wooden railing of the watchtower and stared down into the moat. "As much as I might loathe these blood-drinkers, I founded the Horadrim to fight a far greater threat than they could ever pose. What you have seen here is nothing compared to the suffering this world would endure if the Burning Hells should ever succeed in conquering Sanctuary. *That* is the kind of evil we Horadrim must seek out and destroy, wherever we find it. Enmity may rule this day, but humanity must learn for itself how to stop the suffering of its own making."

Lorath's neck and shoulders tightened, and he gestured over the Blood Marsh. "Do you remember the last time you and I were here?"

Tyrael sighed. "You know I do."

"It wasn't a demon who almost destroyed Sanctuary." A part of Lorath wanted to stop himself from going further, but his frustration proved stronger, and he turned to face Tyrael. "It wasn't a demon who created all this chaos. It was one of *your* kind. It was an angel. The suffering we've seen here is happening everywhere. Do you feel no responsibility for that?"

"I have labored long to defend humanity from demons and angels alike, and I will continue to defend you." Tyrael's eyes flashed with a force that would have made Lorath quail, were he less stirred by anger. "But do you not see? I am now mortal. This body will perish one day, and when it does, I will not leave Sanctuary defenseless. The Horadrim *must* be strong enough to endure."

The thought of losing Tyrael cooled Lorath's temper, though not yet to the point of surrender. "What about justice?" he asked.

"What of it?"

"You were once the archangel of that virtue, yet the Horadrim you founded are still denied it." Lorath nodded down at the people huddled together below them, wounded, frightened, grieving for the loved ones butchered before their eyes. "Where is their justice?"

Tyrael cast his gaze upon the settlers, and he watched them for some time. "You are right," he said at last. "These people *do* deserve justice. But are you certain it is truly justice that you seek?"

Before Lorath could ask what he meant by that, Tyrael turned away and faced the marsh.

"I will take the watch," he said. "Go see if you can be of use to Donan."

Lorath could only shake his head. "Yes, Tyrael."

He climbed down from the tower, and after checking on the freed prisoners, he found Donan near the blood-coated altar, studying an evil-looking tome.

"What is that?" he asked.

"Their scripture," Donan said. "The writings of some corrupt necromancer, though not a true Priest of Rathma. Most of it is meaningless ravings, but there are a few interesting spells. I assume you noted the symbols on the big one's skin?"

Lorath folded his arms. "Briefly."

"That *was* blood magic." Donan jabbed the open book with his finger. "According to this, those symbols were the source of his power. I suspect that's why he didn't show any sign of pain until I pushed him into the fire. The flames destroyed the symbols, you see, and that broke the spell."

"So, mar the symbols, break their strength?"

"I believe so." Donan closed the book. "It's one hypothesis, at any rate."

"I like your hypothesis." Lorath had gone to see if he could be of help to Donan, but Donan had proven to be of greater help to him. "You've given me an idea."

"An idea for what?"

Lorath clapped his comrade on the back. "How to kill the lot of them."

CHAPTER THREE

Together, Lorath and Donan formulated a plan, then went to the enclave's storehouse to obtain the ingredients for a flammable concoction of spirits, oil, and other compounds. They used the blood-drinker cultists' own ritual hearth to brew their downfall.

When the enemy returned two days later, the Horadrim were ready for them. Some of the freed settlers inside the walls had even asked to join the fight and were given weapons from the enclave's armory. The cultists approached the causeway at dusk, driving a train of bound captives before them using cruel whips. Donan stood upon the watchtower, in shadow. Lorath opened the gate, to give the illusion that all was well within the fort and to get the prisoners off the causeway. The few cultists who preceded their prey through the entrance were quietly slain before they realized their encampment had been taken. The bound prisoners who followed them marveled at their unexpected saviors, who motioned for their silence as they ushered them inside. When a young boy passed Lorath, stumbling with delirium from a head wound, he felt his rage stirring again, only this time, it would not be restrained.

The cultists at the rear of the column had already stepped onto the causeway when the last captive reached safe ground. That was when Donan summoned a ball of violet flame into his hand and hurled it down onto the bridge from above, while Tyrael lit the wood afire from the far shore, having hidden himself in the trees. The causeway, soaked with the incendiary brew, went up in a rushing blaze.

The enemy screamed as one in shock, terror, and pain as their melting flesh broke their blood magic. Then the Horadrim attacked. Donan fired a crossbow from the tower while Lorath charged through the gate, swinging his polearm in a deadly arc at all who tried to flee the fire.

Some of the desperate cultists leapt from the causeway into the water, where they landed hard in the deep muck and became mired. Many of them sank and drowned. Donan's crossbow found the others.

Then, as the initial conflagration died down, Lorath attacked, hacking and stabbing any foe within reach of his blade. Behind him came the armed settlers dealing out their own justice, using spears, swords, and arrows to finish off the cultists struggling in the bone-filled moat, but Lorath paid them little mind. The beast of his rage had been released from its lair, and he relished the righteous destruction he unleashed on those who would harm and defile the innocent. He lost himself to the violence, bellowing like the animal he had let himself become, and did not stop his butchery until he met Tyrael near the middle of the causeway. The man had fought his own way there from the shore, cutting off the cultists who had tried to escape that way, and now he held up his hand.

"Lorath! The battle is won!"

Lorath, chest heaving, covered in blood, let out a final roar before collapsing to one knee, clinging to his polearm. Tyrael laid a calming hand on his shoulder.

"Peace, my friend. Your plan worked. The evil here has been defeated."

Lorath closed his eyes and slowed his breathing, easing the rage back into the deep cavern near his heart where it dwelt, ever within him, threatening to rampage if he turned it loose or lost control of it.

When he opened his eyes, he found the settlers staring at him warily, whispering and keeping their distance. Many of them continued to avoid him that evening, when they all stayed together one last night in that place. Lorath could not blame them, though they had no reason to fear him. After he had washed the blood from his hair and his armor with water from the spring, he felt more like himself.

As the Horadrim parted ways with the settlers the next morning, the woman Lorath had seen down in the pit approached him, took his hand, and pressed something into his palm. He looked down at a small wooden talisman the size and shape of a large, thick coin. It bore symbols he had seen back in her village, set beside an image of a woman's face carved in relief with some skill. Vines and leaves surrounded her as if part of her being.

"What is this?" he asked.

"A sign of gratitude," the woman said. "The spirits of this land thank you. I hope that one day you can find peace within yourself, wherever your journey takes you."

The gift caught him somewhat off guard, but he managed to thank her for it.

Soon the Horadrim were trudging back out of the Blood Marsh, retracing their path through the twisting waterways. Lorath clutched the wooden talisman in his hand as they walked, glancing down at it now and then, turning it over in his fingers. For a short while, the sight of the token provided him with a measure of satisfaction and even a sense of calm, the rage within him appeased. But that feeling did not last long. It never did, no matter how great their victories, for Lorath knew that elsewhere across Sanctuary, evil went unchecked, and the innocent suffered. Their imagined cries rang through him, echoes of the suffering he had already witnessed, steadily turning him restless. Within a few leagues, he had shoved the wooden talisman into a pocket, forgotten, his mind fixed on the battles before them. He wanted to ask Tyrael where they now traveled, and for what purpose, but still felt a gulf between them after their disagreement.

He waited until Donan had gone ahead a few paces and cleared his throat. "Tyrael, I . . . What I said to you on the watchtower—"

"You spoke only what you believed to be true," Tyrael said. "I am grateful that you speak your mind. This hunt has opened my eyes."

"To what?"

"I know you, Lorath. This will not be the last time you refuse to look away from the suffering of others. It would be unwise for me to expect different from you. And yet, it is also true that Sanctuary needs the Horadrim to defend it against threats, and we must be intentional in the battles we choose to fight. I have therefore come to a decision. To meet the many needs before us, we must increase our number and strengthen our order."

"How?"

"We will travel to Skovos."

"Skovos?" Lorath had never been to those southern islands, and no one he knew had sailed there recently. But he knew that Tyrael had visited Skovos long ago, and he had also sent a group of Horadrim there some years earlier. They had heard nothing from them since. "You mean to search for the expedition?"

"Their mission was to establish diplomatic relations with the Askari and to reopen the Horadric vault hidden there. We must learn what became of them."

Lorath inhaled as he straightened his shoulders. "I hear the people of Skovos are not . . . welcoming to strangers."

"It is true they are insular and protective of their lands," Tyrael said. "But they are also strong, and their seers are gifted with foresight. I sense we have an important purpose there. It is time we discover what happened to our fellow Horadrim and recover the relics and knowledge from our vault."

Lorath felt some reluctance to leave Westmarch behind, where there remained so much work to be done. Yet he knew the people of other cities suffered just as greatly, and the Horadrim could not be everywhere at once. He decided to trust in Tyrael's wisdom.

After they had left the swamp behind, they made their way to the Fish Road, a winding path that followed the rugged western coastline of the kingdom, connecting the city of Westmarch to Kingsport in the south.

It was not an easy route. The Fish Road skirted the edges of towering cliffs and traversed tide-racked strands of rocky beaches infested with lampreys and other coastal terrors, but Tyrael believed it would be safer than the inland trackways beset by gangs of thieves. Difficult or not, Lorath welcomed the briny breezes off the sea after their confinement in the oppressive, fetid air of the marsh. He preferred the cries of gulls and the chatter of cliff-dwelling gannets to the ceaseless hum of biting insects.

They stopped at the first fishing village they came to, hoping to resupply, but found it deserted. The gray clapboard cottages stood with their doors and windows open to windblown sand. Beach grasses had taken root in some of the corners, and the roof of the former inn appeared to have buckled under the force of some recent gale. A pale crust of salt grew on the buildings closest to the waterline where they faced the spray from crashing waves. The stalwart dock had somehow withstood the battering, but the broken remains of several fishing boats littered the shoreline around it. Unlike at the settlement in the Blood Marsh, they found no signs of violence other than the damage caused by the passage of time, which somehow made the coastal village feel more eerie and haunted.

"It's been abandoned for years," Donan said.

"Most likely since Malthael's culling," said Lorath. They would likely never know the exact number of casualties across Sanctuary, and many of those who survived the Reaping died in the chaos that followed. There were times when it seemed to Lorath that only one in ten had survived. "A small place like this relies on its fishermen for survival. If too many of them were slain . . ." He shook his head. "I only hope the survivors found safe harbor elsewhere."

"A storm approaches." Tyrael pointed at a bulwark of dark clouds moving in from the sea. "We should stay here for the night."

They chose the soundest of the cottages for their shelter and used scraps of wood to try to block up the windows and other openings, but soon a sharp wind began to blow, and some rain still managed to push in through the gaps. Lorath could only imagine how unpleasant the evening would have been had the storm caught them on the open road. Lightning occasionally flashed outside, visible through cracks in the wood, accompanied by thunder that shook the floorboards against his back. Somehow, Donan slept through it all, but Lorath lay awake, staring up into the swaying, creaking rafters.

He wondered who had lived in this shack before it became a derelict hull. Was it a solitary fisherman? A family? Had children run in and out through that front door? Had they watched their mother, their father, their grandparents die at the hands of a reaper?

"Is it the storm that keeps you up?" Tyrael asked from nearby in the darkness. "Or something else?"

"I don't know," Lorath answered.

"What is on your mind?"

"Back on the watchtower, you asked me if I truly seek justice. What else would I be seeking?"

A moment went by, and then Tyrael asked, "Who do you think justice is for?"

Lorath frowned. "For the victims, of course."

"To what end?"

The question provoked Lorath into a sitting position. "What do you mean?"

"When you slew the cultists, did your justice undo the suffering their captives had endured? Did your justice heal the injured? Bring back their dead?"

"No."

"Then how was your justice for them?" Tyrael sat up to face

Lorath. "Some might even say that justice was unattainable because each cultist had only one life to pay in recompense for the many lives they took. But justice is not an equation to balance. Justice is a virtue to serve and fulfill, and that is what makes it so hard to obtain."

"I don't understand," said Lorath.

Lightning flashed outside and glinted off Tyrael's armor, followed a few moments later by a receding clap of thunder. The worst of the storm had passed over them.

"There are many who claim to serve justice," Tyrael said, "when all the while their true master is their anger, their hatred, their fear, their pain, or their powerlessness. Such people seek vengeance, Lorath, not justice."

Lorath lay back down. "In a world this broken, I'm not sure there is a difference."

The next morning, they left the abandoned village under a sullen sky that seemed to threaten them with another storm if they lingered. The coastal road carried them southward, jogging inland now and then through dense conifer forests that offered sporadic views of the ocean below. They had to contend with the occasional pack of spiders or wolves but otherwise managed to avoid any serious confrontations.

Eventually, they came upon an occupied village where the residents had somehow clung to their way of life, though many of the houses sat shuttered and dark as silent monuments to death's toll. The people there appeared fearful and forlorn, with scarcely enough to live on themselves, but they were willing to sell some meager provisions. Lorath intentionally overpaid for a supply of hard bread and oily dried fish, which fed the Horadrim for the remainder of their journey to Kingsport.

Lorath had visited a few times before, many years ago. He knew well its reputation for lawlessness even before the destruction caused by Malthael. The capital port of Westmarch may have boasted a greater volume of legitimate import and trade, but Kingsport made up the difference with illicit smuggling and trafficking of stolen goods. It lay tucked away in a river inlet at the southernmost point of the kingdom's coast. Before the foundation of a royal city there, the sheltered bay had offered a haven to pirates and raiders, who had adapted to the encroachment of the crown on their territory by assuming a thin mercantile guise.

The Fish Road crested a ridge overlooking the city from the west, where the Horadrim paused, unsure of what to expect below. Lorath saw ships secured at the wharf and deeper-keeled vessels anchored out in the harbor. Even from their vantage, he could hear the commotion of the port, the clang of machinery, the shouts and curses of sailors. He could smell the rank odors of rotten fish, mildew, smoke, and oil. The road before them plunged into a labyrinth of streets and alleyways said to hide a murderous thief in every shadow.

"Is this wise?" Donan asked. "I thought we wanted to avoid unnecessary conflict."

"We do," Tyrael said.

Donan shrugged. "It's just that . . . unnecessary conflict seems inevitable in a city like this."

"A fishing dinghy can't make the crossing to Skovos," Tyrael said. "We need a ship. And that city is where we will hire one. Some conflict may be unavoidable."

"At least the port is active," Lorath said. "I suggest we head straight for the wharf."

Their descent followed a winding track of switchbacks down the tiers and levels of the city. The streets were narrow and hemmed in by the leaning upper stories of the half-timber buildings. As with all the settlements they had visited in their travels, they passed many empty houses left to rot, though in Kingsport it seemed that vagrants and squatters occupied several of the forsaken structures. Lorath could feel the gaze of hostile eyes upon them as they made their way downward. He walked with his polearm at the ready, while Donan walked with his staff, and none could miss the great sword at

Tyrael's side. They must have appeared formidable enough to dissuade any would-be thieves from assailing them.

As they neared the market quarter, the streets widened to allow for the passage of wagons, but fewer carts traveled those lanes than the city had once boasted, which left the passages feeling haunted by the loss. Alehouses, brothels, and petty shops began to appear, and the streets grew more crowded with poor mariners wearing clothes fashioned from old sailcloth, but now and then they glimpsed someone wearing finer attire, always in the company of menacing thick-necked guards.

Upon reaching the wharf, Lorath pointed at a dockside tavern calling itself The Bilge. "I imagine we'll meet captains and crew in there," he said.

They went in and found it a typical sort of place, with a low ceiling, thick timbers, and murky light intruding through grimy windows. But as soon as the Horadrim entered, the room fell silent. Lorath peered through the smoky gloom at a crowd of weather-beaten faces. Most stared into their mugs, but a few of the patrons watched them with predatory glares.

Tyrael strode to the barkeep and laid a few coins on the counter. "Your next round is on me," he announced to the room.

"Who's buying?" someone asked from a far corner.

"Three travelers looking to secure passage on a ship," Tyrael replied.

"You can buy your way onto any vessel in the harbor," said an old salt with a crooked nose and a missing ear. "It's the getting *off* bit that'll prove tricky."

At that, the room erupted with laughter.

"Old Pike ain't wrong," said the barkeep, chuckling as he cupped Tyrael's money across the counter and into the waiting palm of his other hand. "Now, do you have a destination in mind? Or are you just looking to get out of Kingsport in a hurry?"

"We are bound for Skovos," Tyrael said.

Thc barkeep glanced up as if he doubted his hearing. Then his thin lips broke into a gap-toothed grin. "Right, right. And from there you're off to the Cold Isles, are you?"

"We do not jest," said Tyrael.

"Then you're mad." The barkeep lowered his voice to a raspy whisper. "If the crossing don't kill you, them Amazons will. No one sails to Skovos."

"No one?" asked Donan.

The barkeep gave him a hard stare. "No one."

"Really?" Lorath drew closer, propped an elbow on the counter, and narrowed an eye. "Are you telling me a fine establishment like this doesn't have a single bottle of Skovos wine in its cellar?"

"Have a care, lad," the barkeep said.

"If you don't have any," Donan said, "we've seen it elsewhere. Do the bottles just wash in with the tide?"

"You should stop asking questions now." The barkeep cast a wary glance at his own patrons. "You wouldn't want to attract the interest of the Harbormaster."

"The Harbormaster, eh?" Lorath said. "Now, who might that be?"

"Keep talking, and you'll find out soon enough."

Donan folded his arms. "What does this Harbormaster have to do with Skovos?"

"That's it. You lot ain't welcome in here." The barkeep made a show of slapping Tyrael's coins back onto the counter with a loud *clink* and pushing them away. "I'll ask you to clear out and never again cross the threshold of my alehouse."

Chairs scraped against the floor as several roughs nearby rose to their feet, ready to enforce the barkeep's order. Lorath looked at Tyrael, who shook his head. A brawl would not be prudent so soon after their arrival in the city. Instead, Tyrael simply took his money back, and the three of them left the tavern.

CHAPTER FOUR

Out in the street, the three Horadrim moved a short distance away from the alehouse and stepped into an alley to regroup, but Donan kept his eye on the alehouse door. The barkeep had obviously feared the presence of an informant among his clientele, and if such a person had been listening in, they now had something to report and might leave the tavern shortly.

"I think I'd like to meet this Harbormaster," Lorath said.

Donan suppressed a sigh of frustration. "What happened to avoiding unnecessary conflict?"

"You saw how that barkeep squirmed," Lorath said. "It's obvious the Harbormaster runs this port. I doubt any ship comes or goes but by their leave. We can keep asking around, and we might eventually find someone willing to talk, if we get lucky, but we'll rouse a lot of suspicion along the way." He turned to Tyrael. "It would save time if we go right to the top, and it might even earn us a bit of respect."

Just then, Donan noticed someone step out of the tavern, the old man with the missing ear. He looked back and forth, turned eastward, and set off in a hurry.

"How do you propose we find this Harbormaster?" Tyrael asked.

"We could follow Old Pike," Donan said, pointing down the wharf.

The other two quickly grasped Donan's meaning, and the three of them left the alley to trail the old man. They followed him along the harbor frontage beneath a leaden sky, making no effort to conceal themselves. Along the way, they passed several ships anchored to the barnacle-encrusted piers extending outward from the wharf into the bay. Donan studied the sailors at work on the different vessels, noting the design and styling of each ship. One appeared to have come from Lut Gholein across the Twin Seas, while another came from Gea Kul, the city where Donan had been born and raised. He looked away from the latter quickly.

Old Pike eventually led them to a large warehouse and disappeared inside. Several dockhands worked on the wharf before it, hauling barrels and crates while plainly keeping their eyes on the Horadrim.

"Do we go in through the front door?" Lorath asked. "Or wait here for an invitation?"

"Let us show restraint and patience," Tyrael said. "They are aware of our presence. I doubt we shall have to wait long."

Donan turned and looked out past the anchored ships to the sea beyond. Somewhere over the stormy horizon lay Skovos. He had read about the isles, of course, but he wondered how accurate his sources would prove to be; much of what was written could easily be dismissed as myth or legend. However, such tales sometimes carried elements of truth forward through the centuries, obscured by exaggeration and symbols. It thrilled him to think he might soon see for himself.

Some time later, Old Pike exited the warehouse in the company of two brutes wielding cudgels and walked directly toward the three Horadrim.

"The Harbormaster would like a word," he said.

"Good." Lorath clapped his hands together. "We were hoping for an audience."

Old Pike smirked. "I think you might regret that."

He and his two associates escorted the Horadrim inside the warehouse, where Donan was surprised to find a tidy, well-ordered enterprise underway. He saw sacks of grain, barrels of dried foodstuffs, objects of fine metalwork, and bolts of silk from Kehjistan. The aroma of raw spices and herbs called to mind the open-air markets of his youth. Cats prowled freely to control vermin, and all the various goods appeared to be stored in clean conditions. Legal or otherwise, sanctioned or not, a part of Donan welcomed the sight of commerce and chose to take it as a sign that perhaps the world had begun its return to the way things had been before Malthael's culling.

At the rear of the building, Old Pike showed them into a private room furnished as opulently as a noble household. Thick woven rugs softened the floor, tapestries and hangings decorated the walls, and incense sweetened the air. A table in the center of the room bore an impressive and mouthwatering assortment of food, including meats, breads, cheeses, and fruits. Old Pike left them without a word, closing the door behind him.

"He didn't take our weapons," Donan said, an oversight he assumed reflected the Harbormaster's confidence rather than incompetence.

Then a woman entered the room through another door, which had been hidden behind one of the hangings. She appeared to be middle-aged, of stout build, with gray hair cropped short. A long scar stretched from her temple to her jaw down one side of her face. She wore long leather boots, flowing trousers, and a blouse of red silk, with a well-used sword hanging from her belt. In one hand, she carried a glass bottle by its neck.

"I hear you have a taste for Skovos wine," she said. "Please, have a seat. Eat, if you're hungry."

The Horadrim each took a chair. None of them reached for any food, though Donan found it difficult to avoid staring at the joint of venison in front of him.

"Shall I open the bottle?" the woman asked.

"That will not be necessary," Tyrael said. "I assume you are the Harbormaster?"

"You assume correctly." She set down the bottle and sat herself at the head of the table, sideways in her chair, with one leg dangling over the arm. "Now that I've seen you in person, I think my assumptions about you were also correct."

"What were your assumptions?" Tyrael asked.

"Not yet," she said. "First, you will tell me why you want to go to Skovos."

"That isn't any of your business," Lorath said.

She laughed, but there was nothing friendly or mirthful in it. "It is most assuredly my business. And as you have seen, I take my business very seriously."

"You seem to be doing quite well," Donan said.

She bowed her head. "It is true I have been very fortunate."

"You have, indeed," said Lorath. "Especially when there are so many starving and suffering."

The Harbormaster reached for an apple, picking up and discarding several before selecting one. "The difference between disaster and opportunity," she said, "is often a matter of perspective."

"The people of Sanctuary have lost much," said Lorath. "Is *death* a matter of perspective?"

"One's perspective on death is certainly important, wouldn't you agree?" She bit into her apple, then looked at the fruit with a wrinkled nose before tossing it back onto the table. "We've all been living with death, haven't we? Ever since death itself came marching down our streets? It's waiting around every corner now. It always was, but now we know it. You can either cower from that or you can get on with it."

"Get on with what?" Donan asked.

The Harbormaster shrugged. "Living the only life you'll ever be given." She sat upright suddenly, placing both feet on the floor. "Now: Skovos. I'm afraid I can't let you go."

"Can't *let* us?" said Tyrael. "Who are you to—"

"I am the Harbormaster," she said with the decisiveness of a drawn blade. "I make sure things run smoothly around here. That's what the good people of Kingsport want, you see? But it wasn't always this way. In the aftermath of the reapers, there were those who thought they wanted chaos. They thought they wanted the freedom to do as they pleased. Take whatever they wanted. Hurt whoever they wanted." She lifted her hand, and with the tip of her index finger, she traced the scar down the side of her face. "Those were dark times. But that is not the kind of world *most* people want. Most people want stability. Predictability. They want the sort of lives that can only be obtained through orderly trade. They don't want to be ruled, but they do want to know that someone is taking care of things."

"And that someone is you?" Lorath asked.

"For the moment," she said. "And when it comes to Skovos, my business is . . . delicate. If you were to cause trouble there, and that trouble were to lead back to one of my ships—"

"What if we use someone else's ship?" Donan asked.

"Mine are the only ships welcome there. Any other vessel would not be treated kindly."

"A moment ago," Tyrael said, "you spoke of your assumptions about us."

The Harbormaster lifted one side of her mouth in a half grin. "On occasion, curious relics have crossed my hands."

"What kind of relics?" Donan asked.

"The kind that call to mind certain rumors. Stories about an ancient order of scholars, wizards, and warriors. Horadrim, they're called. Bane of demons."

Tyrael and Lorath glanced at each other but said nothing.

"Don't deny it. You bear their mark." The Harbormaster spread her hands wide. "Why else would I have invited you here? I would have already disposed of you otherwise, but I wanted to see for myself if I was correct."

The Horadrim were not a secret order. They had been around for too long and had involved themselves in far too many pivotal events in Sanctuary's history to hide their existence completely. But the

Horadrim did keep a great many secrets, and for a variety of reasons, past members had often chosen to veil their identities. Lorath and Tyrael did not appear comfortable with the Harbormaster knowing theirs, but Donan had to admit he felt a slight swell in his chest at having been recognized. It still brought him a measure of personal pride to call himself Horadrim.

"You needn't worry," the Harbormaster said. "I didn't get where I am by making powerful enemies needlessly. I shall leave you to your business, so long as you leave me to mine and respect my authority in Kingsport."

"We do not wish to be your adversaries," Tyrael said. "But our business takes us to Skovos. I assure you, our intentions are noble."

"Oh, I trust they are. But my decision is final, and you would be fools to sail anywhere near those islands. Trust me on that. Now, I do have other matters that require my attention. You are free to eat from my table and leave at your leisure, though if you plan to remain in the city, I would suggest you find accommodations before nightfall. Kingsport wouldn't be Kingsport without *some* lawlessness." She placed both hands on the table and rose to her feet. "It has been a pleasure to meet such esteemed fellows as yourselves." Then she departed the room by the door through which she had come, leaving the Horadrim alone.

They looked across the table at one another, then rose to leave. None of them took any food, but Donan reached for the Skovos wine. When Lorath gave him a questioning look, he explained, "This bottle carries the mark of her trading partners." He pointed at a small stamp on the bottle in the shape of a trident. "We may find that information useful down the road."

They left the room and then the warehouse. Only when they were back on the wharf did they speak openly.

"We will not be seeking permission," Tyrael said, jaw clenched in irritation.

Lorath snorted. "Of course not. But I doubt we'll find a captain here willing to defy the Harbormaster. She has this city locked down."

"We could try Bilefen?" Donan suggested. "Port Justinian has an even harder reputation than Kingsport, which might be to our advantage in this particular situation."

"It's controlled by pirates," Lorath said.

"Exactly," Donan replied. "Most pirates answer to coin above all else."

"Perhaps," Tyrael said. "We will stay here tonight and decide in the morning which path to take."

They found an inn not far from the wharf, situated at the back of a short pocket street and flanked by market stalls. There they secured a second-floor room with three narrow, sagging beds that looked as clean as any of the places they had been sleeping in for the past several weeks. The city's inescapable odor of seaweed and fish pervaded their lodging. The inn had a tavern on the first floor, where they were served an edible soup of clams and onions alongside day-old bread and a hard cheese.

Donan ate quickly, and as the sun had not yet set, he decided to step outside and visit the vendors they had seen nearby. He had little expectation of finding anything of interest, but the time he had spent around the merchants of Gea Kul had taught him that the most surprising discoveries could sometimes be found in the unlikeliest of places.

"I'll be back soon," he announced as he got to his feet.

"Where are you going?" Lorath asked.

"Just a bit of exploration."

Lorath shook his head. "Your curiosity is going to land you in serious trouble one day."

Donan rolled his eyes. "I can handle myself."

"I wouldn't wander after dark," Tyrael said. "I believe the Harbormaster's warning was sincere."

Donan bowed his head in acknowledgment of the request, even though he wasn't worried. "Yes, Tyrael."

The first stall outside the inn sold plain used goods: old shoes, dented pots, clothing ready to be torn into rags. Nothing of interest. The second seller was a bent old man with long white hair that fell to his shoulders in wispy strands. He had spread out his wares across a length of balding velvet like royal treasures. Donan turned over bits of strange jewelry, buckles, a few old daggers, and some broken nautical equipment. None of it struck him as significant or magical, but he could appreciate the workmanship behind much of it.

"Where did you acquire all this?" he asked.

"Down by the shore," the old man said. "I always walk there after a storm. Ships go down, and the sea keeps what she wants for a time. When she's done with a thing, she throws it up onto the beach for me to find."

"Flotsam," Donan said. "Though some of this appears quite old."

"Aye," the seller said. "Ships have been sinking out there since the first boat ever to sail. Centuries of wrecks lie at the bottom of the bay and out beyond. The Harbormaster gets first pick. She always takes the rarest stuff off me—sometimes magical items—but she pays a fair price."

That accounted for the Harbormaster's claim of having seen Horadric relics, though Donan still wondered how such things might come to wash up from the sea. Among the more mundane objects before him, he spotted an old book, which he picked up with interest. It was a slender volume wrapped in soft water-stained leather. Inside, he found almost every page covered in handwriting, with a few drawings, diagrams, and other symbols. It appeared to be a journal, but not in any language he recognized.

"What can you tell me about this?" he asked the old man.

"Oh, well, that right there is the spellbook of a powerful mage from Viz-jun itself—"

"Spare me your nonsense," Donan said. "You found this on the beach?"

The old man sighed and nodded. "It were wrapped in oilskin, bobbing in the rocks. The seawater got to it some, but it's in good shape mostly, as you can plainly see."

"Do you know what language this is?"

"I've showed it around, but no one has been able to decipher it as yet."

The book presented a mystery too tantalizing to ignore. "How much?" Donan asked.

The old man clicked his tongue. "Let me see, now. For something that rare—one-of-a-kind, really—I'd be willing to part with it for a thousand."

Donan laughed. "A thousand? For a book no one can read?"

"Well, we know at least one person can read it, and that's him wot wrote it. That there is a book of importance, you can tell. I know you can tell."

"I'll pay you one hundred for it. And that is being generous."

"Could be more generous," the seller said.

"How long until someone else in Kingsport offers you one hundred gold for a book no one can read?"

The seller smiled in defeat. "You make a fair point there. One hundred it is. I accept Westmarch coin, of course, or . . ." He lowered his voice. "Pirate galleons are also accepted currency 'round here."

"Westmarch coin will do," Donan said, and as he paid the seller, he noticed two men watching him from the entrance to the street. They had not been there when he came out of the inn. He turned his back to them and spoke to the old man. "The two at the corner. Are they the Harbormaster's men?"

The seller cast a furtive glance. "No, no. The Harbormaster's enforcers have no need to hide in the shadows. Those are common thieves. But still plenty dangerous, mind you. They won't be alone."

"I'll be careful," Donan said.

He considered rejoining Tyrael and Lorath inside the inn but didn't want a gang of thieves knowing where they were staying, on the chance they were in league with the innkeeper. He decided to lead them away from their lodging and lose them somewhere in the Kingsport streets before returning. He tucked the book away and bade farewell to the seller, then set off while trying to appear that he paid the thieves no mind.

He wondered for a moment if he had been mistaken and they were not watching him at all, but soon they trailed behind him, keeping a distance of several paces but never out of eyesight for long.

They did not seem particularly adept at subterfuge, so they were either incompetent or overly confident. The latter seemed more likely when the first two men were joined by a woman and a third man. Donan wasn't worried yet, but the level of risk had gone up. The street crowd thinned with each passing moment, offering him less opportunity for diversions and obstacles.

He decided to make his move. He dove down a street to the right and then took the next turn as quickly as he could, racing this way and that, looking for an opportunity to duck and wait. He heard shouts and footfalls behind him, so he kept going while trying to keep his bearings, but the twisting, narrow streets of Kingsport defied his ability to map it on the run. Eventually, he stumbled directly into a dead end, with no way to climb out. Before he could double back, the thieves had blocked the exit.

"You better have enough on you to make the chase worth it," said the foremost of them, out of breath. "That's the only way you get out of here with all your bits attached."

"I'm afraid you'll be disappointed," Donan said, his own chest heaving. "I spent most of what I was carrying on a book you won't be able to read."

"And why's that?" said the thief. "Think we're illiterate, do you?"

"No, it's not that. The book isn't— Never mind."

The four assailants had drawn knives. Donan readied his staff while reaching into a pocket with his other hand. He had been working on something, a bit of trickery Lorath had deemed useless, but this seemed as good a time as any to test it out.

"If my friend were here," Donan said, "he might thank you."

"What for?" asked the woman.

"For proving his point about my curiosity."

Donan inhaled quickly as he pulled the satchel from his pocket, then hurled it at the ground while holding his breath. The volatile compounds in the little bundle exploded, filling the alley with a dense, choking smoke. Then he charged at the thieves, swinging his staff to clear the way. He caught one of them hard, a blow that might have broken the man's shoulder, and felt a hand grasping for him from behind. He spun around, and though his second swing missed, he managed to free himself and ran before the smoke had cleared.

He knew at least three of his opponents would be after him momentarily, intending more than thievery now. He careened downward toward the wharf, which still held the greatest throngs in which to hide, and soon found himself standing before The Bilge. Only hours before, the barkeep there had told the Horadrim not to return, but Donan decided to risk it, hoping to blend in with the evening crowd. As soon as he stepped through the door, he made a hard right, squeezing along the wall, head bowed. He took the first open seat he saw, at a small table occupied by a solitary figure.

"Mind if I sit?" he asked the man.

"Matter of fact," the stranger said, gazing at the floor, "I do."

"Your drinks are on me," Donan said.

The man looked up. His blue eyes had the impenetrable quality of a deep lake frozen over. His brown hair and beard appeared unkempt, with gray at his temples. He wore gray woolen trousers with a matching vest over a linen shirt, all of respectable quality, and all in need of a thorough washing. He gripped his mug of ale as if he thought it might escape.

"Sit," he said, and before Donan had taken his chair, the man had tipped back his mug and drained it, after which he slammed it on the table. "I'll have a Bramwell ale."

Donan looked over his shoulder in the direction of the barkeep. Then he pulled out enough coin to keep his unwitting ally in drink for two days and passed it across the table. "I trust this will suffice?"

The man grunted as he took the money, then heaved himself up from his chair and lumbered away. Donan remained seated, wondering how long he would need to wait in the tavern to avoid his pursuers. He gave little thought to whether the drunken man would reclaim his spot, but a few moments later, the stranger came back to the table carrying two mugs. He set one of them in front of Donan.

"The ale out of Bramwell has been good lately," he said, dropping into his chair.

"Thank you," Donan said.

The man held up his drink, waiting, so Donan picked up his mug and clacked it against the stranger's. They both took a gulp, and Donan had to agree on the quality of the beer.

"Weren't you in here before?" the stranger asked, wagging his finger. "Yeah, I remember you. You're memorable."

Donan set his mug back on the table. "You've been here since then? All day?"

The man shrugged. "Where are the other two that were with you?"

Donan glanced in the direction of the front door. "Back at our lodging."

"You can relax and enjoy your drink," he said. "I won't rat you out. There weren't no cause to ban you, and besides, you bought my silence." The man leaned closer. "I'm Keldon, by the way."

"Donan."

"I'm guessing you didn't come in here to drink, did you, Donan?"

"I was just looking for a place to wait out a pack of street thieves."

Keldon sat back in his chair, and it seemed as if a shadow fell over him. "Kingsport has no end of those," he said. "Did you find yourselves a ship yet?"

"Not yet," Donan said, and added with sarcasm, "I don't suppose *you* have a ship."

"In a manner of speaking, I do."

Donan frowned and pushed his ale aside. "What manner of speaking?"

"Well, you see, the Harbormaster has my ship impounded. So I can't rightly call it mine at the moment, now, can I?"

"Why did she impound your ship?"

"The small matter of a debt."

"What kind of debt?"

Keldon leaned forward over his ale, almost wrapping his arms around it, and looked down into his mug for several long moments. "Where would you be wanting to sail?"

Donan hesitated before answering. "Skovos."

"Ha!" But when Keldon looked up, he quickly seemed to realize that Donan meant what he said, and his laughter faded. "Skovos, eh? The Harbormaster wouldn't like that. She owns those trade routes, and they fetch her a hefty sum."

"Yes, she already informed us of her displeasure."

"And yet, here you are talking with me, alive and everything." Keldon shook his head, puffing out air through his lips. "You're a lucky man."

An idea had begun to form in Donan's mind. "Tell me about your ship."

Keldon took a few gulps of his ale. "The *Arabel*? Prettiest sloop you'll ever lay your eyes on, graceful as a swan."

"And how many are needed to crew her?"

"I can handle her alone in a pinch." He finished off his mug and wiped his mouth across his sleeve. "But two or three is better. She ain't a large ship, but she's swift and sleek as an eel."

Donan pushed his own drink across the table toward Keldon, who accepted it as if it had come newly from the barkeep. "Could she make the crossing to Skovos?"

"That's a rough passage, but I'd wager she could." He offered a wry grin. "Now, I wonder why you'd be asking me that."

CHAPTER FIVE

Night had fallen in full by the time Donan and Keldon reached the inn. They found Tyrael and Lorath pacing before the fire, nearly ready to start a search of the city for him. Donan explained his tardiness by introducing them to the old sailor, omitting any mention of his run-in with the thieves; he generally tried to avoid giving Lorath any excuse to scold or gloat. The four of them sat at a corner table, away from the inn's other patrons, where they spoke in murmurs and whispers.

"Where exactly is your ship?" Tyrael asked.

"The Harbormaster has an estate on Pincer Point, at the mouth of the bay. She has a private boatyard."

"Why does she keep it there?" Lorath asked. "What's so special about this ship?"

Keldon shook his head. "It ain't about the *Arabel* to her. If I were a merchant, she'd have seized my shop. If I were a farmer, she'd have claimed my land. All she cares about is my debt to her."

"Why hasn't she just killed you?" Lorath asked.

"She might, one day." Keldon spoke matter-of-factly, without any apparent fear or interest in that eventuality. "For now, I suppose it suits her purposes to keep me alive."

Donan understood Lorath's and Tyrael's reasons for skepticism, and he shared them, but he also knew that any captain they hired in a place like Port Justinian would be no more trustworthy, and likely much less.

"Why have you not simply left Kingsport?" Tyrael asked.

Keldon said nothing at first, bouncing his leg while avoiding the man's gaze. "I need a drink."

"Please." Tyrael leaned toward the sailor, gazing at him with gentle insistence. "Something has kept you here. What is it?"

When Keldon finally looked up, his eyes and his voice held vast anger. "I'll not leave Kingsport without the *Arabel,* all right? That's all I have to say."

Lorath scoffed. "In other words, you would use us to recover your ship and escape your debt."

"I'd use you?" Keldon scratched at his matted beard. "You think I want to sail to bloody Skovos? That ain't no pleasure cruise, boy. I'd be risking my life alongside yours. So I'd say we're using each other, wouldn't you?" He stood, fists clenched. "You know, I didn't ask for your friend to sit at my table. You don't want my ship, that's fine by me. I'll walk out that door and not give you another thought."

"Wait, don't leave." Donan stood and pressed more coin into Keldon's hand. "Go and buy yourself an ale while we talk things over."

Keldon took the money, but he glowered as he walked away.

After he was gone, Lorath leaned in, shaking his head. "I don't like this. We don't know anything about this man's debt, or how he came by it."

"But you *have* met the Harbormaster," Donan said. "Do you trust her more than you trust him?"

"I don't trust either of them," Lorath said.

"Nor do I." Tyrael steepled his hands, touching his lips in thought. "But I do believe Keldon is a good man. Even good men make mistakes, and I sense that he has suffered for his. I do not think an evil man would continue to carry the weight that Keldon seems to bear on his shoulders."

Lorath propped both elbows on the table and rubbed the knuckles of one hand in the palm of the other. "Well, how can I argue with *that*?"

When Keldon returned, he carried two mugs in each hand. "I regret the loss of my temper," he said, sloshing the drinks as he set them down on the table. "My offer stands: Help me get the *Arabel,* and after that, I'll sail you wherever you want to go. Even to Skovos."

Lorath looked up at him for a moment, then claimed an ale as he stood. "You have a deal." Then Donan and Tyrael did the same, and the four of them sealed their compact with a drink.

Pincer Point lay southeast of the city proper. The Harbormaster's estate occupied a spit of land in the shape of a thick bear claw that extended into the bay. An earthen jetty lengthened and curled that claw to enclose a small personal harbor. The estate itself consisted of several wooden barns and outbuildings surrounding a main hall, which had been built from stone like a fortress to withstand the violent tempests that regularly slammed into the shore. Gnarled and stunted trees grew there, with thick branches and deep roots, a nesting ground for ravens and crawling scavengers. Away from the city's waste and the industry of the wharf, the wind off the sea smelled of deeper currents and more ancient forms of life.

After securing provisions for the voyage, Keldon led the Horadrim there that very night; the moon was bright, he said, and the tides were in their favor. The path they traveled followed the edge of a bluff, with brambly forest on their left and a rocky slope down to the bay on their right. Some distance from the estate, they left the road and climbed down to the water's edge, scrambling over the boulders in the shadow of the bluff, toward the Harbormaster's private boatyard.

As they drew closer, the dark forms floating on the water acquired the shapes of the prows, sterns, and masts of several vessels. Soon, Keldon spotted his ship, anchored to a mooring buoy out closer to the jetty than the shore, and they paused to consider their plan. To reach the *Arabel,* they would have to steal a rowboat anchored to the quay near the estate, on the opposite side of the harbor from the jetty. Donan counted only two guards with torches patrolling the dock, keeping watch over the ships and several stacks of crated goods awaiting stowage, but the lights gleaming from the great hall above suggested that reinforcements would arrive quickly enough if the alarm were raised.

"We will have to do this quietly," Tyrael said.

"We could do with a distraction," Keldon said.

Donan looked at the nearest of the hall's barns. "I have an idea," he said, and after explaining his plan, the others got into position while he crept off on his own.

He threaded his way through the bramble toward the outbuildings, taking note of the surrounding terrain, mapping the escape route he would take when he ran back down toward the docks. As he approached the hall, he could hear voices, coarse laughter, and the clinking of ale mugs through the open windows. By the sound of it, the Harbormaster kept quite a large company of foot soldiers at her personal command.

Donan scouted out a place he hoped would be out of view from any window or guard post, keeping the large barn between himself and the hall. Then he crouched down and held his cupped hands before him as if holding an invisible sphere. As he spoke the incantation, a small tongue of violet flame sprang to life between his palms, and then it swelled into a compressed blaze, churning and lighting up the surrounding thicket and the bare branches overhead. A startled raven cawed nearby as he hurled the burning mass.

The ball of flame arced through the air and struck the barn, exploding in a shower of sparks and viscous fire, igniting the wooden timbers in an instant. Then he turned and ran, scrambling back down toward the dock as cries of alarm rose up behind him.

He made it back through the thicket but paused at the tree line with a view of the wharf, waiting. When the two guards patrolling there left their post to combat the fire, he saw Tyrael, Lorath, and Keldon skulking toward the rowboat, and he broke into a run toward them.

"There!" someone shouted behind him. "Take him down!"

Donan raced harder, head ducked and shoulders braced against the arrows he imagined were now aimed his way. He reached the pier, boots hammering on the wooden planks, but his pursuers had closed the distance fast. Tyrael and the others had already boarded the dinghy, ready to heave away, and Donan leapt from the dock. The impact of his weight set the little boat rocking precariously, but the other three managed to steady it as he rolled over onto his back and looked up at the pier behind them.

The Harbormaster and a few of her thugs had reached the wharf, but not in time. As the rowboat pulled away, the barn blazed behind them, throwing its harsh glow across the entire harbor.

"Keldon!" she shouted after them. "I see you, Keldon, you ungrateful cur! Did you tell them what I did for you? Did you tell them what you did? You Horadrim just threw in with a murderer! He killed three unarmed men in cold blood! You ask him if that's not true!"

Donan hoped the Harbormaster was lying. He and Lorath both glanced at Keldon, who gripped his oar with a clenched jaw, staring hard into the night. It seemed Lorath was about to say something.

"Not here," Tyrael interjected. "There will be time for questions after we are gone from this place."

The Harbormaster and her enforcers did not remain standing on the quay for long. The fire posed a far greater threat, just as Donan had assumed it would, and she had already left to battle the blaze by the time the rowboat reached the *Arabel.* Lorath tied the dinghy to the mooring buoy, and the Horadrim and Keldon climbed aboard the larger ship.

"She's just as I left her," Keldon said. "The winds are with us, girl."

Having been raised in a port city, Donan possessed some knowledge of seafaring and sailing vessels, but only in the abstract. His family's wealth had removed any need to labor on a ship, but even to his untrained eye, the *Arabel* possessed something innately elegant in the sweep of her hull. She was not a large ship, stretching only fifteen paces in length with a single tall mast, but she felt strong. Toward the bow and stern of the vessel, hatchways led down to cabins belowdecks. Much of her timber had been painted a rich midnight blue, with yellow trim and brass fittings that glinted like warm stars in the moonlight.

Tyrael and Lorath appeared to have more familiarity with the complex network of ropes, allowing them to assist Keldon in hoisting the mainsail and the headsail before it, while Donan tried his best to stay out of their way. He felt the rocking of the boat, still mild in the shelter of the small harbor, and for the first time he truly contemplated the voyage ahead of them.

The few times he had been to sea had been short and leisurely. But as the *Arabel* departed from the harbor and the bay, riding out with the tide, he found the waves did not feel completely unfamiliar. Rather, they called to mind the rolling dunes of Kehjistan, and Keldon's ship was not altogether unlike a merchant caravan setting off to cross a vast and forbidding expanse.

Keldon stood at the tiller, setting their course southeast toward Skovos beneath a sky full of stars.

"Now that we're underway," Lorath said, "I'd like to know if the Harbormaster spoke the truth. Did you murder three innocent men?"

"She did not say they were innocent," corrected Tyrael. "She said they were unarmed."

"It's true they were unarmed," Keldon admitted. "But they were *not* innocent."

"Care to elaborate?" Lorath asked.

Keldon stared ahead at the horizon. "No."

Lorath moved into the sailor's line of sight to force a confrontation. Donan stepped between the two men, hoping to pacify the situation, but in doing so, he inadvertently laid his hand on the tiller.

This made Keldon's face twist up with instant rage, though he held himself still and spoke with unsettling calm. "Take your hand off my ship."

Donan almost flinched as he pulled his hand from the tiller, while Lorath came to his defense from behind. "He meant no disrespect, and I think you know that. I also think we're entitled to some explanation. The Harbormaster said you murdered those men."

"Aye, I killed them," Keldon said. "How many have you killed with that wicked polearm of yours?"

Donan could not count the number of cultists and monsters he had personally witnessed Lorath execute, sometimes in a state of such blind fury that Donan became frightened of his comrade.

"I can account for my actions without shame," Lorath said. "Can you?"

Keldon sneered. "I am not accountable to the likes of you—"

"You are right." Now Tyrael stepped forward and placed a steadying hand on Lorath's shoulder. "You are not accountable to us. All we must know is whether we can trust you."

"I have the *Arabel* back." Keldon rubbed his hand along the tiller. "You have my thanks for that. I swear to you, I'll hold up my end of our bargain. You can trust me to sail you to Skovos safely." Then he added, "So long as the seas are in agreement."

CHAPTER SIX

The seas were not in agreement and struck up an argument with their ship not far out of Kingsport, just before dawn. Lorath sealed the hatches, and he had already taken the lines in hand when Keldon gave the order to reef the sails. He and Tyrael managed to lower them before the worst of the winds came roaring at the ship. The swells began to mount, piling high enough to capsize them if they should lose their heading and be caught sideways. It took all four of them at the tiller to hold them on course, the ocean lashing their faces with whips of water. The *Arabel*'s resolute prow cleaved the waves with all the determination of a barbarian's axe, but her keel seemed to flex and groan with the strain.

"We should heave to!" Lorath shouted over the crash of the storm. "Wait this out!"

Keldon's hair hung across his nose and cheeks like seaweed. He stared into the wind without any apparent concern, saying nothing.

"Keldon! Heave to!"

"Don't tell me how to sail!" the captain replied. "She can handle this!"

Lorath had spent some time aboard the ships of Westmarch as a soldier in service to the crown, guarding transports, protecting dignitaries, and fighting pirates. He had watched the sailors at their work, and he had been through storms. He knew something of surviving them.

"Keldon, this is madness!" he shouted. "I'll trim the headsail—"

"No!" Keldon roared. "She is *my* ship!"

Donan stood at Lorath's shoulder, hanging on to the tiller in desperation more than to hold it steady. Tyrael leaned into the storm, blinking through the spray, as if willing their vessel forward, while Lorath felt utterly powerless to do anything to save them.

The waves and the troughs heaved the *Arabel* up and down, yet by some luck, Keldon succeeded in steering them along the safest paths. Several times, Lorath thought the next swell would swamp them or throw them over, but somehow the ship cut through, dauntless, even graceful in its dance through the storm.

Over time, Lorath's arms weakened, then felt as if they had seized up, locked around the tiller whether he would release it or not. The water had soaked through his clothing beneath his armor, and he shivered and trembled at the chill in his limbs. He assumed the sun had risen, but he could not see it. He felt a dragging fatigue in his muscles even stronger than his fear, begging him to surrender, lie down, and rest.

Then, without warning, the wind slowly abated, and the seas calmed. The storm had passed over them, leaving them tossed in its aftermath. They all looked at one another, soaked and miserable. Donan was the first to laugh, which made Lorath laugh. Even Tyrael managed a smile of relief.

"*Now* we heave to," Keldon said, setting the tiller and the sails in opposition so that the *Arabel* came to a stable drift despite the wind. He then went below to check the hull for damage, and Lorath paced until the captain returned a few minutes later, looking pleased with what he had found.

"Are you always that reckless?" Lorath demanded.

"Reckless?" Keldon chuckled. "Most would call it reckless to set sail for Skovos in the first place. If you wanted to avoid storms, my friend, then you should have stayed on land."

"I am not your friend."

"Suit yourself. But I'll thank you not to tell me how to sail my own ship ever again. I know her limits, and I know the sea."

"He did bring us through it," offered Donan.

Lorath bristled with irritation at the younger man's naivety. "We were *lucky*—"

"Mind your helm there," Keldon said. "Luck had nothing to do with it. You asked about my debt to the Harbormaster. Well, it weren't coin I owed her. She wanted me to sail for her because I'm the best in Kingsport."

"And you refused," said Tyrael, sounding pleased.

Keldon blinked, then nodded. "Aye." Then he whipped a smirk at Lorath. "Luck is always at play on a ship, boy, but so is skill and talent, both of which I have in full measure. Don't question me again. That will not be the last storm we encounter."

Lorath thought better of pressing the matter any further in that moment, in part because he didn't doubt the man's seamanship as much as his mental condition. Keldon's decision to plow headlong into the storm had not seemed to be a tactical decision, but rather an act of willful disregard for his own life and the lives of his passengers.

Keldon gave the rest of the ship a looking-over, and when he was satisfied, he declared they could be on their way. "To which of the lovely Skovos Isles would you like to sail?" he asked Tyrael.

"Temis," came the answer.

"Straight to the capital, then." Keldon nodded. "Aye."

They shook out the reef from the sails, and, once trimmed, the *Arabel* plied a southeasterly course at an exuberant speed, as if the ship itself enjoyed being free of the harbor where she had been so long confined. As the leagues passed beneath them and they entered deeper seas, they saw fewer gulls, and the water took on a darker hue. The three Horadrim rested at the bow, letting the wind dry them out after the storm.

"Have you ever been to Skovos?" Donan asked Tyrael.

"Yes," he replied, looking out over the sea ahead of them. "I traveled there almost three centuries ago with four Horadrim: Jered Cain, Iben Fahd, Tal Rasha, and Zoltun Kulle. Together, we built a vault on the island of Skartara." His voice had grown distant, as if pulled away from the present by his memories. "This was before Tal Rasha sacrificed himself to imprison the Prime Evil Baal, and before pride and ambition corrupted Zoltun Kulle. I was still an archangel then. That time now feels as if it belongs to a different age . . ." A few moments passed, and then Tyrael shook himself from his reverie. "Since then, I have had occasional dealings with Amazons. I learned much about more recent events in the islands from a woman named Akara, some years ago."

Lorath cocked his head. "Where have I heard that name?"

"She served as the high priestess of the Sisterhood of the Sightless Eye."

"That's right," Donan chimed in. "Deckard Cain wrote about them. Fierce warriors, by all accounts."

"Yes," Tyrael said. "But some wielded magic. Akara was an accomplished healer and revered spiritual leader, and the Sisterhood did derive its name from a powerful magical artifact."

"The Sightless Eye is real?" Lorath asked. "I'd always assumed it was a myth."

"I have never seen it," Tyrael said. "But I believe it is real. When the Sisterhood left Skovos, they stole the Sightless Eye and carried it with them. I have no idea where it might be now."

"Wait," Lorath said. "Without the Sightless Eye, how are there still seers in Skovos?"

"They have other ways to maintain their gift of foresight," Tyrael answered. "Their caste has its center of power on the island of Philios, while the Amazons occupy Athulua. Temis, where we are sailing, is the city-island that lies between them, where I hope to meet with the Amazon Queen. But we must tread cautiously at court if we are to find our Horadric comrades. I recommend we conceal our true purpose, at least for a time. The Harbormaster recognized us too easily."

With that, the three Horadrim removed the medallions that marked their order, and Tyrael collected the insignias in a leather pouch to be hidden below deck.

"The name of a former archangel might well be known to them," Donan said.

Tyrael nodded in agreement. "I will use a false one."

"We have to get there first," Lorath added, eyeing Keldon at the tiller.

Tyrael seemed to notice the direction of Lorath's glare. "I have confidence in the captain."

"I'm glad one of us does."

They sailed for several days, encountering frequent squalls and storms, but each time, the *Arabel* rode through them without significant harm. Lorath gradually began to accept that Keldon *did* know his ship, as well as how to navigate her through rough seas. On calm nights, they hove to, allowing three of them to sleep belowdecks while the fourth stood watch. The forecastle held two narrow, coffin-like beds and one hammock slung when needed. Lorath did not enjoy his turns alone under the canopy of distant and silent stars. He dreaded the stillness, the halt in movement toward a destination. Without a target, a quarry, the rage within him grew restless, turning in its lair as if chasing its own tail.

On their seventh night at sea, Lorath awoke and went up onto the deck, rubbing his eyes to relieve Donan at the watch. He found the younger man resting amidships in front of the mast, poring over a book by the light of a candle stub. "What's that you're reading?"

"Something I bought in Kingsport," Donan answered, neck bent, eyes on the pages.

"What kind of book is it?"

"I think it's a journal. But it isn't written in any language I recognize."

"You bought a book you can't read?"

"I think it might be some form of code." Donan looked up, forehead creased in frustration. "I'm trying to decipher it."

Lorath yawned. "Sounds like your kind of book."

"What do you mean?"

"I know how you enjoy a puzzle."

Donan returned his attention to the journal. "I suppose I do."

The younger man seemed more drawn to books than Lorath ever had been. Not that he found books unimportant—he knew they held useful information and insights—but he preferred action over study and contemplation. It was a question of priorities. In a world as ravaged as Sanctuary, time spent in the library often felt like a luxury he could ill afford.

Lorath turned and looked behind them, northwest toward Kingsport, which had vanished over the horizon days ago. "I can't help feeling like we're running away."

Donan looked up again. "How so?"

Lorath waved his arm in the general direction of Westmarch. "The fight is back there, where people are suffering, even in this very moment, while we sail away. This feels like a retreat."

"Caldesann wrote that real warriors are proudest of their retreats."

"I cannot understand that," Lorath said. "You put too much faith in the writings of the Horadrim. Just because they're old and dead does not make them right."

Donan closed his book. "Caldesann knew war as intimately as you do. I think he simply meant that a retreat is not always an act of cowardice to be ashamed of. There can be wisdom in retreat. Sometimes, a retreat is the only way to avoid needless bloodshed. Sometimes, a retreat is strategic and necessary to strengthen one's position for a future battle."

"Caldesann became a pacifist," Lorath said. "I have no such desire."

"Nor do I," said Donan. "But I also don't go looking for fights." He stood to go below. "Do you want the candle?"

"No."

Donan blew it out, but before he had left the deck, Lorath heard something that raised his hair on end. It was the moaning of some creature, deep and resonant through the *Arabel*'s timbers, so loud and vast he could not say where it came from. It seemed to be under and all around the ship at once, a bellow in the depths from a mouth he could not even imagine.

The tumult roused Tyrael and Keldon from their sleep, and they rushed up wide-eyed onto the deck.

"What is that?" asked Donan.

"Could it be the ocean currents? A distant storm?" asked Lorath, seeking even improbable answers over the one that he feared.

"Water has many voices," said Keldon. "That is not one of them. That is a sea-beast, but not like any I've heard before."

"Nor I," said Tyrael.

They could do nothing but hold fast and hope the creature took no notice of them, wherever it lurked. Lorath strained to listen for any splashing or changes in the waves around the *Arabel* or any fluctuation in the moaning to determine its position. At one point, he found he was holding his breath and needed to inhale deeply, at which time he smelled something unfamiliar, a faint odor like that of a newly opened tomb, if that tomb were at the bottom of the sea.

"There are legends," said Tyrael. "I've heard a peasant tale about a beast named Kethos, Mother of Deepstriders. But such stories are—"

"Look!"

Donan pointed at the horizon, where a single wave had risen like a mountain, visible even in the darkness, lifted by something immense moving beneath the surface. Lorath watched it in a state of silent, terrified awe as it rolled across his view. Were it not for the fact that the others also saw it, he would have wondered if his imagination had conjured it.

"I think it is moving away from us," said Keldon.

He was right. The moaning sound had diminished, and the mountainous wave soon collapsed out of sight. Not long after that, the wake of the sea-beast set the *Arabel* rocking. Not sufficient to capsize her, but with enough strength that Lorath and the others scrambled for something to hang on to until it had passed.

None of them slept for the rest of that night. None of them took their eyes from the horizon, fearing the return of the beast. When dawn arrived, it brought with it a new storm out of the north, the strongest they had yet weathered, and for the first time, Keldon agreed it would be prudent to hunker down and wait it out.

The ferocious wind howled around them, and the blinding lightning flashed near enough that Lorath worried it could strike their mast. The gale pounded them with so much rain, the bailing of it required almost constant effort. The storm lasted most of that day, pushing them to the point of exhaustion, and when it finally ended, they were left battered and adrift in a dense fog, the air around them listless and warm. Without wind, their sails hung from the rigging, slack and useless.

Lorath had heard sailors speak about dead seas, when the breezes ceased and it seemed that time itself had forgotten about them, but he had never been on a ship so becalmed in the rough waters off Westmarch. "Where are we?" he asked.

"Far off course." Keldon checked his compass. "Can't take proper bearings until the sky clears, but I'd guess west of Athulua."

"What is west of Athulua?" Donan asked.

"Atanos." Tyrael gripped the gunwale, peering into the mist. "A region with an evil reputation."

"I doubt the storm pushed us that far south," Keldon said.

"Let us hope not," said Tyrael.

They could do nothing but wait. The muggy heat caused Lorath to sweat, while the fog painted everything on the ship with a wet sheen, and all the while the specter of the sea-beast hung over his mind. Perhaps it was the languid pallor of their circumstances, but the memory of their encounter with the creature, whatever it was, began to feel like a dream, almost as if it could not have possibly happened as he remembered it. There must have been some trick of the moonlight on the sea, allowing something as ordinary as a whale to take on monstrous proportions.

"Why is Atanos considered evil?" Donan asked.

Tyrael turned from the gunwale and rubbed his palm over his bald head, wiping away droplets of condensation. "The legend takes us back almost to the foundation of Sanctuary, and I myself am unsure how much of it is true. Atanos is a shattered land. According to the myth, it was the place where the angel Inarius and the demon Lilith created humanity. But their union was not to last, as we know all too well. After the conflict that saw Lilith banished from Sanctuary, Inarius destroyed Atanos, sinking parts of it beneath the waves. For as long as the Askari have dwelt in Skovos, the land between Athulua and Celestia has been a cursed place, full of dark tales."

"What kind of dark tales?" asked Donan.

Keldon scoffed. "The kind that smugglers and pirates spread to keep others away from their havens. The kind that superstitious sailors will believe."

Lorath had a different question. "Why did Inarius destroy the island?"

"Anger," Tyrael said. "Shame. They are two sides of the same coin." He faced the gunwale again, resuming his vigil. "As I said, it is an ancient story."

Keldon went to work repairing what needed seeing to after the storm. Donan helped him use scraps of old canvas soaked in pitch to patch a few holes that had opened in the hull, then worked to sew up the sails where they had torn free of their rigging. After that was all done, the four of them could only sit and wait. Keldon eventually went below and came back with an old, scuffed fiddle.

"Fair warning," he said. "The instrument belonged to someone else. I have little musical ability."

He proceeded to play despite that, scratching out a few melodies that caused some wincing and laughter but helped to pass the time.

No wind stirred for the remainder of that day, but toward evening, the fog began to drop away a little, though it still clung to the water and obscured the sky. Keldon climbed the mast to get above it and used the stars to find their bearing. When he dropped back down to the deck, he appeared uneasy.

"I was wrong," he said, now keeping his voice low. "The storm pushed us farther south than I realized."

"Meaning?" Lorath asked.

"We are very close to Atanos." The sailor looked to either side of the vessel. "Too close."

CHAPTER SEVEN

Superstitious or not, they doubled the watch that night so that none of them would be alone on the deck, and they armed themselves. Lorath had no idea what they armed themselves against, but Tyrael insisted, so he held his polearm, listening and peering into the fog that continued to envelop the ship. He stood the middle watch with Keldon, who sat nearby with a seaman's axe across his lap. As the hours passed, Lorath had to blink and rub his eyes or else they would start to see things, as if his tired mind could not abide the soft gray void and sought to fill it with imagined forms and movement. Keldon looked up at the sky more often than he did the sea to either side of the *Arabel*.

Though Lorath had gradually learned to trust the man's command of his ship, the two had not become friends. But the night was long, and the quiet of Atanos unnerved him more than the prospect of awkward conversation. "You mentioned the fiddle belonged to someone else," he said. "Whose was it?"

Keldon took so long to answer that Lorath had almost forgotten his question. "It . . . it belonged to my wife," the sailor finally said.

"Eshella." For a few moments, he seemed becalmed like his ship, adrift in memory. But then he roused himself suddenly and dragged his palm down his mouth and beard. "She's been gone several years now. And she ain't coming back."

Lorath didn't think he would get any more from the sailor, and truthfully, he didn't want to. Keldon irritated him for a reason he could not quite explain, not rationally.

The sailor scraped his thumb across the blade of his axe as if testing its sharpness, and the metal offered a quiet chime against the stillness of the night. "What about you?" he asked.

"What about me?"

"You're old enough to have married. Has there ever been a woman in your life?"

Lorath shifted his footing. "A soldier's life isn't friendly toward marriage."

"Aye, that's true. Nor is the life of a mariner." He looked away into the mist. "And yet, how many spouses go on keeping their sleepless vigils, waiting for their sailors to return from sea? They endure their own kind of storm, I think. Yet they marry us, all the same." A moment passed. "You ain't a soldier anymore, though, are you?"

"Not for the crown," Lorath said. "But I am Horadrim now."

"What, do your lot swear off love or something?"

Lorath chuckled. "No. But it means I have a duty that must come before all else."

Keldon stood, gripping the axe in his right hand while he stretched his back. "Look, lad. This world is harsh. There ain't nothing hopeful nor certain about it. I'd caution you against denying yourself one of its few remaining joys. Though I don't expect my advice will hold much weight with you."

It did not, but Lorath knew he meant well and saw no reason to be disrespectful. "I thank you for your concern."

Keldon gave him a sidelong smirk. "Fine, don't believe me, then. But before you know it, you'll be a lonely old man wondering where your life went."

Lorath returned his smile. "Aren't you a lonely old man?"

"Aye," Keldon said. "I am, indeed. But I know where my life went. It's true I've many regrets, but marrying Esh ain't one of—"

"Shh." Lorath held up his hand, thinking he had heard something while the sailor was talking, but he couldn't be sure. Nothing moved in the fog that he could see, but it sounded as if something had disturbed the water on the port side of the ship. A splash, or a gurgled whisper.

"I don't hear anything," Keldon said. Then his eyes bulged, and he raised his axe. "Look out!"

Lorath spun around as a monstrous pale figure scrambled over the gunwale onto the deck with a slapping sound, dripping water. He barely had time to raise his polearm before the thing leapt at him, but Keldon reacted more quickly, burying his axe in the creature's head before it reached him, smashing it to the deck.

"Drowned," the sailor breathed. "There'll be more." He rushed to the ship's bell and rang it to awaken the others.

The thing at Lorath's feet resembled a waterlogged corpse, with black and blue veins winding through sallow flesh, but it appeared the sea had infected it. Encrustations of barnacles and wriggling worms covered its skin, and bony growths of coral sprouted from its corrupted bones. Its clothes hung in tatters and shreds, tangled with seaweed. Lorath had heard of the Drowned but had never seen one. They were said to be the cursed casualties of shipwrecks, but there were also stories of attacks on coastal settlements, with victims dragged down into the water to join with others like the monstrosity before him.

"Lorath!" Donan shouted, staring at the slain creature. "Are you injured?" He and Tyrael had reached the deck, both wielding their weapons.

"I'm fine," Lorath said. "Thanks to Keldon."

"Prepare yourselves," Tyrael said. "I fear this battle will not go easy."

The four of them took up positions amidships, with their backs together, facing the *Arabel*'s four quarters. Lorath watched the prow. He could hear thrashing in the water now, and distant shrieks.

Shapes moved in the fog that he knew to be real, not figments. From somewhere in the distance a bell rang, its tone deep and haunted, a chilling summons.

"It seems the stories of Atanos are true, after all," Donan said from the port side of the ship. "Do not let them get too close."

"Why not?" Lorath asked.

"I've read there is risk of . . . infection."

"Infection?" Lorath swung his polearm a few times to loosen his muscles. "That's just brilliant."

A moment later, the first wave of Drowned came over the gunwale. They attacked as one, clambering over all sides of the ship. Seawater poured from their open mouths, tongues and teeth ravaged by rot, gurgling out groans and wails. They reached with grasping fingers and wielded weapons tainted by the sea. A moving mass of death. Lorath could focus only on the enemy before him, trusting his comrades to handle their fronts. He swung his polearm, using it to block as much as slash and cleave. The enemy went down fairly easily, seemingly possessed by a mindless tenacity but with little cunning. His comrades also appeared to be holding their own against the first wave, but the enemy had the advantage of numbers. It seemed that for every Drowned that Lorath felled, there were two undead fighters ready to take its place.

"What is the strategy here?" he asked.

The slain had begun to pile up, and the ichor that oozed from their torn flesh mixed with the seawater they trailed aboard, turning the deck slick and treacherous.

"Give no ground!" Tyrael shouted, hewing the Drowned in half with mighty swings of El'druin. "We must outlast them!"

That seemed less likely with each passing minute. The Drowned appeared to come from the bottom of the shallow sea, where an entire army could be lurking for all Lorath knew, waiting for ships like theirs to enter the waters of Atanos.

"Is there no end to these infernal things?" Keldon shouted.

Donan cried out suddenly as he stumbled and dropped to the deck. Lorath lunged toward him, swinging his polearm almost from the end of its shaft, carving as wide an arc as he could to cover both fronts.

"Are you okay?" he asked.

"I think so!" said Donan, climbing to his feet.

Lorath knew it was only a matter of time until one of them fell, unable to rise. Perhaps it would be him. The corpses had stacked up high enough that the attacking Drowned had to struggle over them, but that did not appear to slow them down enough to turn the tide of the battle. The *Arabel* needed to escape, but they couldn't without wind in her sails.

"I'm sorry," Keldon said, out of breath.

Lorath looked to his right. "What are you sorry for?"

"I'm the captain," he said. "I brought us here. To this end."

"It was a storm that brought us here!" shouted Tyrael. "And this is not the end! Now, fight!"

Lorath planned to keep fighting, though he had little hope for a victory. Only a slow defeat. The foul and twisted faces of the Drowned pressed in with their milky, swollen eyes, choking him with the stench of rotten fish. He felt his strength fading. He wondered if he and the others would become Drowned after their deaths, waiting beneath the cold waves to attack the surface world.

Then a horn sounded in the fog, full and deep. The enemy seemed to recognize the noise and turned toward it as the glow of approaching torches cut through the fog. Then came the sound of oars churning the water, the beat of a drum, and a woman's voice calling the rhythm. The silhouette of a ship emerged from the mist, broad with a tall prow, its deck bristling with silent figures armed with spears and javelins. A moment later, flaming arrows came whistling through the air, striking the Drowned as they tried to surmount the *Arabel*'s gunwale. Their bodies hit the water as they fell.

"Who is that?" asked Donan.

Tyrael answered, "Amazons."

The warship rowed alongside theirs, but the attacking Drowned pulled Lorath's attention away from it. A hulking brute had landed on the deck, heavy enough to rock the *Arabel* and so bloated it seemed ready to burst. It swung a length of old ship's timber as a club, easily pushing aside Lorath's strike with his polearm and tipping him off balance. The creature bore down on him before he could recover, but just then a second figure wheeled through the air above the giant. She landed on its shoulders and thrust downward with her spear, a strike so quick Lorath almost failed to see it, but the blade penetrated deep into the brute's chest. Then she launched back into the air and landed on the deck near Lorath as the giant staggered, almost as if it were confused by its mortal injury. Lorath took its head with his own blade and sent the bulk of its corpse backward into the water with a tremendous splash. He turned toward the Amazon to thank her.

"You should not be here!" she said, then leapt across the deck toward the bow. Warriors standing at the stern of the Amazon vessel then threw a grappling line with a heavy hook across the gap between the ships. The woman who had saved Lorath took the line and tied it around the cleats at the *Arabel*'s prow.

"Secure!" she shouted. "Go!"

The warship drum resumed its pounding beat, and the vessel pushed off, swinging its bow outward and around. Lorath looked across the deck and noticed that several Amazons had remained behind on the *Arabel.* A few of them carried large jugs, while the others fought to keep any more of the Drowned from climbing on board.

The line between the two vessels grew taut as the Amazon warship moved into position ahead of them, and Lorath grabbed hold of a rope near the mast.

"Brace!" shouted the woman from the prow.

The *Arabel* jolted and shuddered as the warship lurched her forward, shaking loose the last few Drowned trying to climb onto the deck.

The warrior at the prow stalked past Lorath down-ship toward the stern, obviously a leader among the women. The Amazons bearing the jugs followed her, and they proceeded to empty the contents of their jars into the sea behind the ship. A moment later, one of the Amazons placed a bow in the leader's hands, and then a flaming arrow. She took aim and let the arrow fly. Where it landed, the sea erupted in a blaze, illuminating hundreds of Drowned as they thrashed and burned in their wake.

"That's a nice trick," Lorath said. "We recently used a similar tactic against—"

The woman lunged, a graceful movement that almost captivated Lorath until he realized she now had the point of her spear at his throat. Those Amazons wielding bows had taken aim at Tyrael, Donan, and Keldon, who looked equally stunned.

The leader stood almost as tall as Lorath, and she was close enough that he could smell her sweat. She wore leather armor embossed with a design that resembled an eagle's wings across her chest. The firelight behind the ship caught a hint of red in her braided hair.

"You should not be here," she said again.

"I completely agree with you." Lorath let his polearm fall and held up his empty hands.

She narrowed her green eyes at him. "Are you pirates? Smugglers?"

"We are travelers," said Tyrael, sheathing El'druin as he stepped forward. "We came with a petition for your queen but were blown off course on our way toward Temis."

"Travelers?" she scoffed, turning toward him, at which point something about his appearance seemed to startle her. She recovered quickly. "Only pirates and smugglers travel to Skovos these days. So, I'll ask again, which are you?"

"I am Faysal," Tyrael said. "The man before you is Lorath, and that is Donan. This ship belongs to Keldon here."

"I don't care about your names," the woman said. "Only why you are here."

"We aren't pirates or smugglers," Lorath said. "Search the ship if you like. You will find no stolen goods. No cargo."

"Perhaps you are simply bad at what you do," she said, then gave an order to the other Amazons: "Bind them!"

Lorath winced as he felt his arms pulled and twisted around behind him, and he chafed at the rough rope used to tie his wrists together. The Amazons did the same to Tyrael, Donan, and Keldon after taking their weapons, and soon the four of them were seated on the deck amidships in much the same configuration as before, when they were on their feet fighting the Drowned. The Amazon leader stood near the bow, and ahead of them could be heard the drumming and the warship's coxswain calling the oar stroke.

Keldon cleared his throat. "You may've taken me prisoner on my own ship, but all the same, I'm grateful you came along when you did."

The leader turned around with irritation. "Consider yourselves very fortunate that none of my sisters died rescuing you from your idiocy."

"Fortunate, indeed," Tyrael said. "May we ask what you happened to be doing near Atanos?"

The woman leveled a hard stare at him. "Our duty."

"And you are obviously very skilled at it," Lorath said. "May we ask your name?"

She hopped down from the prow and strode along the deck to stand before him, arms folded. "You may call me Captain. And the next one to ask me a question gets thrown overboard."

Lorath bowed his head. "Understood, Captain."

She marched toward the stern, and after she had passed out of earshot, Donan leaned his head toward Lorath. "Adreona," he whispered.

"What?"

"That's her name. I overheard one of the others say it."

"Then I guess I wasted my question," Lorath said. "I should have asked where they're taking us."

The Amazons cleared the *Arabel*'s deck of the Drowned remains, and after some time, the warship rowed them out of the fog and into the light of a hazy dawn. The waters around them changed character, growing choppy and slapping the hull as the wind returned. A large island lay to the south, rising from the sea in stark cliffs and rocky bluffs, surmounted by open green fields. Atop the spit of highland nearest them, Lorath glimpsed an impressive white temple unlike any he had seen before, hidden among wisps of cloud turned golden by the rising sun.

"We're east of Atanos," Keldon said, "so that'll be Athulua."

Farther to the east ahead of them, Lorath saw two more islands, though they were still too distant to make out details. "Which would make those Temis and Philios."

Adreona signaled the forward vessel, and they came to a halt, slackening the line between the ships enough to untether them. Then the Amazon vessel unfurled a large square sail bearing the image of a sword in gleaming copper, and they turned toward starboard, in the direction of Athulua.

The Amazons that remained on the *Arabel* set to work raising her sails as well. Lorath expected Keldon to object, but the sailor merely grunted as he craned his neck to watch them. It probably helped that the Amazons obviously knew their way around a sloop. The ship was shortly underway, pushing eastward. Adreona leaned against the forecastle, cleaning the head of her spear.

"We sail to Temis?" Lorath said.

Adreona raised an eyebrow. "Is that a question?"

"An observation."

"That's where you claimed to be traveling, is it not?"

"It is," said Tyrael.

"You may wish it wasn't," she said. "Strangers from the continents are not welcome in Skovos. But your fate isn't mine to decide. That will be up to the queen. I hope for your sake that she is sympathetic toward your petition."

CHAPTER EIGHT

Tyrael struggled with doubt, but he could not reveal that struggle to his companions, who looked to him for leadership and guidance. Before departing Westmarch, he had believed with certainty that they needed to sail to Skovos to bolster their number, and yet, their expedition had nearly ended in disaster. Were it not for the timely arrival of the Amazons, they would have all perished, including himself. The Horadrim would have gone extinct in the cursed waters of Atanos, leaving Sanctuary without one of its last remaining defenses against the Burning Hells.

Perhaps he had been wrong about this journey. Perhaps he should not trust his judgment as readily as he once did. He did not doubt that Sanctuary must be protected. He did not doubt Lorath or Donan, who were both men of courage and moral fortitude.

Tyrael doubted himself.

As the *Arabel* sailed to Temis, the Amazons worked to repair the minor damage the enemy had caused, even though the vessel did not belong to them. As Keldon watched them, his expression turned from defensive annoyance to grudging gratitude and respect.

"I don't know why they'd bother making her shipshape when she ain't theirs," he said.

Tyrael was not surprised, thinking back to the Amazons he had known. "I believe it speaks to the value their culture places on sailing vessels, in the same way other cultures revere their horses, or their camels."

"We might share something in common, then," Keldon said.

Lorath laughed. "Our reception thus far doesn't fill me with a lot of hope for that."

"All will be well," Tyrael said, trying to sound as if he believed it.

The sun rose over them as they sailed toward it, warming the deck. Clouds billowed across the steel-blue sky, offering occasional shade, and the wind tasted of salt from the deep sea. Gulls hovered in the air above the ship, and a few descended to perch on the gunwale and other parts of the *Arabel.* Tyrael noted that the Amazons made a point of leaving the birds undisturbed.

As they approached Temis, its features came into view, and Tyrael beheld a mighty metropolis. Though he had been there before, the memory of it had faded, like so many others, as if he were now seeing a place he had only heard described. The island's numerous sharp peaks rose high above the water in a tight gathering, and all but their rocky summits appeared covered in buildings, palaces, gardens, groves, and orchards. It was an ancient center of civilization, built by the Firstborn at the dawn of Sanctuary's creation, but the Askari had made it their home for thousands of years, utilizing and adding to the existing structures until the entire island had become one great city.

"In all my sailing, I've not seen the like," said Keldon.

Lorath and Donan also appeared captivated, though when Lorath shook his head, it did not seem to be from astonishment.

"What is it?" Tyrael asked him.

"They appear to have been spared the evils of our time that have decimated so many other cities."

"We won't know that for sure until we land," Tyrael said. "But even so, would that not be a good thing?"

"For the Askari, yes."

The *Arabel* sailed directly toward what Tyrael assumed to be the island's primary harbor, held in the encircling arms of two towering seawalls, the size of which rivaled the fortifications surrounding the greatest cities on either side of the Twin Seas. Both sections of the wall stood at least fifty feet high and twelve feet thick, crowned with battlements and artillery. At the end of each, a mammoth statue stood twice as tall as the wall, flanking the entrance to the harbor. One depicted an angel, resplendent in plate armor, which Tyrael assumed to be Inarius. The other statue resembled Lilith, the demonic mother of humankind, wearing graceful flowing robes. All who entered the port had to pass between these sentinels and beneath their imposing shadows.

"You worship both angels and demons?" Donan asked.

The Amazon nearest him flashed him a look of confusion. "We do not worship—" She followed the young man's gaze upward, and it seemed she took notice of the statues in a way she ordinarily would not. "The Askari did not make those," she said. "They were built by the Firstborn."

As they entered the harbor, the seawalls choked off most of the wind, and the *Arabel*'s sails began to luff. They moved forward slowly through numerous ships at anchor. Many of them resembled the warship that had rescued them from Atanos, with square-rigged sails and oars. Others resembled the sailing vessels of Westmarch, and still others could have come from Gea Kul or Kurast. The Amazons pulled Tyrael and the other three to their feet but left them bound, facing the city ahead. Before their ship had made it much farther, she drifted to a halt.

"If you will allow a question, Captain," Lorath said, "what now?"

"An unknown vessel has just entered the Great Harbor of Temis," she said. "We will not be here long."

Her prediction proved accurate. Tyrael soon noticed a cutter of perhaps twenty oars speeding their way. When the vessel approached within hailing distance, half the rowers exchanged their oars for drawn bows. When Adreona stepped up to the prow of the *Arabel,* it seemed the cutter's helmsman recognized her.

"Looks like you caught yourself another pirate ship, Captain!" he called. "You could have a whole fleet by now!"

"I don't want a fleet, Parmo!" she called back. "But I would accept better provisions for my warriors, and a legion of reinforcements to relieve them!"

The helmsman laughed. "Not sure I have the power to give you that! Meantime, where do you want this?"

"All the way in," she said, waving her pointed finger in a circle. "We've got four guests to question, and this ship needs a thorough search."

"Aye, Captain!" the helmsman said.

His archers stowed their bows and dropped the blades of their oars back into the water. Then the cutter threw a line up to the *Arabel,* and after the two vessels were tethered, the rowers began hauling both crafts toward the distant piers.

"Guests?" Lorath muttered. "I don't typically restrain my guests, do you?"

"Have patience," Tyrael said. "The Askari are being cautious, as is their right. We have committed no crime, which they will soon discover."

As the cutter towed the *Arabel* closer to the Temis docks, the details of the city became visible. Many of its buildings appeared to have been constructed of pearlescent marble, and others had been given a washing of lime, so that much of the city gleamed white. Rooftop tiles were glazed with blue, red, and other vibrant hues, adding dashes of color that rose up the mountains with the terraces. Here and there, monumental statues stood above the rooftops, depicting angels and demons alike, often near the vaulted domes and pinnacles. Banners waving from towers bore images that Tyrael assumed to represent noble houses, clans, or guilds. From the peak of the largest mountain, in the middle of the city, jutted a cliff-like bastion, an edifice of such prominence and grandeur it could only be the keep of the Amazon Queen. Back when Tyrael had sent the previous expedition of Horadrim to Skovos, a woman named Etara sat on the throne, but much in Sanctuary had changed since then. Other cities and kingdoms had seen their dynasties fall in the wake of Malthael's Reaping. He wondered if Queen Etara still ruled or if another had assumed the mantle.

At last, the cutter pulled the *Arabel* alongside a pier, where dockhands secured her and laid a plank across her gangway. Adreona marched toward Tyrael and his companions and gestured toward the ramp.

"This way, travelers."

Lorath shrugged and went first, followed by Donan.

Keldon seemed reluctant to leave his ship, looking over her deck with his brow low in worry. "I just got her back," he said.

"No harm will come to your vessel in this harbor," Adreona said. "I swear that to you on my honor. And if you are who you say you are, she will be returned to you."

That seemed to appease the sailor enough for him to leave the *Arabel* of his own volition. Then Tyrael walked across the plank onto the pier, and from there the Amazons escorted them in single file along the dock. Adreona led the way, with armed warriors marching to each side and more bringing up the rear. The ordinary men and women they passed gave way with bowed heads, suggesting respect for members of the Amazon caste, though some eyed Tyrael and the other Horadrim with suspicious glances.

When they reached the end of the pier, Adreona led them up a wide avenue paved well with quality flagstones, though the street was not without dips and ruts in need of repair where the surface had cracked and failed. They encountered pedestrians and a few carts pulled by mules, but this quarter of the city boasted no throngs despite it being so near the harbor. The buildings they passed stood in good repair, for the most part; even the many structures that appeared disused had not been abandoned completely to the elements and vermin. Frescoes and mosaics adorned the houses and courtyards they glimpsed down winding side streets, depicting aquatic beasts, ships, horses, and heroic figures. Water fountains trickled and sang, and from somewhere nearby, Tyrael heard the mournful music of a lyre, accompanied by a drum. They passed few shops, and what Tyrael at first took to be a tented food stall turned out to be a ration dispensary, with a line of Askari citizens waiting to receive their allotment.

Adreona halted them as they reached a wall of natural stone at the base of the mountain. The avenue made a sudden turn there, cut into the rock, and climbed upward toward the next terrace of the city, but the Amazons turned in the other direction toward a plain but commanding building that stood like a fortress among the smaller structures around it. Its lower floors had no windows, but loopholes in the upper stories would offer archers a full view of the street below, as would the merlons and crenels running along the top of the tower.

"That has all the markings of a garrison," Lorath said. "Or a prison."

"Both," Adreona said.

The escort prodded Tyrael and the others through the front gate of the fortress, which opened tall and wide enough to admit a column of mounted soldiers. They entered a long courtyard with stables for horses and training rings for Amazon warriors. Columns and doorways lined the walls to either side of the parade ground, but Adreona led them right down the middle toward a keep at the far end. They passed fighters practicing with spears, javelins, and bows so intently that many failed to notice the captives in their midst. Those who did gave the party little more than a dismissive glance. Tyrael admired the martial skill and discipline on display, having always thought the Horadrim would benefit greatly from Amazon members in their order.

They reached the keep, and upon entering it, Adreona showed them down several narrow corridors into a large stone chamber with a single barred window high in the wall. Somewhat surprisingly, the room had been furnished with a few rugs, a table with chairs, several beds, and unlit candles. In one corner, there was a chamber pot, and a long stone basin nearby held fresh water, fed and drained in a constant trickle by way of channels through the rock. Tyrael recognized the engineering as a Firstborn innovation.

"I trust you will be comfortable here," Adreona said as the Amazon escort removed the bindings from their hands. "Food will be brought to you shortly."

"I admit," Donan said, rubbing his wrists, "this lodging is better than I was expecting."

"You haven't yet been found guilty of a crime," she said. "You are confined as a precaution, not a punishment."

"Why confine us at all?" Lorath asked. "You can't really suspect us of piracy, can you?"

"We take no chances with outsiders," she said. "You were found in Atanos, where decent and law-abiding folk don't typically venture. And then you claimed to have a petition you wish to put before our queen. You can't really believe we would allow strangers before her without questioning them first, can you?"

Tyrael could sense that Lorath's temper had been roused, so he interjected before the man lost control of it. "We understand. You are fulfilling your duty. We will try to be patient, though our mission is pressing."

"I don't doubt that. But your mission isn't my mission." Adreona turned and marched toward the door. "Welcome to Skovos," she said as she left the chamber, and then a key could be heard turning in the lock.

A moment went by, and then Tyrael took a seat at the table. Donan did the same, and Keldon fell onto his back in one of the beds, boots propped on the footboard. Lorath paced around the room. Tyrael worried about the change he had witnessed in him following Malthael's culling. He had hoped Lorath's rage would fade with time, but, alarmingly, it had only deepened.

"This city is . . . orderly," Lorath said, seemingly as much to himself as to the rest of them. "It's peaceful. As if Malthael's reapers passed the Askari by."

"I do not believe that is so," Tyrael said. "It is orderly, yes, but did you fail to notice the empty houses? The streets in need of mending? The food rationing? This city should be bustling but has lost much of its populace. The air is heavy with the same grief I have felt elsewhere." He looked over his shoulder toward the door. "Our welcome here speaks to a state of fear and suspicion. The Askari were always an insular people, but they behave as if their islands are under siege."

"In a storm, you batten the hatches," said Keldon from the bed.

Donan nodded. "Perhaps that is the price of order."

"Perhaps," Lorath said.

Tyrael had expected a challenging reception in Skovos, especially after everything the Harbormaster had said, but he had not anticipated captivity. The *Arabel*'s forced detour into the waters of Atanos had certainly complicated their cause, but what they had witnessed there suggested a possible reason for the mistrust. The Drowned had attacked with overwhelming numbers. If the undead army had grown that large and they had taken over Atanos, then all Skovos could be threatened. That would place the Amazons of neighboring Athulua on the front lines, defending against an invasion. It seemed the Horadrim had arrived in Skovos during a time of war. But perhaps that could be turned to their advantage.

"We must respect their laws and customs," Tyrael said. "If we are to pursue our purpose here, we will need their trust. We should look for ways to earn it."

"And I'd like them to earn ours," said Lorath.

A short while later, the door opened, and two Amazon warriors entered with trays of food, escorted by two more armed guards. "Eat," one of them said as they placed the trays on the table, and they left without saying anything more. The trays held the bounty of Skovos that had been absent in the market: grilled brown snapper with crispy blackened skin, soft bread, butter, olives, tomatoes, fruit, and wine.

Lorath picked up an apple and tossed it in the air before taking a bite. "Reminds me of the Harbormaster's table back in Kingsport."

Keldon laughed. "You don't believe her trade with Skovos is legitimate, do you?"

Donan picked up the wine bottle. "Adreona did mention smugglers." Then he pointed at a stamp on the glass in the shape of a trident, the same as the marking on the bottle back in Kingsport.

"I suggest we all eat," Tyrael said. "We would not want to appear ungrateful."

Hunger was one of the many mortal experiences to which Tyrael had learned to adjust, though he could still be caught off guard at times by just how hungry he had become without noticing. He ate an entire fish himself, along with bread, apples, and everything else the trays had to offer. It seemed the others were hungry too, because they managed to clear the table in minutes.

With full bellies, they each claimed a bed and rested, though none of them removed their armor or slept. As the day wore on, the light through the window faded to a red square of sunset against the opposite wall, until that too was gone, and then the chamber descended into a twilight blue. Donan used his flint to light the candles, which offered a warm glow against the night. He sat at the table, bent in study over the book he had purchased. Tyrael felt glad that the young man had something to occupy his active, curious mind.

Eventually, they blew out the candles, and while the others drifted off to sleep, Tyrael did not. Sleep was a mortal need he had yet to master. His mind was simply not accustomed to it, and he often ignored or defied the bodily signs he received from his limbs, lying awake in contemplation. That was why he was still up when the door opened suddenly later that night and a woman strode in, accompanied by three Amazons. She carried a lantern and moved with authority, her chin held high, her thick silver hair falling loose about her shoulders; her guards wore silken tabards clasped with heavy medallions and helmets that suggested a higher rank than the warriors they'd previously encountered.

Lorath and the others woke in startlement at the intrusion and leapt from their beds, ready to fight with their bare hands. The woman appeared to feel no threat from them as she marched to the table and set down her lantern, illuminating the room.

"I am Captain Myrina," she said, "leader of the Askarra Guard and chief advisor to Queen Etara." Unlike Adreona's efficient, battle-worn armor, Myrina's appeared unblemished, gilded, almost ceremonial.

Tyrael rose from his bed. "We are honored to meet you, Captain Myrina. I am Faysal, and with me are—"

"I know your names," she said, looking him over as she spoke, seemingly fixated on his armor. "So, it's true."

"What is true?" asked Tyrael.

Myrina began to circle around him with calm, confident strides, and Tyrael could feel her eyes studying him. Despite his discomfort, he held his ground, eyes forward, trying to appear unconcerned, resisting the urge to turn and face her.

"Here in Skovos," she said, "we are surrounded by the remnants of ancient days. We are quite familiar with the appearance of angelic armor, though only its semblance carved in stone. I have never beheld a man wearing it in the flesh."

"It is . . . uncommon," he admitted.

"How did you acquire it?"

"He is uncommon," answered Lorath.

The captain glanced back and forth between them. "And what brings such uncommon company to Skovos? You don't look like pirates or smugglers. So, what are you? Treasure-seekers? Mercenaries?"

"We are scholars," Donan answered.

Myrina raised a skeptical eyebrow in the younger man's direction. "Scholars?"

"Of a kind," Tyrael answered. "We bring a petition for the queen."

"A petition?" Myrina stepped a bit closer to Tyrael, still keeping a wary distance while looking directly up into his eyes. In hers, he saw pride and layer upon layer of deception.

"On whose authority do you bring it?" she asked.

"By our own authority," he answered. "Does the queen not hear the petitions of the people?"

"But you are not of our people," answered Myrina. "What is the nature of your petition?"

Tyrael now took a step toward her, a calculated provocation that roused her guards to ready their weapons, but she held up her fist to belay them.

"I mean no disrespect to your rank, Captain," he said, "but we will only present our petition to your queen."

The wrinkles around Myrina's brown eyes twitched, and he could almost see her mind working, calculating, strategizing. "Very well," she said at last. "I am satisfied you pose no immediate threat to the queen, aside from wasting her time. You will have an audience in the morning."

With that, she pivoted away from Tyrael and spoke to the others. "My apologies for disturbing your sleep."

Then she marched from the room, and one of her guards grabbed the lantern from the table before they followed her out the door, locking it behind them.

"Well, that was odd," Donan spoke into the darkness.

"You ask me," Keldon said, "she came with a question she never asked. But I think she got her answer all the same."

"Do you think she knows who we are?" Donan asked.

"I don't know," said Lorath. "But I do know that if we're picking captains, I prefer Adreona. This Myrina is obviously more politician than soldier."

Tyrael agreed with that assessment, though he could only guess at Myrina's hidden agenda. Whatever her aim, the presence of the Horadrim in Skovos had unsettled her enough to bring her to their cell in the middle of the night. Tyrael was sure now that his decision to hide their true identities had been wise.

CHAPTER NINE

The other three did manage to doze off again, but Tyrael could not. He sat at the table, staring up at the window as it slowly admitted the gathering light of dawn into the chamber.

The encounter with Captain Myrina had left him troubled. He did not suspect she had guessed his true nature, but his angelic armor had been a subject of some significance to her. It had also seemed to draw Adreona's attention back on the *Arabel,* even if she had refrained from commenting on it directly. He wondered if he should have hidden it somehow, like their Horadric insignia. After all, the Askari lived with ever-present reminders of angels and demonkind. It seemed likely that Tyrael's armor would not be a welcome sight in Skovos and might even be a cause for suspicion. He chastised himself for not considering that sooner, but it was too late now to do anything about it.

It was late the next morning before anyone else came through the door. When the lock turned, it awakened the other three, and then Adreona entered the room, this time without any additional guards.

"I hope you slept well," she said. "I'm here to inform you that the queen will hear your petition this morning." She nodded once, as if to say her job was done, and moved to leave.

"Yes," Lorath said as he sat up, scratching his chin. "We know."

Adreona paused on her way out. "You know? How?"

"The other captain already informed us," answered Donan.

"Captain Myrina?" Adreona came back into the chamber. "She was here? When?"

"She paid us a visit in the middle of the night," Lorath said. "Seemed a bit irregular to us. Does that seem odd to you?"

Tyrael watched Adreona to assess her reaction to learning this, and indeed it seemed to surprise and alarm her, though she did what she could to quickly hide it, straightening her back and her expression.

"Of course not," she said. "I would never question a fellow captain. You may refresh in the basin. I will return for you shortly."

After she was gone, Lorath looked at Tyrael. "Maybe you're right. Perhaps all is not as orderly in Skovos as it first seemed."

"Are you surprised?" asked Donan. "I would expect to find political scheming in any royal court."

Keldon had gone to the basin to wash, and he spoke between splashes of cupped water against his face. "Anywhere there's power or money at stake, you'll find either politics or violence."

"Sometimes both," Lorath added.

Tyrael spoke with a gently commanding tone. "Let me do the talking when we have our audience with the queen. I'm even more convinced it would be wise to reveal as little as possible until we understand more about the situation here. I'm not sure who we can trust quite yet."

Lorath went to take his turn at the water basin. "I am more than happy to let you speak for us."

When Adreona returned, she brought an escort of six Amazons, all armed and looking grim. Four of them carried sets of manacles linked with chains.

"Come now," Lorath said. "Is this really necessary?"

Adreona clasped her hands behind her back. "I'm afraid there can be no compromise where the safety of the queen is concerned."

"We will consent to this one more time," Tyrael said with a hard glance at Lorath, then offered his wrists to the nearest guard.

"The outcome of your audience will determine whether it is the last time," said Adreona.

Lorath grunted an objection and extended his wrists, as did Donan, but Keldon did not, instead returning to sit on the foot of his bed.

"If it's all the same to you," he said, "I think I'll wait here."

Adreona frowned. "Why?"

"Well," the sailor said, "I ain't party to their petition. I don't even rightly know what they're after. I'm just the captain of the ship that brought them here, and I'm looking to leave Skovos just as soon as you give her back to me."

Tyrael was somewhat surprised at Keldon's assertions but could not fault the man. The sailor had carried out his side of the bargain they had made back in Kingsport. He was not a member of their order and had no personal stake in their mission.

"I see." Adreona took Keldon's manacles from the Amazon holding them and stepped toward his bed. "Did these men press you into service on your own ship?"

Keldon looked affronted. "Absolutely not."

"And did they threaten or coerce you into sailing here?"

"They did not."

"Then you are not innocent in your trespass. You will accompany them whether you are part of their petition or not, because your fate is tied to theirs." She glanced down at his wrists.

Keldon rolled his eyes with a sigh and raised his hands, which Adreona secured with the manacles. Then the Amazons marched the four of them from the chamber.

They did not take the same route as the day before but traveled deeper into the keep until they reached the first of many stone staircases, which carried them up through the inner passageways of the city and the heart of the mountain. They ascended corridors built by the Askari and walked through vaulted halls cut from the dark gray rock by the Firstborn. Tyrael recognized the geometric patterns and severe angles of the columns. The air smelled of ancient dust, as if the stone itself had undergone a form of granitic decay. No one spoke as they passed through those high chambers, but their footsteps filled the space with echoes that returned to them like whispered voices from the past.

The corridors brightened as they left those stygian depths and approached the end of their climb, where white limestone and marble replaced the dark rock. Twenty Amazon warriors guarded the final archway that marked the lower boundary of the queen's palace, arrayed in the style of armor worn by Myrina's guards the previous night. It seemed to Tyrael that a division had formed within the Amazon ranks between warriors like Adreona and those in silk.

Adreona led them up into a vast and airy basilica. Colossal carvings in relief lined the walls, above which high windows of stained glass shone with prismatic light. The carvings depicted motifs similar to those seen in the city below, but on a grander scale, and with greater artistry. Horses galloped, warships sailed, and warriors hunted and fought, portraying events from the islands' past, all surrounded by friezes of fish and seashells. Some of the panels showed monstrous beasts of myth emerging from the waves, bringing to mind the creature they had encountered during their crossing. Banners hung from the round columns, bearing emblems and sigils embroidered in gold and silver thread. But upon closer inspection, Tyrael noted that many of the pennants appeared frayed and faded. Several of the carvings had areas of wear, with cracks and chips. The mosaic tile floor needed repairs, cleaning, and polishing.

They had entered the basilica through one of its several side entrances. To their right stood massive doors of iron and wood, fitted with bronze panels into which intricate images had been hammered. They represented the queens who had ruled over Skovos throughout its long history, the seers on one door and the Amazons on the other. Tyrael assumed them to be the main doors to the palace, which visitors would approach from the outside after climbing upward through the city, but they were closed now and barred with a beam the size of a ship's mast. On the opposite side of the chamber stood doors of slightly lesser size but equal beauty and decoration, no doubt leading to the queen's throne room.

Amazon guards stood at regular intervals throughout the basilica, wielding spear and shield, though Tyrael could not say whom they would be called to defend against. The chamber was empty, its main doors shut to the public. There were no gatherings of scheming nobles, guild masters, or courtiers as one might expect to find in the anteroom before the throne.

"This way," Adreona said, her voice echoing.

She led them toward the inner doors, which opened at their approach, groaning on their ponderous hinges. They entered a chamber that appeared in some respects less ornate than the outer basilica but in other ways more—the carvings in relief had been replaced by slabs of richly colored marble with inlaid patterns of precious stones and iridescent abalone shells. Whereas the anteroom made its impression at once, appreciation for the throne room grew the longer one stood within it noticing the details, the craftsmanship, and the cost.

As in the basilica, Amazon guards stood at every pillar, which lined the length of the room on both sides. At the end of the chamber, a dais rose to a modest height beneath a soaring rotunda. The striking thrones that rested upon it appeared almost surreal in their juxtaposition against the finery that surrounded them.

Both were made from ancient wooden planks, thick and as deeply grained as driftwood but polished to a shine by endless centuries of cleaning and care, though that was only part of what made them unique. On one of them, in place of a traditional backrest, a ship's mast rose twenty feet into the air, where it terminated at a jagged break; on the other, a ship's rudder formed the top rail of the chair. Tyrael had heard the story of the Askari thrones but had never known whether to believe it. According to the legend, when the daughters of Philios first sailed to Skovos, great sea monsters had attacked and broken their ship upon the rocks. The wood from their vessel was later used to fashion two thrones: one for the Amazon Queen, and one for the Oracle Queen, corulers of their new island kingdom. The chairs before Tyrael certainly appeared as if they could have come from a shipwreck.

A woman of advanced age sat in the throne with the mast, wearing armor more highly wrought and gilded than any Tyrael had yet seen in Skovos. She sat up tall, with a regal bearing somehow amplified by the rustic nature of her throne, rather than diminished by it. Her white hair flowed beneath a golden circlet like rapids over a fall. No one sat on the throne with the rudder over its backrest. Captain Myrina stood at attention between the two seats.

Upon entering the chamber, Adreona and her Amazons bowed. Tyrael followed their example of deference, as did Keldon and the other two Horadrim.

"The petitioners may step forward!" Captain Myrina called, her voice resounding against the stone.

Tyrael moved toward the dais, and his comrades followed, until two guards extended their spears to block their approach. The four of them stood shoulder to shoulder nine or ten paces from the throne.

"You stand before the Mast," Myrina said, "which is upheld by Etara, Amazon Queen of the Askari." She gestured to her left. "You also stand in the presence of the Helm, which represents the guiding foresight of the Oracle Queen, who by tradition dwells in her temple on the island of Philios."

"We are honored," said Tyrael, bowing his head once more.

"Why are they shackled?" asked the queen. Her warm voice crackled around the edges but retained much of its former strength, like an ancient stone wall baked by the sun.

"It is for your safety, my queen," said Adreona from behind them.

Etara waved off her words. "Release them."

"Your majesty." Adreona stepped forward. "I would recommend against—"

"I said, release them."

Adreona hesitated, frowning.

"Your queen gave you a command," Myrina said.

Adreona closed her eyes, exhaled, and bowed. She then marched to stand before Tyrael, footsteps echoing, and proceeded to unlock his manacles. She let them fall to the ground with a loud clang and then did the same for Lorath, Donan, and Keldon. When she stepped away from them, she took up a position near the dais, watching them, rather than returning to the rear of the room.

"That's better," Etara said. "Why were they bound in the first place?"

Myrina leaned toward her. "Suspicion of piracy, my queen."

"Still?" Etara asked. "I thought the Askarra Guard had searched their ship and found no evidence."

Adreona cleared her throat. "That is correct, your majesty."

Etara said nothing for a few moments, then turned her attention from her officers to Tyrael. "They told me that one of you wore an angel's armor, but they did not tell me how you obtained it."

"The armor was part of my inheritance," he answered. "A gift of my lineage going back countless generations."

"I see," said the queen. "Much like this throne of flotsam on which I sit." She leaned forward. "I am satisfied that you are not pirates or smugglers. But you are *someone,* aren't you? You have a remarkable presence. What is your name?"

"Faysal, your majesty."

"And why are you in Skovos, Faysal?"

Tyrael adjusted his words to speak as much truth as he deemed prudent. "We are scholars, your majesty. Historians. We have been traveling throughout Sanctuary, assessing the widespread devastation following the events of several years ago."

Etara sat back on her throne, touching her index finger to her lips. "To what end?"

"We want to understand what was lost," Tyrael said. "We wish to assess how people are rebuilding and to preserve what useful knowledge we can."

"Your endeavor is virtuous," Etara said, emphasizing the word in a way that filled it with significance. "Here in Skovos, we do not follow Akarat or Skatsim. We do not put our faith in external powers but trust in ourselves as we strive to follow the Three Virtues: life, courage, and wisdom. I am pleased that your mission seems guided by all three."

"I hope it is, your majesty."

"What is it you seek from me?" the queen asked.

Tyrael glanced at his companions, then said, "From what we have heard, and the little we have witnessed, Skovos has recovered better and more quickly from the Reaping than any other city or people we know of. We seek your permission to travel your islands, to learn from you, so that we might understand how you have achieved this."

"In other words," Adreona said, "they wish to spy on us."

The queen frowned at her. "That seems a rather hostile interpretation, Captain," she said, which brought a flush to Adreona's cheeks.

"My queen," Myrina said, "Adreona has served valiantly on Athulua for many years, leading our forces in the fight against the Drowned. It is only natural that she would look for threats and enemies, out of habit."

Tyrael sensed that Myrina intended that statement as some form of veiled insult, even though it seemed exculpatory, but he still had no guess as to what the captain's private motives might be.

"I suppose that is true," the queen said, turning toward her advisor. "How would *you* answer these scholars' petition?"

Myrina regarded them for a few moments. "I do not believe they pose a threat. They have broken no laws, and were they to do so, they would be punished accordingly. Until then, I see no reason to deny them."

"Your majesty." Adreona dropped to one knee, bowing her head. "May I speak?"

The queen nodded. "You may."

Adreona stood and gestured toward Tyrael. "I do not wish any harm upon these strangers. That is why I recommend we return them to their ship and escort them safely from Skovos. After they have left our waters, they may sail where they choose. These are perilous times, my queen. The threats we face—"

"That is enough," Etara said, her gaze turning hard. "We will speak no more of that here."

Adreona's mouth snapped shut, and it seemed to require tremendous restraint for her to keep it that way; the muscles in her jaw and neck remained drawn. The queen watched her for several moments, then spoke in a resonant, formal tone.

"I have made a decision. As with all that we Askari do, we must be guided now by the virtues we cherish. Faysal, you and your scholars may remain in Skovos, but there are conditions for my continued forbearance."

Tyrael nodded. "We will abide by such conditions as you set, your majesty."

"In service to courage," she continued, "one of you will accompany Captain Adreona to Athulua, where you will fight to defend our islands."

Adreona looked up suddenly, as if to object, but held her tongue.

"In service to wisdom," the queen went on, "I ask that Faysal remain in Temis, for I am curious about him and his scholarly travels. There is much I wish to discuss. Finally, in service to life, one of you may travel freely throughout our islands to learn more about how we have preserved the lives of our people."

Tyrael balked at the idea of separation but did not have the grounds to object. Their circumstances had placed them at the mercy of the queen, and she had rendered her judgment in a way that did not allow for negotiation.

"Where does that leave me?" Keldon asked.

The queen furrowed her brow. "Who are you?"

Myrina answered, "He is the captain of the ship that brought them here."

"I see." Etara tapped her foot, as if she had grown suddenly impatient with the proceedings. "You must remain in Skovos, I'm afraid. You and your vessel will be required to sail the others away from here when the time comes for them to leave. You may choose which of the three you will accompany."

"Thank you, your majesty," Keldon said, without even attempting to feign sincere gratitude.

"May we confer amongst ourselves, your majesty?" Tyrael asked.

She inclined her head. "You may."

The four drew closer together in a huddle, whispering as quietly as they could.

"I vote we leave," said Lorath. "Return to Westmarch, where we're needed."

"I think we're needed here," Donan replied. "The Drowned are an evil of unquestionable danger. And you said yourself, things aren't as orderly as they seem. But I do regret dragging Keldon into this."

"You got me my *Arabel* back," the sailor said. "We're even."

"I agree with Donan," Tyrael said. "Yes, we must accomplish what we came to do, but I feel there is a darkness in Skovos, beyond the Drowned. I have only fragments, glimpsed like passing shadows. Our aid in this moment may prevent the isles from falling fully into ruin—as so much of Sanctuary already has."

Lorath stared at his boots, arms folded, shaking his head. Then he looked up and said, "I guess that means I'm going with the Amazons to Athulua."

"Why you?" Donan asked.

Lorath shrugged. "You like puzzles. If anyone can find out what happened to the Horadrim, it's you."

Donan accepted this with a reluctant nod.

"Then we are agreed," said Tyrael. "All that remains is for Keldon to decide which of you he will accompany. Or would you rather stay on Temis?"

The sailor thrust his hands into his pockets. "Guess I'll go with Lorath."

"Me?" Lorath said. "Why?"

Tyrael felt some surprise at Keldon's choice as well. The sailor knew firsthand the peril he would face on Athulua, and it had seemed during the crossing that he got along better with Donan.

"No offense," Keldon said, "but I'd rather not sit around on Temis having audiences with the queen, and between the other two choices, I'd rather go where the fighting is."

"Fair enough," said Lorath.

CHAPTER TEN

Aside from Tyrael's assignment, Queen Etara seemed uninterested in their activities, so long as her requirements were met. Of the possible tasks, Donan had privately hoped to go in search of the missing expedition, but not because he wanted to avoid the dangers of Athulua and the Drowned. Rather, he relished the mystery and the hunt, the puzzle of it, though he worried the others would think him cowardly if it seemed he wanted to escape the fight. He even wondered if Lorath had volunteered only because he believed Donan inadequate to the challenge, or, worse, to protect him.

Adreona had seemed quite displeased with the arrangement imposed upon her. Donan assumed she would have objected to any of them coming with her, but it seemed particularly irksome to her when it was Lorath who stepped forward.

At the conclusion of their audience with Queen Etara, they wasted no time. With Adreona's approval, it was agreed that Keldon could sail Lorath and Adreona to Athulua on his ship, to keep the vessel closer to him, instead of leaving it in the Temis harbor. Donan was glad for that, since the *Arabel* seemed so important to the sailor.

They were to leave immediately, and Donan and Tyrael decided to see them off down at the wharf.

They left through a wicket in the palace's main entrance, leaving the larger, more impressive doors barred. Outside, the grand portico offered staggering views of the city and the harbor below, where rowed ships skidded across the sparkling water like insects. From that vantage, Donan could see several of the other Skovos islands, both near and distant. He knew that Philios lay behind him, out of view on the other side of Temis. To the southeast lay an isle covered in lush forests from which a soft mist seemed to emanate. The wind from that direction smelled almost perfumed with floral fragrances and plant life.

"That is Lycander," Adreona said, having noticed the direction of his attention. "It is a wild place, of abundant beauty, occupied by artists and philosophers. Young Amazons train to hunt in its forests, keeping the island's residents safe."

"I'll remember that," Donan said.

She turned and pointed in the opposite direction, to the northwest. "That is Athulua, which we passed sailing here. Beyond it lies Atanos." She glanced at him sidelong. "I don't think I need to remind you against traveling there. Beyond Atanos lies Celestia, which you can almost see from here."

"What is that island like?"

"Somewhat abandoned," she said. "I seldom have reason to go there. Seers from Philios keep an astronomical observatory on the coast."

Beyond Celestia, dark clouds hung in the sky, but as Donan studied them, they ceased to resemble a thunderstorm and looked more like rising smoke. "What is that beyond Celestia?"

"That is Skartara," she said. "It's a volcanic island. Eruptions from Mount Hefaetrus render most of it uninhabitable. I can't imagine you will have any reason to travel there."

"I'm grateful for your advice," Donan said.

"Then let me give you a little more. We Askari are proud, with an ancient and noble heritage. If you are treated with suspicion or distrust, please remember that we have endured great misfortune and loss. Trust can be dangerous in times like these, and we are reluctant to risk it. But if you prove yourself worthy of our trust, you will find no warmer people."

"Thank you for that, Captain."

Adreona gave him a subtle nod. "I wish you safety on your journey, wherever it takes you."

They descended through the city along its paved streets and numerous switchbacks. Donan noted the aspects of Temis that Tyrael had observed—boarded-up dwellings, empty shops, disrepair—and he came to the same conclusion: Malthael's reapers had indeed laid waste to Skovos, just as they had throughout Sanctuary. Yet conditions in Skovos did seem far better than in Westmarch, or Lut Gholein, or Entsteig, and Donan wanted to understand why. That question would not be his primary mission, but Tyrael's mild deception about their real purpose contained a degree of truth.

Down at the wharf, they found the *Arabel* safe and secured to the same pier where they had left her, deck and rigging well ordered. Those who had searched her for evidence of piracy had apparently taken care to put her back to rights. The day was sunny and calm, and in the water around the docks, Donan saw striped sheepshead fish searching for crustaceans. A few Amazon warriors met their party near the ship. They brought the Horadrim their packs, along with Donan's staff and Lorath's polearm. They did not have El'druin with them.

"Your sword is in Queen Etara's safekeeping," one of the women said.

Tyrael seemed unsurprised. "Is it, now?"

"She asks that you reclaim it from her."

"You may inform her I will do so shortly," he answered.

Lorath came over and took Donan's shoulder in a firm grip.

"Your first mission on your own," he said. "Are you ready?"

Donan sighed. "I was on my own when you found me, or have you forgotten? I know how to take care of myself. You don't need to worry about me."

"Then I won't. And you don't need to worry about me, even though I *am* sailing to a battlefront."

Donan laughed. "Looking for a fight."

"Always."

Though they jested, they had both spoken a truth. "Tread carefully, Lorath."

Then Tyrael approached and clasped Lorath's forearm. "Send word as you can. And avoid unnecessary risk—"

"I know, I know," Lorath said. "Farewell, both of you."

By that time, a cutter had arrived to tow the *Arabel* out of the Great Harbor. Lorath, Keldon, and Adreona boarded the ship, and soon they were underway. Tyrael and Donan remained on the pier, watching them grow distant. Gulls shrieked overhead, and a large cloud moved in front of the sun, plunging much of the city into shadow.

"Do you think the members of the previous expedition are still alive?" Donan asked.

"I do not know," said Tyrael, "but I have hope."

"If they are, they must be living in secret, given the reception we have received."

"The same thought had occurred to me."

"What else can you tell me about them?"

Tyrael looked up as if searching his far-reaching memory. "There were five Horadrim. I appointed a Xian woman named Sho-Ren as their leader. She had left her home to study in the Yshari Sanctum and became a mage of some skill. I remember her as someone with a very firm but even temperament."

"A mage?" Donan considered that for a moment. "I think I will start on Philios."

"Why there?"

"Just a hunch that a mage would be drawn more to the Oracle than the Amazons. That's all I have to go on for now."

Tyrael nodded. "Your reasoning is sound."

"What will you do here? Aside from placating the queen?"

"I plan to listen."

"What for?"

Tyrael turned toward him. "The secrets Myrina is keeping."

Donan nodded, scanning the harbor. He had lost sight of the *Arabel* among the other ships. Keldon and Lorath would soon be sailing toward Athulua. He decided it was time he embarked, so after bidding Tyrael goodbye, he wandered the streets of Temis until he found a narrow shop selling provisions, although of limited supply. The merchant wore his hair in oiled plaits and his face shaven, and his greeting was in a vernacular that Donan failed to understand. This seemed to irritate the vendor, but he grudgingly switched to the common language of the continents to ask, "What do you want?"

"My apologies," Donan said. "What were you speaking just then?"

"Coin-tongue."

"Fascinating." A dedicated language of trade suggested more robust commerce in the islands' past, a time when they had exchanged commodities and goods with many nations and peoples. "I'm here for food and supplies," Donan said. "I'll be traveling in Skovos for a time."

"You can see what I have," the merchant said. "My shop is not what it was, and not what it should be."

"What should it be?"

"Are you here to buy, or are you here to talk? I am here to sell, and that is all."

"I'm . . . here to buy," Donan answered.

He quickly selected some victuals that would last him long and keep well but soon realized he should have agreed on the prices beforehand. The merchant wanted to charge much more than Donan would have expected to pay, even in an overpriced market, and the man could not be haggled any lower. Back in Gea Kul, the merchants at least tried to justify their gouging with elaborate excuses and stories of misfortune, but the Skovos vendor seemed to feel no shame at all, as if Donan were in the wrong to expect any different. He paid the man but was left wondering if an Askari would have received the same price or if he was paying an outsider's premium.

He left the shop and continued through the city. Perhaps it was the lingering residue of that encounter dimming his perspective, but afterward it seemed that every eye he met looked back at him with suspicion and even outright hostility. He had planned to purchase a few more things, such as a length of good rope and perhaps a tarpaulin to sleep under if he were ever caught in the rain, but he gave up on these and returned to the docks, hoping to buy passage on the first ship to Philios.

On one of the piers, he saw dockhands unloading sacks of grain from an Askari cargo vessel, and the goods all bore the trident stamp he had noticed on the wine bottles. They labored under the watchful gaze of several Amazons who wore the armor and silken tabards of the Askarra Guard. He approached one of the warriors with his query, but she seemed confused by it.

"I suppose there might be a ship that could carry you," she said. "But most people take the Eye."

"The Eye?"

"The Bridge of the Eye. It's on the northeast side of the island."

Donan thanked her and set off in that direction, crossing Temis in a meandering orbit beneath the palace, keeping to the base of the mountains. The journey took the better part of that day and carried him through silent and empty quarters of the city. Though the dust of crumbled limewash gathered in unswept corners and house upon house stood vacant, it was easy to imagine a fuller time, when children splashed in the fountains, neighbors called to passersby from their windows, and hawkers trundled along the streets with their carts of fresh fish or garden produce.

Then Donan came to an open field that confounded and halted him. A wall surrounded it, with arched entrances at its four corners. Neighboring buildings shoved right up against it, but no crops grew there, not even grass. He saw no tools, no marks in the dirt, no signs of planned construction. No indications of any purpose at all. An unused field in the middle of a city made little sense, especially considering the apparent paucity of food. The enclosure lay before Donan like a riddle, demanding he divert from his path to solve it. When he stepped into the field, he noticed its utter stillness. Not even insects chirped or buzzed. The silence almost had a presence, the potent inverse of something deafening, a void that seemed to swallow all noise.

Though unsettled, he took a few steps inward, looking around, and saw a woman kneeling in the shadow of the field's wall. Her dark clothing and veil had prevented him from noticing her until then. It took him a few moments to decide whether to approach her, but his curiosity won out.

"Pardon me," he said, keeping his voice hushed, without knowing why. "Can you tell me, what is this place?"

She looked up at him. The veil obscured her features, but through its gauze he could see smooth cheeks, bronze hair, and wet eyes. "You are a mainlander."

"Yes," he said, "I am. I hope I haven't caused offense with my question."

She lowered her face. "You do not offend me. I wish more people knew and understood, but few come here anymore. Few want to remember."

"Remember what?"

"The night the reapers came. They swept through the city without mercy, without regard for age or station. They took my children. They took my husband. I wish they had taken me." She spoke wearily and without emotion, without any vitality at all behind her words.

Donan swallowed, almost choking on the dry air as the sun drew sweat from his brow. "I'm sorry," he whispered, which sounded pathetic and inadequate as soon as he said it.

"There were so many to bury," she said. "So many corpses. The city reeked of death. Something had to be done." Her head swiveled from side to side. "This was once a market square. They tore up the paving and dug a hole, deep, down to the waterline. All the dead went into it."

Donan looked again at the field, which was large enough to contain thousands and thousands of bodies. "A mass grave."

"They call it the Field of Sorrow." She made a choking sound between a sob and a laugh. "I call it the Field of Shame."

"Why?" he risked asking.

"Because they never speak of it. It reminds them of their failure. They want to forget it even exists."

"Who?"

She looked upward, toward the royal palace that loomed over the island. "The queens. The Oracle didn't warn us. Captain Myrina and her Amazons did nothing to protect us. We had to defend ourselves, but my husband was a potter. An artist. He had never—" Her head fell, and she said nothing for several long moments. "The reaper struck him down in an instant."

Her account threatened to dredge up memories Donan could not afford to indulge. He also found it difficult to believe that Etara and Myrina had done nothing to defend Temis during Malthael's assault, but he knew enough about grief to keep those doubts to himself.

"I am glad that you remember him," Donan said. "And your children."

"I remember because I can't forget. There is a difference."

Donan bowed his head. "So there is."

She labored to her feet like a woman much older than she appeared beneath her veil. "I must go now."

"I appreciate you speaking with me," Donan said. He felt a desperate desire to help her somehow, and on an impulse, he reached into his purse for a few coins, which he extended toward her. It was a clumsy gesture.

"What am I to do with that?" she asked, looking down at the money in his palm. Then she turned and drifted across the field to depart through an archway on the far side. It was some distance, and she was unhurried, but Donan waited where he stood until she had gone—it felt disrespectful to leave before her, though she never looked back at him. Then he exited the Field of Sorrow by the nearer archway through which he had entered and resumed his course.

The island of Philios ascended from the sea as a mountainous plateau many times the size of Temis, with soaring cliffs above a rocky, battered shore. Over eons, the endless crashing of the waves had steadily carved deep caves into the island's foundations, and according to a legend Donan had read, it was in one of those caves where the first seer discovered the Sightless Eye. Atop the plateau rose Mount Karcheus, an extinguished volcano named for a mythic companion of Philios, the summit of which reached high enough to breach the clouds and wear a crown of ice throughout the seasons.

The sun had fallen well into its afternoon decline when Donan reached the bridge that connected the island of Temis to neighboring Philios. He had beheld few constructions to rival it in size and engineering achievement; it was plainly of Firstborn origin. The sharp arches of its double arcade threw swords of light onto the water below, and its massive stone columns stood at wide enough intervals to admit the largest ships between them. It spanned a wide sea channel, and towered high above the churning water.

Donan could see light traffic on the upper tier of the bridge but none on the lower tier, which he assumed to be an aqueduct bringing meltwater from Karcheus into the capital city. He made his way up through the winding streets until he attained the same level as the lower bridge, and from there it was a simple matter of asking directions.

Askarra Guard stood watch over the entrance to the Eye, collecting tolls and turning away those who could not pay them. They seemed to apply more scrutiny to Donan than they did anyone else nearby, but they ultimately accepted his coin and let him pass.

The bridge was as wide as a market thoroughfare, with enough space to allow horse-drawn wagons to pass one another going different directions without risk to the pedestrians on either side. From a distance, he had wondered about the stability of the construction, given its age, but now that he stood upon it, the masonry felt as secure as solid rock. Even so, he avoided looking down to the sea below. He shared the bridge with only a few other travelers, but he joined their flow and left the city-island of Temis behind him.

CHAPTER ELEVEN

Lorath said nothing to Adreona as the cutter rowed them from the harbor out into open water, and she said nothing to him. After they passed under the colossal statues of angel and demon, they worked together to raise the *Arabel*'s sails, but neither of them spoke more than the few words necessary to set the rigging. Lorath genuinely felt no anger toward her, despite their brief imprisonment at her insistence, and despite her desire to banish them from Skovos. He did not resent her personally for the relative prosperity of Skovos compared to other cities and regions in Sanctuary. Yet he sensed her anger toward him, radiating off her like heat ripples off an Aranoch horizon, and in truth he found that more than a little unjust.

They had the wind at their back, out of the southeast, and the *Arabel* galloped with glee across the waves. Once they were underway, Lorath took up a position near the stern, next to Keldon at the tiller. Adreona stood on the other side of the captain. Keldon seemed quite content with the silence, but Lorath was not. Eventually, he had to speak his mind.

"Captain," he said, "this arrangement may not be what either of us would've wanted, but you can trust me. I swear I will do my best to fight for you and—"

"I don't want you to fight," she said, as if the words had been waiting on her tongue. "Not for me, and not for Skovos. I want you to stay out of my way. I don't have time to be your minder."

Lorath worked to keep his pride in check. "Look, I did not want to come to Skovos in the first place. But now that I'm here, your queen has commanded me to fight. That's what I was doing before we sailed to your islands, and that's what I plan to do while I'm here. I could be of help to you."

"I doubt that," she said. "I plan to keep you where you can do no harm."

"Do you often disregard the orders of your queen?"

That finally turned her head toward him. "Queen Etara did not give any command as to *how* you would fulfill your duty. There are many tasks within our ranks, and all of them are important. All of them are performed in service to the islands we safeguard."

"Why am I sensing latrine duty in my future?"

"Perhaps you should be with the seers instead of troubling me."

"We're luffing," Keldon said between them.

Lorath looked up, then moved to trim the mainsail, while Adreona saw to the jib. After that, they resumed their silence for a time, until Adreona spoke with a somewhat gentler manner than before.

"This isn't personal," she said. "How can it be, when I don't know you?"

"If you did know me, you would—"

"Please, I am trying to explain something."

Lorath closed his mouth and nodded.

"You are strangers," she said. "You are unfamiliar with our customs, but you do know something of the threat we face, since that threat would've killed you if we had not arrived when we did."

"And I'm grateful you—"

"I'm not finished. I said you know *something* of the threat, but you don't know all of it. The Amazons lost many, many warriors during the Reaping. We were slaughtered, and our legions have not recovered. Meanwhile, the Drowned have only grown their ranks. My forces are barely holding the line. If we should break . . ." She paused, as if momentarily seized by that thought. "So, you see, our position is fragile. We cannot risk any weakness or disruption, no matter how well intentioned. As I said, I don't know you, and it is because I don't know you that I cannot afford to trust you with the lives of my troops."

"I understand," Lorath said.

"Do you?"

"I do. I was a soldier. I understand the importance of troop cohesion and the danger of a weak link."

She tilted her head. "I'm glad to hear it."

"Put me to work in whatever capacity you deem best." Lorath had accepted he would get nowhere convincing her with words. "I can dig a hole as well as anyone."

"I never doubted *that,*" she said.

They had come to a workable understanding, at least for now, and the tension between them eased. Even Keldon appeared somewhat more relaxed at the tiller. Lorath did not look forward to the menial tasks he would soon be assigned, but he knew that he could earn Adreona's trust in time, if not her respect. He wondered only if they would be in Skovos long enough for him to achieve it.

As the *Arabel* approached Athulua, Adreona directed Keldon away from the island's main commercial port and toward a fortified Amazon harbor farther along the coast. There they sailed into a shallow bay, where thick tree trunks had been sunk deep into the silt to form an enclosing palisade out in the water. But this fortification had not been raised against storm surges and tidal swells. It was a martial defense. At their approach, a sea-gate opened in the wall to allow the sloop entrance into the harbor.

"This was built after the Drowned attacked our fleet at anchor," she said. "They managed to sink several ships before we even knew they were down there."

"That shows greater intelligence than I thought the Drowned possessed," Lorath said.

"Yes. They seem to be getting smarter."

Inside the palisade were many dozens of tall-masted warships secured to rows of floating docks like ranks of soldiers standing at attention, waiting for their orders. As in the Great Harbor of Temis, the seawall thwarted the wind, and a rowboat approached the *Arabel* to tow them in. The delay and extra labor set Adreona pacing the deck.

"Your ship needs oars," she said to Keldon.

"Never required them before," he answered. "The wind never stops a-blowing off Westmarch."

Where the palisade met the shore, the wooden fortification became a wall of stone that continued overland, securing a large patch of earth with a central keep much like the garrison where they had spent the previous night. Beyond the wall to the west, highland fells brooded over a rolling farmland of pasture and crop.

"This stronghold is called Fort Galina," said Adreona. "Named in honor of an Amazon captain. It was from this fastness that she defended Athulua against a pirate armada three centuries ago."

The tug rowed them to a floating pier not far from the fort's main wharf. After securing the *Arabel,* they marched from their dock to the shore, where they were met by several warriors. Some of them eyed Lorath and Keldon with suspicion, others with curiosity, others with derision.

The foremost of them bowed her head to Adreona and said, "It's good to have you back, Captain."

"Believe me, Tavie," Adreona said, "it is very good to be back."

The woman grinned. "I take it you did not enjoy your time among the silks?"

"I did not."

Tavie appeared slightly younger than Adreona, with dark skin and sharp cheekbones. She wore her black hair in thick, twisted locs, each ringed with bands of silver; the emblem of a serpent coiled across her armor. She craned her neck to look at Lorath and then raised her eyebrow at Adreona in an unspoken question.

"Yes, our guests," Adreona said with a deep sigh. "This is Lorath and Keldon. The queen has shown forbearance toward these mainlanders. They will be with us for the time being. They'll need rations and billet, preferably somewhere I can keep an eye on them."

"Very good, Captain. But if I might ask . . ."

"Yes, Shieldmatron?"

Tavie leaned in. "What will they be *doing* here?"

"Queen Etara sent us to help you," Lorath interjected, "in whatever ways your captain sees fit to use us."

The intrusion earned him a glare from Tavie, while Adreona simply ignored him and strode away in the direction of the keep. Lorath, Keldon, and the Amazons all fell in behind, but Tavie quickened her pace to march beside her.

"I have not decided what to do with them," Adreona said, loudly enough for Lorath to hear behind her. "For now, put them to work in the stables."

Then it was Keldon who glowered at Lorath. "I should've gone with Donan," he said.

To reach the keep, they passed through the encampment that surrounded it, and everywhere Lorath looked, he saw the familiar signs of an active military campaign. They passed sheds for storing and dispensing supplies, both food and other equipment. They passed infirmary tents where healers tended to Amazons—some of them grievously wounded, it appeared. They passed training areas, though they were not as numerous or as large as at the garrison in Temis. They passed the kitchen, the ovens, and the mess tent where warriors sat eating their food rations. From somewhere inside the fortress walls, Lorath heard the metallic hammering of a smithy, and he smelled smokehouses curing fish and pork. They passed orderly columns of tents used as personal quarters, outside of which Amazons sat sharpening their blades. A small group of them made music together on flute, lyre, and hoop drum.

All along the way, Adreona received the sincere welcome and affection of the warriors under her command, and she took the time to speak with many of them, calling them by name. Between those interactions, she had Tavie catch her up to speed on the fort's activities. Lorath tried to listen in without making his interest obvious.

"How many patrols in the field?" she asked.

"Three," Tavie replied.

"Are they all on schedule?"

"Yes, Captain."

"Any Drowned incursions to report?"

"No, Captain."

"Any news from the Athulua Garrison?"

"No, it's been calm."

"I don't like that word," Adreona said. "It invites the storm."

The keep itself stood near the fort's main gate, where warriors upon the wall faced the land beyond armed with spear and bow. In a nearby courtyard, Lorath saw the stables and animal pens where he expected to soon be working. Chickens roamed freely outside their coop, pecking at hard ground compacted by the accumulated weight of innumerable foot- and hoof-falls.

The entrance to the keep forced them through a narrow corridor with a raised portcullis at each end. Along the passageway, Lorath looked up into murder holes in the ceiling, through which hot sand, boiling water, or deadly substances of a magical variety could be poured onto invading enemies.

At the end of the corridor, they entered the great hall at the center of the keep. Three levels of columned balconies looked down on the chamber from above, each lined with doorways. Glass deck prisms had been installed in the roof high above as if it were the upper deck of a ship, admitting a strained greenish light into the hall. The air smelled of dry stone and incense. A few rugs lined the floor, bearing the stains and patterns of wear that came from long use, and the banners hanging from the balconies appeared dingy and gray. The wooden benches and tables had many notches and dents but were otherwise oiled and well cared for. The appointments gave Lorath the impression of former glory, enjoyed during periods of greater status and priority for the fort.

A battle plan covered the largest of the tables at one end of the hall, and Lorath sauntered over toward it. The map portrayed all of Athulua and a portion of Atanos, with labels for Askari settlements and tokens representing the placement of Amazon troops. Adreona had been honest when she said they had suffered losses—their forces were spread thin. On Athulua's northern coast was a site labeled TEMPLE OF COURAGE, which he assumed to be the structure he had seen in the clouds while sailing to Temis. Near the middle of the western shore, he noted a fortified position, which he assumed to be the garrison Tavie had mentioned, as well as a marking near it, set just off the western coast, portraying the image of a flame.

"You are needed in the stables," Adreona said, standing behind him.

Lorath accepted this with a slow nod, then looked around the hall. "Did Keldon already head out there?"

"He asked my permission to work at the dock instead, which I granted."

"I see."

"Welcome to Athulua."

She turned and strode away toward Tavie and a waiting group of warriors. Lorath took another glance at the map and then left the hall.

He found the stablemaster in the fort's barn, leaning against a thick timber post with her arms folded, watching over a dappled gray mare with her foal in one of the pens. The little white colt stood firmly on its spindly legs as it nursed. The stablemaster appeared older than many of the warriors Lorath had seen in the fort, her black hair threaded with pewter. Instead of armor, she wore brown woolen trousers and a leather vest over a linen shirt. A puckered and ragged scar ran the length of her left forearm and disappeared up her rolled sleeve.

"Almost gives one hope," she said as Lorath approached.

"What does?" he asked.

She nodded toward the foal. "New life. Brief as it may be on this island."

Lorath was reminded of something Tyrael had once said about mortality. "Every story comes to an end, but that doesn't mean it's not worth telling."

The stablemaster looked at him fully then, her brown eyes flicking back and forth between his. "I like that," she said. "You must be the new stable hand."

"Reporting for duty," he answered.

"I've been told to keep you busy."

"To keep me out of trouble, you mean."

"Why? Are you much trouble?"

"I won't be for you."

"Glad to hear it." She unfolded her arms and extended her hand for a shake. "I'm Tanna. The proud mother there is Zerae, and the little one is Arjak. He's only two months old, but he'll grow into a fine warhorse one day. And you are?"

"Lorath."

"Been around horses much, Lorath?"

"I have."

"But I don't imagine you've mucked out many stalls."

"What makes you say that?"

"You carry yourself like you know how to use that polearm on your back." She made a show of appraising him. "I wonder if you've got what it takes to wield a shovel or a pitchfork."

"My father was a blacksmith," he said. "I'm not afraid of hard labor."

She laughed. "We'll see about that."

She spent the next few days trying to prove him wrong. Lorath had hoped that the same muscles used for swinging a polearm would help him heave a shovel, but he quickly discovered that was not the case. The fort kept a herd of more than thirty horses for scouting patrols and messengers, as well as a large drove of swine and a few goats for their milk. At the end of each day spent feeding the animals, cleaning the stables, and hauling barrow after barrow of manure from the fort to the dung heap outside its walls, he fell into bed exhausted. He had been given the loft above the barn for his quarters, and he awoke on his pallet each morning with stiff limbs and joints. The intensity of the labor did much to quiet the beast within him but could not silence it completely. He never saw Keldon, though he heard the sailor had been hard at work himself assisting the shipwrights and dockhands. Lorath saw Adreona only in passing as she marched through the camp, and she seemed to pay him no mind at all. He began to wonder if he truly would be spending his stay in Skovos as a muckraker. Fortunately, he made a much more favorable impression on Tanna. He and the stablemaster got along well, often working side by side for long stretches, speaking easily, though infrequently.

On the fifth day since he had arrived at Fort Galina, she called him to her in the midafternoon, and they settled on a bench near the chicken coop for a rest. She had a honey cake and a wineskin, which she offered to him. He gratefully accepted both, gulping the wine down first without really even tasting it.

"Easy there," she said. "There's work yet to be done before this day is through."

Lorath wiped his mouth on his sleeve. "I'll be fine. But thank you for this."

"You're welcome. Now, eat the cake."

Lorath's daily rations consisted of the same plain food received by everyone else in the fort, as far as he knew—bread, cheese, porridge, beans, sometimes fish, sometimes meat—so he relished the rich sweetness of honey on his tongue. A few chickens had bobbed up close to his feet, clucking and hoping for crumbs to fall.

"Where did you get this?" Lorath asked.

Tanna shrugged. "Cook owed me a favor."

"And you wasted it on me?"

"Are you saying I shouldn't have?"

"No, I—"

"Relax. Just enjoy it. You've earned it." She rubbed the scar on her left arm. "I know how frustrating it is to be held back from the fight."

Lorath had been curious about Tanna's history since meeting her. Until this moment, she had kept their conversations far away from the personal, but sitting here with him in the sun, she seemed less guarded. "How long have you been the stablemaster?"

"A few years."

"And before that?"

She sat up straighter. "I was a shieldmatron. I fought the Drowned on the front line dozens of times, killed hundreds of them. Until the day one of those undead bastards almost took my arm. But luck and a bit of magic were on my side." She raised her arm and flexed her fingers. The muscles beneath her scar rippled and tightened irregularly. "I can't carry a shield anymore. Not reliably. And if my war-sisters can't rely on me, I endanger them."

"I'm sorry—"

"I don't want your pity." She snatched the wineskin from him and poured several gulps down her throat. "I've been fortunate."

"How so?"

"Maybe you've heard the expression that an Amazon warrior never grows old? Most people think that's about dying in battle, but it's not. The truth is that some Amazons take their own lives when they reach the point where they can't fight anymore." She waved toward the encampment with the wineskin, spilling some on the ground. "For many of us, this is all we've ever known. What are we going to do, become farmers? Weavers? Fishwives?"

"I imagine that would be difficult," Lorath said.

"Difficult? For many, it's impossible. They can't imagine another life. They don't *want* another life."

"It seems you did."

She looked down at the chickens pecking curiously at the wet dirt where the wine drops had fallen. "After I was injured, the pain in my arm would keep me up at night. I'd lie in my cot, right down there in that same healers' tent, and I would think about ending it all. But one day, Captain Adreona came to me, and she gave me a gift."

"What was it?"

"She told me that she and my sisters still needed me. She said that if my days of fighting to defend life were at an end, then perhaps it was time I start helping to bring it into the world. She knew I'd always had a way with horses. She told me the stablemaster position was waiting for me as soon as I was healed. And that was her gift. She offered me a way to stay here, in my home, and serve the virtue of life."

"And the virtue of courage," Lorath added.

"What do you mean?"

He wondered if he had overstepped. "I think it takes great courage to face and accept one's limitations."

She leaned her head back against the coop. "I hadn't thought of that."

Neither spoke for a few moments. The remainder of Lorath's honey cake had gone uneaten while he listened to her story. Tanna suddenly reached over and broke off a piece, which she popped into her mouth and chewed.

"The captain is wise beyond her years," she said.

"I'm beginning to see that."

"I know you're frustrated. I would be too, if I were you. There are still days when I grip that pitchfork in my hands like it's a spear, and I yearn to be back on the battlefield. But I think you might have misunderstood Adreona."

"How so?"

"You think she's keeping you here because she doesn't trust you, and maybe you're right. But I think she might be keeping you here to save your life."

CHAPTER TWELVE

The next day, a storm swept in, dragging sheets of rain over the fort. Lightning flashed up in the highlands, sending growls of thunder rolling down into the valleys. Most of the work Tanna had planned for the day would have to wait for the weather to clear, which meant that Lorath had little to do except the daily feeding of the pigs and milking of the goats. Upon finishing those chores, he rushed back to the stables, hopping over the runnels that carried the deluge down through the camp to the harbor. He was already soaked by the time he reached the barn and found Adreona inside, leaning over Zerae's stall, admiring mother and foal.

She glanced his way as he entered. "I forget how peaceful the stables are."

Lorath strode to stand next to her, wiping the water from his face and pushing his wet hair back from his brow. "I take it you don't spend much time here."

"My duties leave little room for it. But on a day like today . . ."

The sound of the rain against the roof overhead reminded Lorath of the strikes by his father's ball-peen hammer. Arjak nursed, appearing unconcerned by the storm. "Strong little colt," he said.

Adreona watched the foal with sadness in her emerald eyes. "I knew his father. He was strong too, but the Drowned still brought him down. I wish I could protect his son from a similar end. If only innocence were a shield against fate." She smiled at the youngling, then turned toward Lorath. "I hear good things from Tanna regarding your work here in the stables."

His laugh had a sarcastic edge. "How flattering."

"It should be. You're a soldier." She gestured around the barn. "This can't be easy for you. But it seems you are not ruled by your pride, and that is a good thing. To be honest, you've surprised me."

"I plan to keep surprising you. I have much more to offer, if you'll let me—"

"Let's not get ahead of ourselves, all right? You are to remain here, Lorath, performing good and needed work, which I appreciate."

He wanted to argue, but he thought about what Tyrael would advise, and he bit his tongue. "Yes, Captain."

Adreona gave him a nod and departed from the stables, but a dissatisfaction lingered in Lorath's mind the rest of that day and into the next. With each shovelful of manure, he grew more frustrated, thinking of things he wished he had said, until he could keep silent no longer. He left the barn and crossed the yard in the direction of the keep, determined to press his case. When he entered the great hall, several Amazons looked up at him from dice and card games. He scanned their faces but did not see Adreona.

Shieldmatron Tavie stood at the end of the room, leaning over the large map with some kind of ledger in her hands. She appeared to be checking it against the map, but she glanced up briefly from its pages at Lorath's approach.

"Is there something you need?" she asked.

"There is." He worked to keep his voice sounding calm and reasonable. "Would it be possible to speak with the captain?"

"Why?"

"There is a matter I wish to discuss with her."

"What matter?" She traced a line in the ledger with her finger and then moved some of the troop tokens across the map to a new position near the Athulua Garrison.

"I would rather discuss it with her," Lorath said.

She looked up from the book. "I am afraid that will not be possible."

"May I ask why?"

"Because Captain Adreona is not here."

"Where is she?"

Tavie returned her gaze to the map. "Nowhere that concerns you."

Lorath's anger rose like heat up the back of his neck, but he did what he could to steady himself, knowing quite well that losing his patience with Tavie would get him nowhere.

She moved another token, and another. Lorath noticed that many of the Amazon forces on the island now appeared to be coalescing around the garrison. He pointed at that location on the map.

"I assume she's gone here?"

Tavie closed the ledger, then nodded.

"Why are all the troops gathering there?" he asked.

"Our scouts have reported an increase in Drowned activity. The captain went to conduct an inspection of our readiness for an incursion."

"Personally?"

She hesitated just long enough for Lorath to sense there might have been a disagreement between her and Adreona. "Yes, personally."

"I take it the captain likes to handle most things herself."

"Her approach is very . . . direct."

He pointed at the map again. "How long does it take to get there?"

"It is a few days' ride over the highlands."

Lorath had seen Adreona just yesterday, which meant that she had left only that morning. Assuming she remained at the garrison for a time performing her inspection, she would not return to Fort

Galina for perhaps several days. Which was fine. He could muck stables for a little while longer.

"What is that?" He pointed at the fire emblem he had noticed off the coast the last time he studied the map.

"That is the great watchfire."

"Watchfire?"

"Our ancestors built it to help keep the Drowned at bay."

"How does it work?"

Tavie sighed with impatience. "It burns?"

"But—"

"Look, it's really very simple. Much of our coastline is protected by cliffs and other natural features." She used her finger to draw an invisible line down Athulua's western coast until it landed on the Athulua Garrison. "This is the weakest point. A valley there offers access to the island's interior, which is why we established a fort there, and why the ancient Askari lit the watchfire. The Drowned are weak to fire. You remember how we used fire-oil to free your ship from their attack? The watchfire is more than that. It burns with a power that repels the Drowned. For the most part."

"For the most part?"

"The watchfire is a deterrent. There are times when the Drowned become emboldened, stronger, or simply more ravenous. They push through." She used her fingers to draw a path from the water, over the fort, and into the valley. "The watchfire limits the number of enemies that can get past at any one time, which allows us to meet them and stop the incursion."

"How often do you resupply the fuel?"

"Never."

"Why not?"

"The fire is of a . . . magical nature."

"It doesn't burn out?"

She tucked the ledger under her arm. "It hasn't yet."

Something in the way she said that caused Lorath to ask, "What happens if it ever does burn out? Can you relight it?"

She said nothing at first. "Unfortunately, the method used by the ancient Askari to create the watchfire has been lost to time. If it burns out, it will be on the Amazons to hold the line."

She held her chin up in defiance as she said it, but Lorath saw doubt in her eyes. He looked again at the troop placements on the map. If the Drowned ever got past them, Athulua would fall, but he did not need to point that out. Tavie obviously knew it. He finally began to see what Adreona had meant when she spoke about the fragility of their position. Any weakness, any imbalance, any gap in the wall, and all Skovos could be lost.

"I know this much," he said. "If anyone can defend Skovos, it is the Amazons. I thank you for your time, Shieldmatron. I will return to my duties in the stables now."

With a bow of his head, he left her.

Lorath spent the next few days laboring with the animals. Most of the mares spent their time in pastures and paddocks outside the walls, but the stallions had to be kept apart from them, and from one another. They lived in the barn, which meant they required daily grooming and exercise. Lorath would have liked to saddle and ride them, but that privilege belonged to the Amazon warriors. He was tasked with cleaning the stalls while the horses went outdoors. He did not relish that task, but he did enjoy the time it allowed him to spend watching Arjak with his mother.

The foal had grown noticeably, even in the short time since Lorath had started working in the barn, and it possessed a confident and curious temperament. When Lorath entered Arjak's pen, the foal approached to smell him and even accepted a gentle scratch around his withers while his protective mother looked on.

"Tanna was right about you, little one," Lorath said. "You will grow into a fine stallion."

"I see Adreona meant what she said."

Arjak startled at the voice and kicked his hind legs. Lorath turned to see Keldon leaning his folded arms over the wall of the stall.

"About you working in the stables," the sailor added.

Lorath replied with a sardonic chuckle. "You have no idea what you've been missing,"

"I think I do." Keldon looked around the barn. "Though I will say it's a lot drier than where I've been spending my days."

"I take it they've kept you busy."

"Aye. A shipwright's work is never done. That's the odd thing about a boat. From the moment it touches the sea, the sea is doing everything it can to destroy it."

Lorath lifted the latch and exited the stall, closing the gate behind him. "Do you still wish you had gone with Donan?"

"Naw." Keldon flicked the idea away with his hand. "I might feel differently if I had to work here—never been at ease around horses. But I have quite enjoyed attending to these lovely Amazon ships. I've even managed a few improvements on my *Arabel*."

"You really have been busy."

"Aye." He glanced around the barn, as if checking to see whether they were alone. "Still, I am beginning to wonder how much longer we'll be here. I see messengers come and go from Temis. Any word from Donan or, uh, Faysal?"

"Nothing yet," Lorath said. "But I do plan to speak with Adreona about our circumstances when she returns."

"And say what?"

"Still figuring that out."

"Well, I wish you luck with that." Keldon turned to leave through the nearest barn door. "If you need me, you know where I'll be."

"Likewise," Lorath said.

He returned to his work, feeding the horses and pigs, and finished out the day somewhat less drained than on those first nights at the beginning of his servitude. He had slept only a few hours when he was awakened in his barn loft by shouts and voices coming from outside. The horses whinnied in their stalls below him, similarly disturbed by the noise. The thick darkness told him that dawn was still several hours away. He rose from his pallet and crept across the floor in his stockings, then peered down at the courtyard through a gap between slats of wood.

An Amazon messenger had arrived on horseback. She stood next to her mount, surrounded by warriors holding torches. A moment later, Tavie rushed from the entrance of the keep to greet the messenger, and a leather sleeve passed between them. They spoke, though Lorath could hear nothing of their conversation, and then Tavie pulled the message from its sleeve. Her eyes widened as she read it, and within moments she was calling orders.

Something of urgent importance had happened. Lorath pulled on his clothes and scrambled down the ladder to the floor of the barn. On his way through the door, he bumped into Tanna as she came in.

"Good, you're up," she said, looking somewhat disheveled. "We need to saddle a fresh horse."

"Why?"

"To carry a message back to the front."

"But—"

"There's no time to explain." She pointed at a roan stallion with a black mane. "Saddle him up. Now."

Lorath did as he was told, as quickly as he could. The stallion seemed to sense the tension in the air. He snorted and chuffed, nostrils flared, but there was also an eagerness to the stamping of his hooves as Lorath laid the saddle over his back.

"You want action as much as I do," he murmured.

As he led the horse from the barn into the courtyard, he saw Tavie return the leather sleeve to the messenger, who then hurried over to take the reins from Lorath and mount the stallion.

Tavie had followed her and laid her hand upon the horse's neck, looking up at the Amazon in the saddle.

"Courage be with you, sister," she said.

"And with you," the messenger said. Then she wheeled the horse around and charged off at a gallop through the open gate. Tavie stood and watched until the night's darkness swallowed both horse and rider.

"What has happened?" Lorath asked.

"See to her horse," Tavie said. "Her name is Thistle, and you'll need to walk her. She has ridden long and hard." With that, she marched away without looking back.

Lorath considered following her, but a hand on his arm stopped him and gently turned him around.

"Do as she ordered," Tanna said. "I'll find out what's going on."

Lorath accepted this with difficulty, but he eventually took Thistle's reins and walked her through the gate, out into one of the paddocks. The mare was still breathing heavily, and she seemed agitated at having been left in a strange place with a strange handler. Lorath spoke calmly to her, and he stroked her shoulders, wondering where she had come from and what she had seen. After she had settled and her breathing had fallen to a normal rate, he walked her back into the fort, then into the barn. He gave her a stall next to Zerae, where he removed her saddle and brushed her down, then fed and watered her, the whole while watching for Tanna's return. When the stablemaster finally appeared, she looked troubled in a way that Lorath had never seen.

"It's a Drowned incursion," she said. "But it sounds dire. The Athulua Garrison is surrounded. Besieged."

"What about Adreona?"

"She's hiding out with a small patrol outside the barricades, in a cave near a rock formation called the Pommel. The warriors inside the garrison can't escape, and Adreona won't leave them. But she doesn't have the numbers with her to break the siege and drive back the Drowned."

"Then we need to send reinforcements—"

"*We?*" Tanna snapped. "What do you think Tavie is doing? She'll be leading a mounted company at first light. A second force will travel by sea." She clenched her teeth and shook her head.

"What is it?" Lorath asked.

"Even if they push the horses until they're lame, by the time they get there it might be too late."

"Surely the warships will reach them sooner."

"If they could sail the whole way, yes. But they'll be rowing through the dead waters of Atanos. If they're attacked on the way, it might even take them longer."

A war horn bellowed out in the camp, calling the Amazons to battle. The sound of it seemed to rouse something in Tanna. She straightened her back and inhaled deeply, her eyes keen and her expression grim. "You and I have work to do," she said. "We need every mount saddled and ready to ride by dawn. That's only a few hours away."

Lorath nodded. "Then let's get to it."

Together, they pulled in every horse from the pastures, some of which had to be carefully awakened. They offered all of them hay, but no grain, given the long ride they would soon be undertaking. The late-night feeding seemed to confuse them, but most of them ate; a few horses refused, perhaps disquieted by the unusual activity in the fort.

When each horse was ready, Lorath led them outside into the courtyard, where he handed them off to waiting Amazons. By the time the sky had entered the blue hour before dawn, they had saddled all but the incoming messenger's horse, Thistle, and Zerae, who stood with her head high and ears pricked forward, alert to the bustle around her and her foal. When Tanna went to saddle her, Lorath objected.

"Arjak isn't fully weaned," he said.

The stablemaster's mouth tightened. "Shieldmatron Tavie called for every available mount. That includes Zerae."

"Why not Thistle?"

"She isn't rested. We can't risk her going lame halfway there. Zerae is strong."

"But Arjak could die without her."

Tanna clenched her fists, but not in anger. It seemed she wanted to stop them shaking, from either exhaustion or some inner turmoil.

"He's eating hay now," she said, but she sounded as if she were reassuring herself. "I'll give him goat's milk while his mother is away. He's tough. He can survive until she gets back."

Lorath knew he wasn't thinking or behaving rationally. He knew that Adreona would need every spear she could muster, which meant that Tavie needed every horse. But he had come to care for the foal more deeply than he had realized, or perhaps it was simply the idea of innocent life that the foal represented. "And if Zerae doesn't come back?" he asked.

"Then Arjak's brief story may come to an end. But let us hope for the best, eh?"

Lorath nodded, but his resolve faltered when they went to remove Zerae from the pen. Arjak tried to follow his mother, clinging to her side, almost underfoot. Lorath had to break the foal away and push him back into the stall. Zerae put up an argument then, twisting her head against the bit, but Tanna calmed her and pulled her away. Arjak whinnied and nickered as he paced around the stall, clearly in distress.

"She'll be back," he said. "I'll do everything I can to take care of her."

Then he helped Tanna saddle Zerae, planning to ride her himself. But when he asked the stablemaster to hold her reins while he went up to the loft to put on his armor and retrieve his other gear, she looked confused.

"Why do you need your armor?"

"Because I'm riding west."

She offered him a sympathetic smile. "I don't think you are."

Lorath took the reins from her and led Zerae from the barn into the courtyard. More than thirty Amazons stood near their mounts or sat high in their saddles, arrayed in their armor and helms, with spears and javelins strapped to their backs. In the chill morning air, the breath from the horses' nostrils turned to a cloud of steam. Lorath searched the company until he found Tavie standing among them, determined to waste no more time begging for permission.

"I'm coming with you," he said.

"No," she said, "you are not."

"You cannot stop me."

"You're right. I cannot stop you from following us on foot. But you will not be riding with us." She snapped her fingers and motioned to two Amazons, who marched up to Lorath and pulled Zerae's reins from his hands.

"I can help you," Lorath said.

"You already have." Tavie leapt up into the saddle of her mount. "You have done what Captain Adreona ordered you to do, and I can ask for no more than that." Then she shouted to those with her, "My war-sisters! We ride!"

The sun's fire had begun to push reds and oranges over the horizon, and the Amazon cavalry thundered west from the fort with its golden light at their backs. Lorath watched them go, hoofs kicking up dirt and mud behind them, barely containing his rage. The beast within him roared in its lair, rattling his ribs and echoing down his bones.

"I know," Tanna said, having walked up to stand beside him. "I know. I wish I were going with them. And for what it's worth, I would have asked you to ride beside me." She clapped a hand on his shoulder. "But that is not our lot."

"I determine my own fate," Lorath said.

He pulled away from her and returned to the stable, where he went to saddle Thistle, the last horse remaining. Tanna had followed him, and when she saw what he was doing, she placed herself between him and the horse with folded arms and planted feet.

"Don't be a fool," she said. "This horse should already be lame, the way she was ridden. If you take her, all you will succeed in doing is killing her and stranding yourself leagues from where you're trying to go."

Lorath threw the saddle to the ground and shouted, "I have to do *something*!"

"Something often feels better than nothing." The voice came from Keldon, who now stood in the barn doorway. "Even when it's the wrong thing." He looked over his shoulder in the direction of the harbor, shaking his head. "I just watched a fleet of Amazon warships row to battle. That was a sight I'll not soon forget."

The appearance of the sailor distracted Lorath from his anger long enough for him to realize that his plan to ride Thistle would have most likely failed, just as Tanna had suggested. He did not know what else to do.

"Why are you so eager to join a fight that isn't yours?" the stablemaster asked. "Do you wish to die?"

"It's not that," Keldon said as he stepped into the barn. "There's a rage in him needs quenching. And I think there's a woman he wants to stand alongside."

"No," Lorath said. "It isn't about that. It's about justice and fighting evil wherever we find it."

Keldon shrugged. "Then let's go fight."

"How?" Lorath demanded. "There aren't any horses left to ride."

"Horses?" The sailor scowled, but a moment later, his expression turned into a grin. "Who said anything about horses?"

CHAPTER THIRTEEN

Evening had arrived by the time Donan had crossed the Bridge of the Eye, leaving behind the dense city of Temis for the more rural island of Philios. A few roads stretched away from the bridge in different directions, cutting through farmland and dry scrub. With the sun setting, Donan decided to see if he could find lodging somewhere nearby for the night. He set off down an easterly trackway, asking the few locals he encountered where he might find an inn. They directed him onward, but at one point, he felt as if someone were watching him. Glancing back, he caught sight of a few Askarra Guards in the road.

Their presence was surely not unusual, and at first Donan paid them little mind, but as he made his way, he noted how the Amazons kept pace with him. He thought it a bit paranoid to assume they were following him but decided to take no chances. He hurried ahead, and upon reaching the inn, he found it also boasted a small crowded tavern, with a few candlelit tables spilling out onto the street. Donan quickly and quietly slipped into a seat in the back, hidden from view. The innkeeper served him a plate of cheap shellfish with bread and a few olives, along with watered-down wine.

As Donan ate, the Askarra Guards marched by, sweeping their haughty gaze from one side of the street to the other. He imagined they were searching for him, but it was also possible he had misread the situation completely. The townsfolk seated around Donan fell silent as the Amazons passed, but as soon as the warriors had moved on, the gossip began.

"When will they leave?"

"When there's nothing left to take."

"I hear it might go up to eight-tenths."

"Hard to even live on two-tenths, let alone turn a profit."

"But how can they justify that?"

"You know how. Peace and order."

"I said it then, and I'll say it now: no one gives up power once you give it to them."

"I say it's time we—"

"Shh."

A man nearby had noticed Donan sitting in silence behind them, and that ended the conversation as swiftly as the presence of the Askarra Guard. Then the townsfolk all took turns stealing glances at him, some furtively and some quite openly. He tried to meet their curiosity with a pleasant demeanor.

One of them finally asked, "Who might you be, mainlander?"

"My name is Donan."

"What brings you to Philios, Donan?"

"Curiosity," Donan said, adhering to the story Tyrael had given the queen. "I am traveling the whole of Skovos to learn from the Askari."

"Learn what?" another of them asked.

"You may not know this," Donan said, "but your islands are doing much better than other parts of Sanctuary. Aranoch, Westmarch, Khanduras . . . there is still much bloodshed and suffering elsewhere, almost as if the reapers still walk among us. But here in Skovos, you enjoy safety and stability."

The mood of the crowd shifted and tensed, as Donan suspected it might, given the topic of their conversation moments ago.

"I'm here to witness how this has been accomplished," he added.

At first, no one said anything in response to that, but then one of the more outspoken men leaned toward him. "Stranger, you just witnessed it."

"What did I witness?"

"Those Amazons in silk. The Askarra Guard. The queen formed them after the Reaping. They take everything, or nearly everything, and then they dole it back out to us like they're the ones who grew it, or made it."

Donan remembered the trident stamp he had seen.

"And they expect us to be grateful to them for it!"

"Careful, Ammon," someone said.

"Why should I be careful with the truth?" the man asked.

"Because that's not the whole truth, is it?" said a woman nearby. "You're forgetting how it was after the Reaping. You aren't talking about the looting, or the pirates, or the Drowned."

"That was the deal we struck," said an old man with white hair as thin as cobwebs. "We wanted peace, didn't we? We wanted things to go back to the way they were, and we traded our freedom to get it. *That* is the whole truth of it."

No one spoke for a time after that, but gradually, smaller, hushed conversations sprang up again at the different tables. Donan bade them all good night and retired to his room, having received at least partial answers to some of the questions the Horadrim had been asking since arriving in Temis. The Amazons had likely helped to keep Skovos an orderly society even before Malthael's attack, but in the chaos afterward, Queen Etara had tightened her grip. The relative prosperity in Skovos had come with a price, however. Whether that price had been worth paying seemed a matter of perspective.

The next morning, Donan awakened to the sound of a cock's crow. He lay in his bed, which was not so uncomfortable as to drive him from it, with his eyes closed, imagining himself in a different time and place. His sleep had been restless. His conversation with the villagers kept his mind and body turning because there were no easy answers. Donan opposed the idea of tyrannical rule, and yet the Askari lived in far greater safety than the people of Westmarch or Lut Gholein. He could not decide for himself what price would be too high for him to pay.

At last, he rose from his bed, dressed, and went downstairs. For breakfast, the innkeeper served him a boiled egg, a slice of bread, and butter churned with a hint of honey. She appeared to be about the age his mother would have been, with threads of silver in her dark hair. It seemed she ran the inn on her own, which he took as yet another sign of the upheaval resulting from Malthael's Reaping. Donan had already paid a fair rate for his night's stay, but having learned more about the financial circumstances of the common folk, he gave the innkeeper a bit more coin on his way toward the door. She seemed perplexed by his generosity, and even a bit suspicious, but she accepted it.

"Where are you traveling to from here?" she asked.

"I am hoping to speak with the seers."

"Ah." Her eyes rolled a bit as she turned away from him. "Of course you are."

"I take it that doesn't surprise you."

"Not really, no." She pulled a rag from an apron pocket and used it to wipe down an adjacent table. "You're hardly the first traveler to come here hoping to get a glimpse of the future."

"Can you blame them?"

"I suppose not."

"But it doesn't interest you?"

She stood up straight and wiped her forehead with the back of her hand. "What doesn't?"

"Speaking with the seers?"

She chuckled. "Why would I want to go and do a thing like that?"

Her dismissive attitude puzzled him. "I think most people would be drawn to learn something about their future."

"Many people are," she said. "Just not me."

"And why is that?"

"You think it comes free?"

"I don't know."

"Well, you ought to, if you're heading that way." She dropped the rag onto the table she'd been cleaning and motioned for him to sit. Then she took a chair next to him, one elbow leaning on the table, the other hand propped on her thigh. "Firstly," she said, "you'll have to walk the pilgrimage path to reach the seers. You won't know what your individual path looks like until you're on it, but it often extracts a heavy toll. After that, there's the cost of the message they give you."

"They expect payment?"

"Not of coin," she said. "You have to hear the message."

Donan wondered how hearing the message could be a cost. "Surely that is the whole reason for going—"

"You'd think so, wouldn't you? But consider this: What happens if they tell you something you don't want to hear? You can't just forget you've heard it. You have to live with it every day after. Or what if they speak a riddle, which they are known to do? Some visitors have been driven quite mad by their sophistry."

"I see."

"Or let's say they give you a vague kind of warning. 'Take care around water,' or some such. You'd spend the rest of your life in fear, hiding from the world."

"Do they give warnings of that nature?"

She picked up her cleaning rag. "I've heard stories."

"And where do I find this path that I must walk?"

"If you're still determined to go after everything I just told you . . ." She sighed. "Take the western road from here, and before long you'll come to another road leading north toward the mountain. Follow that for the better part of a day, and you'll eventually reach a shrine. A seer dwells there. She'll know which way to send you. What is your name, traveler?"

"Donan."

"My name is Alenia, and I wish you luck, Donan."

He thanked her and departed from the inn, after which he found the western road she had mentioned. He paused at a public fountain to fill his waterskin and then set off into the countryside. A warm, arid breeze stirred dust into swirls across the paved road, which had not been maintained well in recent years. Weeds and seedlings had taken root in the cracks between paving stones, and eroded dirt and sand had buried the edges. Locusts snapped and thrummed, leaping from one tussock to the next. The sun felt hotter than it had on Temis, or perhaps Temis had simply offered more shade. The narrow cypress and short scrub trees found along the Philios road provided little relief, and sweat soon dripped from Donan's brow into his eyes.

Before long, he turned north on the road Alenia had directed him to take, an unpaved, hard-beaten track heading upward in the direction of Mount Karcheus's distant snowcap. Low stone walls lined sections of the road, fencing off unkempt farms and cottages. Olive groves grew thick and gnarled, with some of the most ancient trees appearing centuries and even thousands of years old. Rows of grapevines rippled over the surrounding slopes and terraces, but many appeared withered and barren.

Donan met few Askari along the way, and those he did encounter avoided meeting his gaze, friendly as he tried to make himself appear. A few of them even stepped off the road a fair distance from him, waiting until he had passed before resuming their own journey. At such times, Donan recalled what Adreona had told him about the people of Skovos and chose not to take offense.

Toward midday, he spotted a large cedar tree and decided to seek shelter from the sun beneath it, where the air felt heavy with the wood's fragrance. He ate a little of the food he had purchased in Temis the day before, then he pulled out the journal.

He had determined that the author of the book wrote it using coded text, rather than a known language, which meant the journal required deciphering instead of translation. Donan had read coded volumes in a Horadric library utilizing their accompanying ciphers, but he had never broken a novel code himself. The process would take time, and although the journal still felt like an object of importance, he was aware that it might not end up containing anything of interest. It was the challenge that excited him, more than anything else.

He had thus far been looking only for patterns, letting his eyes roam the pages while keeping his thoughts pliable, simply letting the arrangement of symbols suggest possibilities. If it was written according to a code where each single symbol corresponded to one he knew, then word length would be consistent, and frequently used words would appear more regularly. Of course, that rested on the assumption that he knew the author's original language to begin with, which was not guaranteed. He wished there had been time for Tyrael to examine it more closely, since he possessed a vastly greater knowledge of such things than Donan. Perhaps when they had accomplished their purpose in Skovos, they could look at it together.

With a sigh, Donan put the book away and resumed his trek. The road rose and fell with the rolling foothills surrounding Mount Karcheus, and there in the hinterlands he noticed more overt signs of previous violence and destruction. The doors of some cottages hung in splinters from their rusted hinges, and the scorched remains of farm buildings moldered. In the pastures and pens, the scattered bones of sheep, goats, and other animals lay stripped and sunbaked.

Donan had run out of water by the time evening approached, and the back of his neck felt broiled. The mountain appeared nearer than at the beginning of his climb, but its steepest slopes still lay several leagues away. He had begun to scan his immediate surroundings for a sheltered place to stop for the night, preferably out of sight from the road, when he noticed a stone structure peeking over the next rise.

Upon reaching it, he discovered what could only have been the shrine the innkeeper had mentioned. The building was a towering rotunda set against the base of a solid rock escarpment, its domed roof clad in slate shingles cut in the shape of reptilian scales. The outer stonework had been chiseled to resemble the stacked coils of a serpent, with its head and gaping mouth forming the entrance to the shrine's interior. Donan approached the doorway but stopped himself before going inside, feeling vaguely apprehensive.

He almost turned away, but suddenly a bent old woman stood before him, draped in layers of fine muslin robes. Beneath her headdress, a veil covered most of her face, but the skin around her eyes appeared wrinkled and ancient. She seemed to emanate an uncanny presence that Donan found both frightening and intriguing. She fit the description he had read of the seers, which claimed that to gain the gift of foresight, initiates sacrificed parts of their own bodies. He wondered what kind of disfigurement lay concealed beneath the woman's shroud.

"I am the Keeper of the Fang," she said, her voice creaking like aged leather and somewhat muffled by her veil. "I bid you welcome."

Donan bowed his head. "Thank you."

"You have come seeking your path?"

"I seek the seers," Donan said.

"You have found one. Come." She waved him toward her and went back inside the rotunda.

Donan took one last look at his surroundings. From somewhere nearby, he heard the evening churring of a nightjar, but he detected no sign of any other person near the shrine.

Inside the rotunda, he found a clean dwelling lit by oil lamps. Heavy chairs of olive wood surrounded an altar hewn from marble, on which sat a stack of bowls and a mortar and pestle. A wooden screen offered privacy for a part of the chamber, around which Donan could see the corner of a bed. Bundles of dried flowers, herbs, and mushrooms festooned the rim where the walls met the dome overhead. Ghostly images could be seen across the ceiling, but the paint had flaked and faded away until little remained but faint vestiges. A spring-fed fountain gurgled into a pool on the far side of the chamber, set into the wall below a mosaic depicting the all-seeing eye. Next to it, an iron door appeared to lead deeper into the mountain.

The woman grunted as she eased herself into one of the chairs. "Would you like to begin?" she asked.

Donan stood where he was. "Begin what?"

"Your path. Every soul has one. If you would know the future, you must first understand your past."

"Forgive me," he said, "I didn't actually come here seeking divination."

She tipped her head a little. "Then why have you come?"

"I am . . . a scholar," he said. "I'm searching for a group of my colleagues. They came to Skovos some years ago."

"Scholars, you say?"

"Yes. It is possible they made contact with the seers. They may have even spoken with your queen."

"If *you* wish to stand before our queen and speak with her, you need only walk the path before you."

Donan sat down in the chair opposite her. "Perhaps my associates came to this shrine. They would have been led by a woman named Sho-Ren. She was a mage from Xiansai. Do you remember her?"

"Alas, I do not," she said. "But I am young, and I have not been serving as the Keeper of the Fang for very long."

"Young?" Donan said before checking his surprise. "I'm sorry, I didn't mean—"

"I take no offense," the seer said. "I would guess I am not much older than you."

"But—"

"Our gift of foresight is received by exchange of our own vitality. Our lives and our bodies become sacred offerings."

Despite Donan's desire to be respectful of her, he now felt a powerful curiosity to see beneath her shroud, which he did his best to suppress. "Would I be able to speak with the Keeper who served before you?"

"I am afraid her eyes are shut."

Donan assumed that phrase to mean the previous seer had died. "Then I suppose I must speak with your queen, if I may. And that means I must walk a path?"

She inclined her head in agreement.

"Your journey begins here, at the mouth of the serpent, and it ends in the belly. It will not be easy for you."

Donan assumed the path involved more than simply walking a road like the one that had brought him to the shrine. "What must I do?" he asked.

She folded her hands in her lap. "You must be bitten and swallowed by the serpent."

"That sounds . . . uncomfortable."

"For many," she said, "the process is unbearable."

"Then what happens?"

"The serpent will show you your past." Donan had always preferred to leave the ground behind him undisturbed; he could do nothing to change the past, and therefore it served no purpose to revisit and dwell on it.

"Have you walked this path?" he asked.

"I have not. Initiate seers make a different pilgrimage."

Donan looked toward the exit, out into the twilight, and contemplated leaving the shrine. After all, he had no evidence the previous Horadrim had come this way. He had no confirmation they had even set foot on Philios. He wondered if time wasted on this mysterious path would be better spent searching elsewhere, but even as he considered that notion, he recognized it as an expression of his fear, not his intuition. Tyrael had agreed with this course, which meant that Donan would be wise to see it through.

"Let us begin," he said.

CHAPTER FOURTEEN

The seer rose from her chair and brought one of the bowls from the altar over to the fountain. She ladled some of its water into the bowl, then pulled down some of the flowers and herbs from where they hung overhead. She brought all of this back to the altar, where she selected some of the dried blossoms, leaves, and mushrooms and ground these into dust using the mortar and pestle. An aroma of grass, spice, and earth filled the chamber as she spooned some of the powder into the spring water.

After stirring it all together, she set the bowl on the altar before Donan. "When you are ready, drink."

Donan looked at the swirling liquid with suspicion. "What is it?"

"We call it Venom of the Serpent."

"Venom?" The herbal ingredients had infused the water and turned it the sinister color of verdigris, granting it properties of which he could only guess. "What will it do to me?"

"It will show you the past," she said.

"But what will it *do* to me?"

Donan's mouth had gone dry, and he could hear his own racing heartbeat in his ears. He feared whatever effects the potion might have. He could find his faculties diminished, or it might render him unconscious, and he would be vulnerable, helpless, without control over himself. A breathless panic set in, and he began to believe the liquid before him might be poison, and the seer might be an alchemist of malevolent will.

"It will not harm your body," she said. "But you may harm yourself if you fight against it."

"I am afraid," Donan whispered.

"As you should be," said the seer. "To walk the path of one's fate requires great courage that many do not possess. There is no shame in turning away from it. I cannot force you to drink."

Each moment that Donan delayed only increased his doubts and anxiety. He knew if he waited much longer, he would push the Venom away and leave the shrine, never to return. But then he heard a gentle distant voice—not the seer's, a more familiar voice—and it whispered to him, "Drink. Drink it."

Donan picked up the bowl and tipped its contents into his mouth, gulping it down before he lost his nerve. The liquid tasted pungent, bitter, and sour, burning a little as it slid down through his chest and into his stomach.

"Well done," the seer said. "Now, come with me."

She offered him her hand, which he took. Her bony fingers felt warm, her skin dry and papery, and she led him from the altar toward the iron door. From within her robes, she drew forth a heavy key. The ratcheting of the turning lock echoed loudly, as though an endless space lay on the other side of the iron plates and rivets. Donan noticed no effects from the potion yet, but he attuned himself to every shift, every sensation, every signal in his body as the seer opened the door. The metal groaned as if it had not been asked to move for some time, and Donan saw a tunnel and stairway that led downward into the abyss.

"Do you see the way?" she asked.

"I do."

"You must follow it."

"But . . . there's no light."

"I assure you," she said, "the journey would be no easier with a lantern or torch. Go now, and may your eyes be opened."

Donan knew that turning back now was not an option. He could only go forward. So, he bade farewell to the Keeper of the Fang and set off down the stairway. Light from the shrine tumbled after him for several steps, but then the door groaned once again as the seer closed and locked it behind him.

His eyes widened in the darkness, straining to grab hold of any glimmer, any discernible shape, and when they found none, they created their own sparks and shadows. He reached out his hand for the rock wall and felt a smooth, cold surface. He used this to steady himself as he took another step downward, and then another, and then another, proceeding slowly, surrounded by the sound of his own breathing. The passageway initially followed a straight course, but then it began to turn and wind. Donan relied on his hands to feel the direction of the path before he took each step downward, and at times, it felt as if the course's descent spiraled back on itself. He had not gone far before he began to see the curve of the walls and the angle of the stairs, which at first he suspected was a trick of his eyes. However, the clarity of his sight only grew until he realized some distant, unseen source of light had begun to reveal the path around him.

Not long after that, the passageway joined with a much broader, rounder tunnel that appeared more natural in origin, and it ran close enough to the surface of the mountain for cracks and openings in its roof to allow in shafts of moonlight. Donan followed it upward, thinking the ground felt somewhat unsteady, only to realize the potion had taken hold; his balance and his focus drifted. The tunnel smelled of earth and something else, a kind of musk he recognized only in the deepest reaches of his ancestral memory but could give no name. As he ascended, the air became humid, and he could hear the trickling of water. Tree roots penetrated the ceiling and grew down the walls, curving like the ribs of the great serpent that had swallowed him. Then Donan began to see things that were not there and could not be there.

The tunnel became a corridor through the grand market of Gea Kul. He stood beneath the awnings and canopies of merchant tents, which reached overhead from both sides to enclose the avenue and shield customers from the relentless sun. Donan looked up at their captivating stripes and patterns of vibrant color as if he were a child again. He smelled meat sizzling somewhere over open coals, the sweet aroma of freshly baked flatbread, the heady fragrance of raw spices, the perfume of rose oil, the sharpness of human sweat, and the tang of animal dung, all stirred together by the heat into the scent of his home.

Donan navigated the maze of tents, ducking and dodging his way through the crowd, until he arrived at his mother's shop on the edge of the square. The piles of rugs within filled him with pride because of the way others spoke about their quality. His mother didn't do the weaving anymore—she could afford to hire the labor of others—but she had created the intricate designs and oversaw their manufacture. Her talents had afforded him a life of luxury and education, and he had measured his growth into manhood against the height of those piles.

Then Donan heard his mother's voice, and she emerged from the shop's back rooms, alive again and looking as she always had. She wore a fine blue satin dress, as if she had wrapped herself in the sky, with an emerald necklace the same color as her eyes. He rushed to embrace her, shocked into speechlessness by the sight of her.

"Hello, my son," she said. "I wondered if you would drink."

"Drink?" Donan finally recognized the subtle voice that had beckoned him to drink back in the shrine. "But how—?"

"I reside in your memory," she said. "And I am always calling to you. It is you who cannot always hear me." Then she gave him a stern, disapproving look that he knew well. "Sometimes, I think you even ignore me on purpose."

"I—I don't mean to—"

"Yes, you do." She laughed, and the sound of it trembled his heart.

"Every boy sometimes pretends he can't hear his mother calling. The important thing is that you are with me now."

"Why?"

"Because I am about to die."

A savage wind tore down the street and into the shop. Donan looked outside as night arrived like an onrushing storm over the city.

"No," he whispered.

Moments later, screams erupted in the market, full of pain, anguish, and confusion. People ran past their shop in all directions, faces contorted in terror.

"Go, my son!" His mother grabbed him and pushed him toward the back rooms. "Hide! Quickly!"

He almost fled, just as he had that night years ago, but this time, he stopped himself. "No," he said. "It is you who needs to hide, Mother. Those are Malthael's reapers out there, and one of them will kill you."

"But you didn't know that, did you?" she said. "You heard a commotion in the market, and you were afraid. You did what I told you to do. You knew nothing of angels or reapers or the Horadrim."

"But now I do." He readied his staff, preparing himself for the enemy that would soon enter the shop. "I have learned much since you last saw me. Now, get behind me, Mother."

She placed a calming hand on his shoulder. "Donan, my son. You cannot alter what has happened. To confront the past is not to change it—"

"No!" He shook her hand off in anger, tears clouding his vision. "I should have protected you. I should have known."

A horrid wailing filled the shop, and then a ghastly death maiden stepped into the doorway, trailing streams of spectral power, a dark void beneath her cowl. She glided toward Donan's mother wielding a scythe, seeming not to notice him at all. For a moment, Donan stood paralyzed, until the reaper swung her blade. He tried to block the blow with his staff, but the enemy's weapon passed through his as if he were not even there.

The strike cleaved his mother's head from her body, just as it had the night she died, her blood staining the beautiful rugs surrounding her. The maiden then turned and stalked from the shop, and Donan collapsed to his knees, sobbing, utterly powerless.

"I should have protected you," he said.

"Is that why you avoid thinking about me?" His mother's head spoke from where it had fallen. "My son, even when you ignore your past, you are still shaped by it. Never forget that though my death is a part of your story, so also is my love for you."

When Donan opened his eyes, he was kneeling in the tunnel, covered in dirt, but not where he had been at the beginning of his vision. He wiped his eyes and his cheeks, finding them dry as he staggered to his feet. Sunlight had replaced moonlight through the gaps in the ceiling, and he had apparently somehow traveled the length of the passage. He could see another iron door farther up the way, where the path came to its end.

He stumbled toward it, disoriented, still reeling from the images drawn from his memory by the Venom, still trying to find his way back fully to the present. The door opened as he approached it, and on the other side stood a seer wearing the same style of veil and robes that the Keeper of the Fang had worn.

"I welcome you," she said. "You have walked a harrowing path, and you may now rest. Come."

She motioned him into a natural, cavernous chamber that had been expanded and shaped with such artistry and skill that Donan could not tell which features had come about through human effort and which had been produced by erosion and the strange weathering of time. Torches and braziers cast a warm flickering light across the walls. Columns carved to resemble serpents coiled and twisted, creating arched doorways and passages. Mosaics adorned the cave walls, but their imagery differed from what he had seen on Temis. The artwork in the palace and the rest of the city had seemed preoccupied with myth, heroic deeds, and the natural world of predator and prey. The seers, on the other hand, seemed to be preoccupied with the contrast and balance between light and dark, angel and demon, as if they had embraced the Firstborn heritage of their island without falling to worship either lineage. The gentle trickle of rivulets and fountains filled the cavern.

The seer guided him to a bench of stone carved into an alcove. "Please, sit."

Donan did as she asked, still somewhat dazed.

The seer then brought him a cup of water from a nearby fountain. "You must be thirsty."

He was parched, but still he looked carefully to make sure she had given him ordinary water before he drank it. "I would like to speak with your queen," he said, handing back the empty vessel.

"Of course," the seer said as she took the cup. "But there is no hurry. If you would prefer to rest—"

"Please, I mean no disrespect, but I am pressed for time. I wish to speak with her as soon as possible."

"Very well," the seer said. "Please, wait here."

She left him alone, departing through one of the arches, and he lay back against the wall, pressing the heels of his palms against his eyes. He could still hear his mother's voice. He could still smell the perfumed oil she used in her hair. He could still feel the calluses on her hands that never softened, even after she stopped working at the loom. He could still see her severed head lying on the purple rug, staring up at him. The Venom had wrenched him back to a night he never let himself remember, and that angered him. He could not say the Keeper of the Fang had deceived him—he should have expected as much from something that promised to show him his past—but she could have forewarned him.

"The queen will see you now."

Donan pulled his hands from his eyes to find the seer had returned. He rose from the bench and followed her beneath a few arches, down a corridor that flowed through the rock like a snake through grass. They passed a wall on which were hung a collection of masks fashioned from precious metals. They glinted in the torchlight with hollow eyes, each unique in its design. Some were adorned with elaborate headdresses, while others were more plain, but all possessed an intimidating presence. Then they entered a throne room, and here the character of the cavern took on the qualities of Firstborn architecture that he had observed back on Temis, dark stone carved into severe facets and angles. The writhing serpent motif had been inlaid into the floor, surrounding Donan as if preparing to wrap him in a scaly embrace and devour him.

At the end of the room, polished metal had been cleverly wrought into the shape of a great radiating eye, and at its center stood the Oracle Queen. She wore a mask of silver, polished until it reflected like a mirror. The black and white threads of her robes had been so finely woven, they seemed to shift back and forth in undulating shades of gray. Braziers cast orange firelight onto several stoic seers, all waiting upon their ruler.

Donan approached the throne and bowed his head. "Your majesty."

"I welcome you, Donan," she said with a voice that sounded ancient, powerful, and perilous. "You have walked your path, and now you come before me with questions."

"I do," Donan said.

"What do you wish to ask?"

"I have come to Philios in search of . . ." He was about to lie and represent himself as a scholar once more but found himself unwilling to deceive the Oracle Queen; he sensed it would be foolish to even try. "I belong to an order," he said.

"Yes, the Horadrim."

He paused, not surprised but a little awed. "Yes, your majesty. Some years ago, an expedition of Horadrim journeyed to Skovos, and we have had no word from them. I come before you asking if you might know anything about them or where they might be."

The queen was silent for some time, her mirror mask betraying no expression or reaction. "I had forgotten about them," she finally said. "A mage led their party. What was her name?"

"Sho-Ren."

"Yes. She hailed from Xiansai. She came before me, just as you have done."

"What did she ask you?"

The queen shook her head. "When I receive a supplicant, I hold their question and its answer in sacred trust."

"I meant no offense," Donan hastened to say. "I only wish to find her. Do you have any knowledge of where the Horadrim may have gone?"

"I remember they wished to settle on Philios for a time, and I allowed them the use of an Amazon fortress that our sisters of the spear had forsaken. That was the last I heard of them."

Donan thought it unlikely the expedition would still be living there after all this time without sending word, but it thrilled him to at least have a solid foundation on which to begin his search. The discovery was worth the terrible vision he had endured.

"May I go to this fortress to look for them?" he asked.

"Of course you may," the queen said. "It is located some distance east of this sanctum."

"You have our deepest gratitude, your majesty."

"I am pleased to assist you how I may. The Horadrim serve a noble purpose. When you leave here, seek out my sister. She is an innkeeper near the Bridge of the Eye. She will aid you in your search."

"I believe . . . I have already met her." It surprised Donan to learn of the true connection between the innkeeper and the seers. Based on the conversation they had shared, he doubted she would be inclined to help him, but he thanked the queen and backed away from her to depart.

"Do you have no other question for me?" the queen asked.

He bowed his head again. "With respect, your majesty, I did not come here seeking divination or foresight."

"That does not mean you have no question."

Donan had little desire to ask her about his future, but he did wonder why he had been made to relive the worst night of his life. "The path I walked," he said. "If I may ask, what was the purpose of the vision it showed me?"

"That is for you to answer," the queen said. "The Venom of the Serpent shows you the memories of your past that define your present, for the past and the present together define your future. That is what some may call fate."

"I see," said Donan, even though his understanding remained incomplete.

"Would you know something of *your* fate?" the queen asked.

Donan was about to refuse once again but decided he did have a question he wanted to ask, after all. "Can you tell me, will we Horadrim achieve our purpose in Skovos?"

The Oracle Queen went still for several moments, head dipped low, almost as though she had fallen asleep. Donan waited, unsure of what was happening. Then the queen sat up straight, as if a charge of energy had raced up her spine, and when she spoke, she did so in a resonant tone that filled the entire chamber.

"One queen shall fall, and two shall rise! One queen shall throw the spear, and another queen shall retrieve it! One queen shall call the beast, and another queen shall free it. Thus, shall Skovos be saved."

CHAPTER FIFTEEN

Tyrael made his way, unhurried, back up through the tiers of the city until he reached the palace gates. He expected to enter through the same wicket by which they had all left not long ago but instead found Captain Myrina waiting for him outside it. She was accompanied by an escort of Amazons wearing silken tabards.

"Have your comrades departed?" she asked.

"They have," Tyrael said. "I am here to reclaim my sword. I was told the queen has it in her keeping and that she wishes to speak with me."

"Yes, she will trade your sword for a bit of conversation. I hope you will not find the terms of the deal too burdensome. Please, come with me."

Instead of walking Tyrael like a captive under guard, Myrina fell in beside him as if he were a respected acquaintance. Together, they left the portico and main gate of the palace, traveling the lanes and squares that followed and abutted its high walls. Though Tyrael had traveled to Skovos before, and he had walked the streets of Temis, he had little memory of them. Disconcertingly, this was not an isolated lapse. It seemed that when his eons of angelic existence had been compressed into a fallible, mortal mind, some of his memories had become lost or inaccessible.

The captain walked with her hands clasped behind her back, her chin high. The townsfolk they passed gave the Amazons a wide, deferential berth. Tyrael noted how some of them appeared quite cowed.

"As I'm sure you've guessed," said Myrina, "the queen is likely to ask you more about your armor. And your sword."

Tyrael nodded. "I hope she will not be too disappointed when I have little more to say."

"She will be." Myrina offered a slight grin. "But not to worry. I suspect she also wishes to inquire about your travels. We Askari have always been an insular people, but our self-imposed seclusion has only grown in recent years, out of necessity. I think Queen Etara would welcome news from other parts of Sanctuary."

"You seem to know her well."

"I do, and in that way, I am fortunate. Not every daughter can claim such affinity with her mother."

Tyrael startled at that revelation. "Queen Etara is your mother?"

"Yes, she— Did no one mention that to you?"

"No one."

Myrina seemed surprised by that but also somewhat pleased. "People often assume that my parentage has afforded me a rank beyond my talents. If anything, I have had to work harder. Queen Etara is my ruler before she is my mother, just as I am her captain before I am her daughter. We both have our duties to Skovos."

"Does your rank mean you will be queen one day?" Tyrael meant for the question to be mildly provocative, to see how the captain answered it.

"I am next in line," she said, without hesitation but also without any apparent pride. "But not by birthright. Our monarchy is not hereditary. By tradition, the seniormost captain becomes the next queen, which is a much more civilized method of coronation than in centuries past. At one time, ancient laws allowed any Amazon warrior to challenge the queen for the crown. Thankfully, such combat has been unheard of for a very long time."

They arrived at a secondary entrance toward the rear of the palace complex, heavily fortified but not so grand as the main gates. The doors opened at their approach, admitting them through a passage into a broad cobbled courtyard surrounded by high walls and overlooked by Firstborn towers and statues of angels and demons. In addition to many doorways and corridors branching off the courtyard, an ornate archway stood on the far side with a view of greenery beyond.

"Before we go any further," Myrina said, "you should know I will not risk any harm to the queen. If you give me the least sign that you are a threat, I will not hesitate to kill you."

"Are we not past this?" asked Tyrael.

"In times like these, we are never past this."

With that, she led him across the courtyard and through the archway. They entered a private garden hemmed in by thick cypress. Honeybees lighted among roses, flowering herbs, and citrus trees, and the distant plucking of a lyre could be heard, as if from a tower window above. They followed a winding gravel path through plant beds, hedges, and trees, eventually arriving at a central fountain sculpted to resemble leaping dolphins. Nearby, Queen Etara sat at a lacquered table with El'druin laid across her lap. She had removed her armor and now wore a flowing peplos dress, secured at the shoulders with golden pins.

As Tyrael approached her, he bowed his head and said, "Be careful with that sword, your majesty. I would not want you to cut yourself. Despite its age, the blade is keen."

The queen arched an eyebrow. "It is foolish to think an Amazon needs your advice on handling a blade. Even an old warrior like me."

"Of course," Tyrael said. "I meant no offense."

"And I took none. Come, Faysal, sit with me."

Tyrael claimed the chair opposite her across the table, while Myrina took up a position directly behind him.

"Might we have some privacy, Captain?" the queen asked.

Tyrael refrained from turning to look, but a moment later, he heard Myrina's grudging footsteps move away, far enough for them to have a discreet conversation but near enough for her to intervene should she feel the need had arisen. A lark in one of the trees began to sing over the trilling of the fountain. The setting, lovely as it was, felt odd in contrast with the relative privation seen elsewhere.

"I hope you do not feel too ill-treated," the queen said. "With our history of fighting piracy, we must take certain precautions, you understand."

"I do. You must protect your people, and Skovos faces many threats."

She frowned slightly. "To what threats are you referring?"

"Piracy, smuggling, the Drowned."

The queen flicked her hand dismissively. "Myrina assures me that smuggling is only a very minor problem, and as for the Drowned, you are thinking of what Captain Adreona said earlier." She continued without waiting for confirmation. "She is excessively preoccupied with our defenses. I think our experience with the reapers has left her expecting attacks at all times, for which I suppose I cannot fault her. However, I think she occasionally . . . overstates the danger, which risks causing a panic among the people. We have faced the Drowned for millennia, and we know how to deal with them. Still, it is better to be overprepared than underprepared."

"That is true."

"The important thing is, Skovos is strong enough to meet whatever challenges we might face. As you astutely observed, we have weathered the near destruction of Sanctuary better than other nations."

Tyrael could plainly see she derived a measure of pride from that, which he decided to exploit to learn more. "I remain very interested in how you have achieved your recovery. Can you tell me about the Askarra Guard?"

"Yes, we formed them after the reapers to help us restore order. We deployed them to all the islands, dispensing swift justice against those who sought to exploit the turmoil for their own gain. They have been instrumental in safeguarding our supply chains of food and other goods so that none go hungry. Their presence is a great reassurance to the people."

The Askari civilians Tyrael had seen thus far seemed more intimidated than reassured, but he thought better of mentioning that. "And you find the Askarra Guard are still needed? The Reaping happened years ago . . ."

"Captain Myrina assures me they continue to be of vital importance to Skovos."

The way the queen spoke gave Tyrael the impression that she relied on Myrina for much of her information and decision-making. He suspected it was the captain who managed the daily functions of the Askarra Guard, and likely much of the administration throughout the islands. He wondered whether Etara was truly aware of the challenges facing her people.

"Enough about all of that." The queen traced her finger along El'druin's spine. "I am curious about you and how you truly came by your armor."

"There is nothing more to tell than what I have already told you."

"Really?" she said. "I thought perhaps you might be a paladin."

"You are perceptive," said Tyrael. "Some might say I am akin to a paladin, though I would not claim that title for myself, nor have I sworn myself to any such order. I have known paladins, and some can be . . . overly zealous."

"That is true. Here in Skovos, we've never had many followers of Akarat, nor worshippers of the Light. Our people are free to pray how they choose, of course. We do not forbid the practice of Zakarum or Skatsim or any other faith. But prophets and missionaries often have a difficult time making converts of the Askari. We are quite fulfilled in our adherence to the virtues laid down by our ancestors."

"Those virtues have guided you well," he said.

"And now I suppose you will want your sword," she said. "It is a remarkable blade. Also angelic, is it not?"

"It is," he said. "I have had it for so long, it feels as though it is almost a part of me."

"I feel the same way about my spear, the Thorn of Skovos. It is inscribed with runes that make it a fearsome and powerful weapon, but it has been many years since I wielded it in battle."

"Perhaps you may yet again."

The queen laughed. "I think, Faysal, that you are a flatterer. No, my fighting days are done, and I am content to leave the battles in younger hands."

Skovos had changed. Tyrael could remember an era long ago, admittedly a harsher time, when the Amazon Queen who could not lead her army into battle lost her throne. He would not celebrate a return of the islands to that way of life, but he also could not help but feel the Amazons had lost something when their warrior queen seemed so disconnected from the needs of her people.

"I don't know if you have already found lodging for yourself," Etara said, "but we have secured quarters for you within the palace." She gestured at the garden around them. "You are welcome to stay as my guest and enjoy the grounds at your leisure."

The invitation surprised him, considering his relative anonymity and the welcome he and the others had initially received. He suspected a hidden motive. "I wonder what I have done to warrant such generosity."

"You intrigue me," she said with a shrug. "I do not need to have a seer's sight to know there is something exceptional about you, even beyond your rare armor and sword."

"Now it is you who flatter me," Tyrael said.

The queen rose from her chair and made a show of offering him El'druin, holding the sword by its blade as she extended the hilt toward him. "I thank you for speaking with me," she said.

Tyrael stood with her and gently accepted the sword from her hands, feeling a subtle and familiar surge of connection between the weapon and himself as soon as he touched it. "It was my privilege," he said.

"And now I bid you good day. But I hope to speak with you again soon."

She turned and strode from the garden by a different route than the one Tyrael had used to enter it. Myrina approached him after her mother had gone and said, "If you will accompany me, I would like to show you something that I think will be of interest to you."

The captain guided him from the garden back to the courtyard, then down one of its branching hallways, which shortly deposited them into a small, shaded cloister. An octagonal white tower dominated the enclosure, a Firstborn construction like much of the palace. They followed the columned perimeter of the cloister and entered the tower through narrow pointed doors.

Inside the building, Tyrael found an impressive library, the air heavy with the scent of old paper and parchment. A sweeping staircase connecting its five levels followed the angled curvature of the wall around and around, rising from the base of the tower to its conical peak high above their heads. Wooden shelves filled with many thousands of books and scrolls lined the entirety of the structure's interior, except where slender windows interrupted the collection to admit slashes of light. Several heavy desks and lecterns occupied the ground floor, covered in stacks of books and maps.

A heavyset man wearing plain brown robes looked over the balcony of the third level, an open tome in his hands. "Welcome, Captain Myrina," he said, speaking with a gentle voice further softened by all the sound-absorbing leather and paper.

"Greetings, Keeper," the captain replied.

"Wait there, I'll be right down." The man then carefully closed the book and replaced it on the shelf before beginning his descent down the staircase. His footsteps sounded more like shuffling scrapes than thumps against the floor.

Myrina turned to Tyrael. "This tower holds the Askari royal archive and library. Not all, but much of it."

Tyrael wondered why the captain had brought him here. "It is an honor and a pleasure to be admitted here," he said, and he meant it.

"It is a pleasure to have you here," said the heavyset man as he came down the last flight of stairs to the ground floor. He was shorter than either Tyrael or the captain, with blue eyes, a mass of long blond hair, and, unlike other clean-shaven Askari, a close-cropped beard.

Myrina gestured toward him with a formal flat hand, leaving the other behind her back. "Faysal, this is Maziel, Keeper of the Archive. Maziel, this is Faysal, the mainlander I told you about."

"I was informed you are a scholar," the librarian said.

"I do have a deep interest in history and lore," Tyrael replied.

"Then I trust we will have much to discuss."

"Discuss?"

"Yes," Myrina said. "I thought the two of you might find common ground." She swept her hand in a disinterested arc, taking in the tower. "Perhaps some of the volumes here will contain answers to your questions about our history."

"I would be very pleased to explore your archive," Tyrael said.

The captain nodded. "Then I shall leave you to it. When you are ready to retire for the evening, I'm sure Maziel can show you to your guest quarters."

"I'd be happy to do so," the librarian said, with a slight bow at the waist.

With that, Myrina departed at a brisk clip, leaving the two men alone. A moment passed between them full of the library's silence.

"Thank you for tolerating my presence," Tyrael said. "I suspect the captain sent me here to keep me out of her way. I hope I will not cause too much disruption to your work as the keeper of this archive."

"Not at all," Maziel said. "I wish more people took an interest in our history, but to be quite candid with you, I'm seldom visited or consulted."

"That is unfortunate."

Maziel's glance seemed to linger on El'druin. "If you'll pardon me," he said, "you give the impression of a soldier more than a scholar."

"Can one not be both?"

"I suppose it's possible, if one lives long enough." He looked down at himself. "It's too late for me now to start winning sword fights. But I knew my proper place from an early age." He stepped away from Tyrael and went to one of the desks, where he began to sort and straighten the piles stacked upon it. "I started in the archive as a young man, assisting the previous Keeper. When he passed, I was offered his position."

"It seems an enviable occupation."

He looked up from the desk. "I'm glad you think so," he said, as if it were the first time he had ever heard anyone express that sentiment. "As a scholar, do you have any specific areas of focus or interest?"

Tyrael had begun to wonder if the archive might help revive some of his memories from the last time he was in Skovos. The first Horadrim had traveled more openly as powerful mages and it was likely their activities had been mentioned. It was even possible that evidence of Sho-Ren might be found in the records. "At present," he answered the librarian, "I am curious about relations and diplomacy between Skovos and other nations, factions, guilds, and other groups."

"Diplomacy is always an interesting topic," said Maziel. "The willingness of our queens to engage with other parts of Sanctuary has gone through periods of fluctuation. Skovos has been a much more open society at certain times in the past, more so than it is now. Come with me."

He shuffled toward the staircase, and Tyrael followed him. Together, they climbed to the second level of the tower.

"Below us on the ground floor are maps and atlases, along with non-Askari texts about other peoples and places. That is where you would find the writings of Abd al-Hazir, for example. On this floor, we keep all the royal Askari records, which would include decrees, treaties, trade agreements, and official annals and chronicles. You might start here."

"What do you keep on the upper floors?"

"On the third floor just above us, you'll find books written by Askari historians. Not official accounts, mind you, but they're often more detailed and textured than the dry renderings of palace scribes. On the fourth level, we keep our more . . . subjective texts. That's where you'll find journals and memoirs, private correspondence, collections of folktales, that sort of thing."

"And on the fifth floor?"

"That is where we shelve materials related to the Firstborn."

Tyrael looked at him in surprise. "You have Firstborn writings?"

"Not a large collection, but yes. That is also where we keep the work of Askari scholars who have made a study of Firstborn architecture, relics, and so forth. As you might assume, much of it is highly speculative."

"I see."

"Do you have a particular time period you're interested in researching?"

Tyrael did not want to reveal too much about his true interest in the Horadrim, so he decided to let the librarian believe he had guided him where he already wanted to go. "A moment ago, you mentioned a more open period of diplomacy in the past?"

"Yes, the eleventh century comes readily to mind. That period saw Kurast become the capital of Kehjistan under Emperor Tassara, the conquest of the west by Rakkis, and the rise of the Zakarum church. I'd assume those powers all sent emissaries to Skovos, for which there would be some records."

Those events also happened to follow the founding of the Horadrim, very near the time of their first visit to Skovos. "You are quite knowledgeable, Maziel."

"I live in a library," Maziel said. "I'm expected to be knowledgeable."

"I suspect your knowledge of Skovos history gives you a unique perspective on recent events."

"Such as?"

"The formation of the Askarra Guard, for example. Such divisions within the Amazon ranks are rare, historically, are they not?"

Maziel's demeanor turned hard and blank. "Unprecedented challenges call for radical solutions." He then ushered Tyrael around the course of the walkway to a section of shelves on the far side of the tower. "I would suggest you begin your reading here."

With that, the librarian returned to the stairs and climbed back up to the third floor, while Tyrael began his search.

CHAPTER SIXTEEN

After bidding farewell to Tanna, Lorath made his way through the encampment down toward the docks. He found that a company of Amazons had stayed behind to maintain and defend the fort, going about their various duties and chores as if nothing had changed. When Lorath had been a young, inexperienced soldier, he probably would have considered them the lucky ones, and he might have felt some envy toward them, even if he refused to admit that to himself or anyone else. But that was before he joined the Horadrim, and before Malthael changed the world. Now Lorath was eager for the battle and glad to be heading toward the front; perhaps Donan was right, and he really was perpetually looking for a fight.

By the time he reached the wharf, it appeared that fifteen or twenty warships had departed the harbor, judging by the empty slips. He marched along the dock and then out onto the floating pier where the *Arabel* sat at anchor. Keldon moved about the top deck, preparing her to sail.

Lorath stowed his gear aboard and said, "I'll go find a rowboat to tow us—"

"No need," Keldon said. "Cast off, and I'll show you."

Confused, Lorath did as the sailor ordered, freeing the *Arabel* from her moorings and pushing off from the pier. Then Keldon called him down to the helm, where he stood at the tiller, and Lorath noticed a new wooden spar reaching up and over the aft cabin from the stern like the shaft of a heavy oar, its end secured to the deck by a line.

"You remember Adreona said the *Arabel* needed oars?" Keldon said. "Well, I rigged her for sculling with help from the blacksmith—she forged the metal fittings. All you have to do is pull it back and forth with that line. The weight of the oar and the machinery should do the rest."

"The captain is wise. You really have kept yourself busy."

"Aye," Keldon said. "Now, get us moving."

Lorath took hold of the line and hauled it from side to side as directed. The motion took some effort, but within a few moments, the sloop pushed forward. They seemed to crawl at first, inching away from their berth. But as Lorath kept heaving the oar, the ship gained speed and enough momentum that he had to ease off in places so Keldon could steer them through the surrounding docks, out into the open harbor. Lorath wondered if the guards at the sea-gate would even allow them to leave, but it seemed Keldon had already come to an understanding with them. The gates opened before they had reached them, allowing them to glide through without the need for Lorath to break the rhythm of his stroke.

Outside the fenced harbor, a strong wind swept around the island. Keldon showed Lorath how to cinch a line on the sculling oar to lift it out of the water, and then the two of them set about raising the sails. Before long, they were underway, plying northwest along the eastern coast of Athulua.

The *Arabel* made good time. As they rounded the island's northern headland, with its cliff-top temple of white towers, they turned to

the southwest, and Lorath glimpsed the Amazon fleet in the far distance, sailing into the misty sea east of Atanos. Under normal conditions, Keldon's sloop might have overtaken the heavy square-rigged warships, but the Amazons supplemented their wind power with the stroke of their oars.

"They'll get there ahead of us," Lorath said.

"I'm guessing we'll still have our share of fighting to do, if that's what you're worried about. Or is there something else that troubles you?"

"Such as?"

"Could it be you're concerned about a certain Amazon captain?" The old sailor raised his brow in a knowing, suggestive way.

"I'm concerned about the Askari who will die if an undead army conquers this island."

Keldon bowed his head in acceptance, but with a wry smile. "She won't thank you for rescuing her, you know. A woman like that ain't looking for a savior. What she wants is an ally."

"Then that is what we will be."

On they sailed, and that afternoon they reached the boundary of fog that lay upon the water like a sickly, dissipated cloud. Their first encounter with that dead sea had been accidental, driven by the will of a storm. This time, they sailed into those shallow, sluggish waters knowingly, but at least Keldon now had a chart for navigation. As the mist closed in around them, Lorath felt smothered and cut off from the rest of the world. He attended to every wave and splash, listening intently for signs of the Drowned in the water around their boat. The wind slackened but did not die completely this time, allowing them to push on slowly by sail.

Night came without incident, but the going was more perilous with their field of vision limited by the darkness and the fog. Lorath lit an oil lantern and hung it from the prow, keeping watch for obstacles that might not appear on the map that Keldon had acquired back at the fort. Ordinarily, they would've hove to and waited for dawn, but with every moment potentially counted in lives lost, they could afford no such delays.

The next day arrived, and the fog began to thin, allowing them to glimpse more of the surrounding sea and rough terrain. The pieces of land that rose above the water appeared cracked and broken, waterways and channels running through them like fissures through shattered crockery. Jagged shards of rock jutted upward among boggy sumps and marshy hillocks, and ravens and other carrion eaters screeched from hidden perches. The feeble currents and waves did little to circulate the water, allowing waterweeds and slicks of algae to bloom in stagnant basins. Even more so than the Blood Marsh, the sea near Atanos gave Lorath the impression of a cursed land, utterly wasted and destroyed. A fitting home for the Drowned.

Keldon tried to keep the *Arabel* to the deeper channels marked on his nautical chart, but there were times when Lorath had to man the sculling oar, which allowed them to better navigate the twisting corridors of tortured stone. The slowness of their pace at times drove Lorath mad—the rage within him yearned to swing his polearm, not a sculling oar—but they passed another day, and he hoped that the third would bring them to the battle at last.

That evening, Lorath lit the lantern again and kept watch at the prow, though the fog continued to thin, and the moon could be seen fading in and out of desultory clouds.

"Narrows up ahead," Keldon called from the stern. "According to the map, that is."

Not long after, two low shelves of craggy rock emerged from the mist, stretching out of sight to the east and west, with an ominous cleft between them. If Lorath looked at the feature like a soldier, the choke point was not unlike the entrance to a keep, which set him on edge.

"I don't like that," he said. "Can we sail around?"

"Depends on your eagerness for a delay," Keldon said. "I think the Amazons will have come this way."

Lorath conceded this through his silence, but he remained alert as they approached the two shoulders of land and then sailed between them. The cliffs were not tall, but they loomed high enough over the ship to afford the advantage of elevation to any assailants who might be hiding, waiting to attack. Lorath gave so much of his attention to watching the rims above them that he almost missed a disturbance in the water.

First one lump floated by, like a piece of pale driftwood, and then another, and another, until their ship was surrounded. Lorath leapt across the deck for his polearm, ready to fight the Drowned he expected to board, but none came over the gunwale.

"I think these undead are dead," said Keldon, craning to peer over the stern.

Lorath looked again. The old sailor was right. Even in the darkness, he could now see that the corpses in the water had all been burned and chopped apart. Amazon arrow shafts protruded from many of the bobbing lumps of charred flesh. Milky eyes looked up at the *Arabel* without seeing, and a residual film of oil coated the water with an iridescent sheen.

"Glad to see your time in the stables did nothing to dull your instincts," said Keldon. "The warships were attacked here."

Lorath gripped the gunwale, shaking his head. "I'd rather have been wrong. An attack here shows clear strategy, as if the Drowned really are displaying some level of intelligence."

"It looks like the Amazons gave them one hell of a fight, though."

"And cleared the way for us," Lorath said.

The wind had subsided, so they switched to sculling and pushed their way through the charnel waters. Lorath watched for Amazon bodies among the remains of the enemy but saw none. That meant either the warships had suffered no casualties on their way through or they had reclaimed their dead to prevent them from joining the Drowned. Lorath hoped for the former.

They transited the strait and continued onward, steadily sailing south. Toward dawn, the pulsing, chaotic glow of many fires reached through the fog ahead of them like a fitful sunrise on the wrong horizon, accompanied by the thunder of distant explosions. Lorath began to hear faint sounds of battle, which only grew louder with each league they traveled. The clang of metal, war cries, the hateful shrieking of the cursed, the screams of the dying, all soon reached his ears. He felt his blood quickening, his rage rearing as they bored through a final bank of mist, and the battle came into view.

The Athulua Garrison occupied a promontory wedge jutting outward from the coast. Any force attacking that post directly from the sea would have to scale a daunting face of natural cliffs surmounted by a wooden palisade. Even though a few Drowned could be seen attempting the climb, it did not appear they posed a threat to the encampment. On the other side of the fort, an earthen wall protected its landward front, surrounded by fields at the mouth of the shallow glen Lorath had seen on the map, and there the enemy had massed for an assault on the main gates.

A thin barrage of burning missiles and explosive shells rained down on the Drowned horde, causing some damage to their ranks. However, the newly arrived Amazon warships had plowed directly into the Drowned-infested waters, surrounding the promontory with a defensive crescent of fire and steel. Their efforts appeared to have pushed the enemy forces back, preventing additional Drowned from joining the force attacking the eastern wall.

Lorath hurried to help Keldon lower the sails, letting the *Arabel* drift a safe distance from the violence. It did not appear that Tavie's cavalry had arrived yet.

"There's another sight I've not beheld," the sailor said. "You wanted a fight, lad, well, there it is. What's the plan?"

Lorath considered their options for a line of attack. "We won't be much help on the water," he said. "We have no incendiary weapons, and the Amazon warships appear to have that front in hand."

Keldon regarded the mob at the gates with skepticism. "I don't mean to injure your pride, but I doubt the two of us can turn the tide of that land assault, either."

"Not yet," Lorath said. "First, we need to find Adreona."

"In that mayhem? How? Why?"

"Her message said she and her company had holed up in a cave near a place called the Pommel." Lorath scanned the surrounding terrain, and it did not take long to spot a large rounded feature of rock standing like a saddle pommel partway down a sloping ridge on the far side of the glen. "There. That must be it, but we'll have to make our way there on foot. Put to shore here. Any nearer and I think the Drowned would be on us."

Keldon's ship had a fairly shallow draft, which allowed them to drop anchor close enough to wade ashore. From there, they skulked up the pebbly beach into a thicket of scrub oak and juniper. A few farms long since fallen into ruin lay between them and the garrison, offering stone fences and overgrown shaws to hide behind while they skirted as far around the Drowned horde as they could manage. Even at a distance, the ringing of unholy bells filled Lorath with a chilling dread, and the reek of rot and bilge wafted over him whenever he turned to survey the enemy's strength.

There were hundreds of them. Hooded juggernauts and grotesque tidewalkers towered over simpering, vicious wretches, while the decayed corpses of former sailors brandished cutlasses and clubs. Unlike the Drowned Lorath had heard of in other parts of Sanctuary, some of these wore pieces of armor and jewelry that appeared to be of Firstborn style and make. They moved with unnatural lurches, rasping voices issuing from gaping mouths. They could not be reasoned with. They could not be appeased. They knew only mindless hatred and sought only to kill and destroy. Anyone facing such horror could be forgiven for fleeing in terror at the first glimpse of it, yet Adreona and her Amazons had not run. They remained valiant in tireless defense of their people.

Eventually, Lorath and Keldon reached the mouth of the glen. The vestiges of a trackway from more ancient days could still be seen in a winding descent from the nearer northern ridgeline down to the field before the fort. The current road followed the valley floor and led directly across the field to the main gates; Lorath assumed Tavie and her riders would arrive by that route.

To reach the Pommel, he and Keldon needed to cross the road out in the open, several hundred paces behind the horde, which they managed to do without being seen. From there, they started up the ridge on the southern side of the glen but found it to be an unstable slope of shale. So, they skirted around it and picked their way through more abandoned homesteads until the Pommel stood above and behind them. Lorath could not yet see any cave. As they made their way through overgrown fields and pastures, the sounds of a secondary skirmish reached them, much closer than the main horde.

"Do you hear that?" Keldon asked.

Aside from the cavalry, Lorath knew of only one Amazon company on land outside the walls of the fort. "Adreona," he said, and he broke into a sprint toward the fray.

Keldon followed him. They passed the remnants of several outbuildings and then came upon a party of six Amazon warriors in a degraded farmyard, their backs against the splintered hulk of a fallen barn, surrounded by Drowned. Lorath glimpsed Adreona among them, and at the sight of her, he felt a powerful urge to rush to her defense. But he resisted this impulse in favor of a clearer strategy, choosing instead to draw the enemy's attention with a roar.

The Drowned turned in surprise to face him, and then several of them attacked. Within moments Lorath's polearm had taken off heads and limbs. He ducked their confused, haphazard blows and swung his blade in all directions, fighting to break through their line. The Drowned outnumbered the Amazons two or three to one, but Lorath's distraction had disoriented the enemy for the few moments Adreona's company needed to go on the offensive. Their renewed war cries only heightened his own vengeful rage, but then he saw a juggernaut, swinging a colossal flail, bearing down on Adreona.

Lorath shouted her name and barreled toward her, unthinking, shouldering enemies aside to reach her. He came up behind the brute and slashed low, cutting deep into the monster's flanks, severing its hamstrings. The thing wobbled and collapsed to its knees, still taller than Adreona. She drove the behemoth onto its back and killed it with a spear thrust into its skull. Then she looked at Lorath over the corpse.

"You should not be here!" she shouted.

Lorath hadn't known what to expect from her when she saw him. He knew he had defied her orders, but he had hoped she would be at least somewhat pleased to see him, and perhaps even grateful for his aid.

"You just don't know when to quit, do you?" she said, then turned away from him without waiting for a reply. By that time, the other Amazons had slain the rest of the Drowned, with some help from Keldon. The old sailor stood with his chest heaving, out of breath, several corpses at his feet.

"Back to the cave," Adreona said.

She led them from the farmyard toward the hill behind it, then up onto a goat path that climbed the slope, using the terrain's natural depressions and folds to keep them out of sight from the ground below. After several switchbacks, they crested a bluff with a crevice in the rock set back from the ledge. This opening admitted them into a large natural chamber the Amazons had obviously been using for some time. Crates and sacks of supplies filled the corners, furs and other bedding lined the floor, and the cold ashes from an old cook fire sat near the mouth of the cave. Upon entering, Adreona first checked each of her warriors for wounds, and after she confirmed they were all relatively uninjured, she rounded on Lorath with disciplined anger.

"Now. You will explain yourself."

He folded his arms. "Your message arrived at Fort Galina, calling for aid. I watched Tavie ride out with a company on horseback—"

"When did Tavie ride out?" she asked.

"Two days ago."

"How many?"

"Over thirty. Every mount fit to carry a warrior."

"Thirty won't be enough. To break this siege, we'll also need warriors from the fleet to come ashore, and every spear inside the fort." She strode to the mouth of the cave and looked out. "When I saw our ships, I had hoped to finally leave this cave and join them. The Drowned cut us off."

"We have a ship," said Keldon. "She's anchored north of here."

Adreona shook her head. "Tavie's coming changes things. We

need to stay here and warn them. Otherwise, they might come charging out of that canyon and straight into an army of Drowned."

The first hint of an idea took shape in Lorath's mind. "The canyon . . ."

"What about it?" asked Adreona.

"The southern slope is shale," he said. "How unstable is it?"

Adreona pinched her chin in thought, as if the plan forming in Lorath's thoughts had leapt to hers. "An avalanche?"

"The glen is a choke point," he said. "Like the passageway into your keep. You draw the Drowned in, and then you bury them."

Some of the other warriors in the cave had been listening, and when Adreona turned toward them, they nodded and shrugged their openness to the possibility.

"The warships are cutting off reinforcements from the water," Lorath went on. "Leave them there. You just have to worry about the Drowned forces already on land. Even if you don't kill them all, you could definitely soften them up."

"How do you trigger an avalanche?" Keldon asked.

Lorath had not yet solved that problem.

It was Adreona who put forward the answer.

CHAPTER SEVENTEEN

"We have what we need," Adreona explained. "We have the ingredients for Askari fire. If we ignite it at the top of the hill, that should trigger an avalanche of the shale."

"We need something to lure the Drowned into the trap," Lorath said. "For this plan to work, we need them to commit in numbers."

"That's where Tavie comes in," said Adreona. She then wrote orders and sent two of her warriors as runners, tasked with intercepting the cavalry on the road to warn them of the plan and to instruct them in the role they must play as bait.

"What can I do to help?" Lorath asked.

"You can stay out of our way," she said.

Lorath had no idea what more he could do to make Adreona trust him, and he had begun to accept that perhaps she never would. Until she did, he was forced to sit back and watch as the Amazons brought out volatile oils from the goods stored in the cave. They blended these and poured the mixture into jugs and bottles, which they then fitted with fuses, and when they had a sufficient quantity, they made to leave the cavern to plant them across the top of the ridge. Lorath rose to accompany them, but Adreona stopped him.

"You will wait here."

He could bear it no longer, and his frustration found its way into his voice as a growl. "I will not be left behind again. I am not a child in need of your protection."

"And I don't think you truly understand what it means to be an Amazon. I have taken an oath, Lorath, and I will lay down my life if that is needed to fulfill my oath. I am a guardian of Skovos and all who dwell here. At this moment, that includes you, which means you are under my protection. But for some reason, you insist on making that very difficult for me."

Lorath chuckled.

"Something about that amuses you?"

"No, no," he said. "Or, at least, it doesn't amuse me for the reason you might think. It's just that I'm usually the one saying that. I respect your oath, because I have taken one as well."

"What oath?"

In that moment, Lorath almost told her that he belonged to the Horadrim, but instead he thought back to what Keldon had said about what Adreona was looking for. "My oath isn't important right now. Your oath is, and I am only here to help you carry it out. For Skovos. I don't need your protection, and you certainly don't need mine. I am here to fight for you, *with* you." She seemed to be listening to him, and he took a step closer to her. "I won't be left behind again. You'll have to tie me up, and even then, I'll just break free and follow you."

"You really *don't* know when to quit, do you?"

"Some might say that's an admirable quality."

She looked like she would go on refusing him if she could find another argument, but she had none. "Fine. You can accompany us to the ridge."

Lorath bowed his head in victory, and when he looked over at Keldon, the old sailor gave him a wink.

They left the cave and followed a different path that continued north along the bluff, in the direction of the Pommel. From that height, they had a view of the siege in the water below them. The warships surrounding the promontory appeared to be holding the line against the Drowned. Their decks appeared orderly, with ranks of archers and warriors standing at the ready, but the flames seemed to be doing most of the deterrence. That vantage also afforded Lorath a glimpse into the garrison, where Amazons fought from the walls against the enemies that tried to assail them. The action appeared diminished in size by the distance, the roar of battle a faint disturbance, but Lorath knew well the horror that the Amazons trapped down there would endure.

Adreona shielded her eyes with her hand, looking even farther westward, where the perpetual haze over the sea of Atanos obscured the horizon line between the sky and the broken land.

"I can't see the watchfire," she said, pointing. "It should be out there, less than a league beyond the fort."

"How easily can it be seen during the day?" Lorath asked. "Perhaps the fog is shrouding it?"

"It's usually visible." She lowered her hand, brow furrowed in doubt.

"If it has somehow gone out," Lorath said, "that would explain how this Drowned army got through."

"The watchfire has never gone out," Adreona said. "If it has, then we could be dealing with a greater threat than any we have faced since before it was lit. This incursion would only be the beginning." She turned northward and resumed their trek along the path, but she kept casting searching glances toward the sea.

The trackway they traveled ran parallel to the line of the ridge high above them until it wrapped around an escarpment where they could look down the slope of shale into the valley. The Pommel stood over them like a sentinel, as tall and broad as a castle tower but balanced on a tapered throat due to some curious quirk of weathering or erosion.

From that position, they had a view of the road as it came down the highlands from the east and wound its way through the glen, but most important, they could see around a bend the Drowned could not. It was there Tavie would halt and wait, assuming the messengers reached her, but Lorath could not see her cavalry yet.

The Amazons carrying the incendiary jugs and bottles fanned out along the top of the shale slope, sending some of the loose stones sliding downward. They then began to nestle the Askari fire deep into the slippery fragments, so their blasts would upset as much of the unstable rock as possible. The fuses would give them only a few minutes to get clear of danger.

"What if they don't work?" Keldon asked.

Lorath answered, "Then at least the narrowness of the valley will prevent the Drowned from flanking us."

"Us?" Adreona asked.

Lorath turned toward her. "I thought we settled this."

"What I thought," she said, "is that you would stay up here on the ridge to make sure the avalanche is triggered as planned. I am entrusting you with this. If the Drowned take the bait, it is up to you to light the fuses when the rockslide will take out as many as possible."

Lorath wanted to fight. He wanted to slay the Drowned in retribution for the suffering they had caused and the lives they had taken. He would have tried to go with Adreona into battle, but she had planted an uncertainty in his mind that immediately took root: Someone did need to stay behind to ensure the success of the avalanche. Their victory depended on it, and the idea had been Lorath's to begin with. So, he took up the small torch and watched as Adreona and her Amazon warriors continued eastward along the ridge, deeper into the valley, leaving him behind with Keldon to light the fuses. By the time Adreona had made it beyond the slope of shale and begun her descent to the valley floor, a small dust cloud had risen beyond the last bend in the road, coming toward them. Shortly thereafter, that cloud rounded the fold, and Tavie's cavalry rode into Lorath's view, still out of sight from the Drowned down on the field. The riders halted at the expected point, which meant Adreona's messengers had reached them. Tavie held that position for several minutes, perhaps resting and regrouping after their long journey, readying themselves for the battle ahead.

The pause gave Lorath time to consider all the ways their stratagem might fail. Even if the Askari fire succeeded in triggering an avalanche, what if the rockslide remained a minimal event, doing negligible damage below? What if it did too much damage and harmed the Amazon forces? What if the Drowned saw through the ruse and refused to enter the canyon at all? These questions and many others filled Lorath with sudden doubt about the likelihood of the plan's success, but then Tavie and her cavalry initiated their slow march forward, and he could do nothing but be ready to enact his part.

The Amazons blew on their war horns. Their bellowing echoed up and down the glen, seeming to multiply, creating the auditory illusion of a greater force than they actually possessed, a full and triumphant sound that rang off the walls, as if that clarion alone could bring the stone down.

The horns drew the attention of the Drowned. Their rearward ranks turned to face the threat that had suddenly appeared behind them, some even moving a few paces in the direction of the glen. Lorath scrambled to get in position to light the first fuse, waiting and watching, but the enemy failed to attack, their few maneuvers appearing furtive and defensive. They had not yet taken the bait, and the cavalry paused its advance at the mouth of the glen, directly beneath the shale slope.

Keldon sucked his teeth. "Perhaps those infernal creatures are cleverer than we credited them."

Just then, one of the horses broke from the line, and Lorath recognized Zerae. Adreona rode her, charging the Drowned army alone, wielding a bow. Lorath could hear her voice raised in war cries. She sat high in her saddle firing arrow after arrow that all found their marks, galloping as if she meant to drive right into the heart of the Drowned army. The enemy forces howled and moved to receive her, but at the last moment, she veered and raced down the length of the Drowned line, still shooting arrows from her bow. Then she veered again, this time riding back to join her waiting cavalry. The Amazons blew on their horns again, taunting their enemies.

The Drowned had been roused and now gave chase, like an unthinking swarm pouring forward as one body, committing almost their entire number. Lorath and Keldon readied to light the fuses. The Amazon cavalry held its position, firing volleys of arrows into the charging Drowned army, then suddenly turned and galloped eastward as if in retreat, deeper into the glen. The enemy kept coming, and a moment later their vanguard crossed the mouth of the valley.

"Hold," Lorath said.

They waited until the first third of the enemy force breached the glen, and then they ignited the first fuses, scrambling over the shale from one incendiary vessel to the next. When the first ones blew, they shot fire, splinters of rock, and clouds of oily smoke into the air. They loosed a cascade, but nowhere near the size the Amazons would need down below to bury the enemy. Almost without thought, Lorath snatched up a jug and darted upward.

"Get clear!" he shouted at Keldon over the crashing of falling shale.

"What?" the sailor said, but then he seemed to realize what Lorath planned to do and rushed out of the way. "You're mad!"

Lorath bolted up the ridge, ignoring the charges blowing behind him, until he reached the narrow base of the Pommel. He had no idea if this would work, but the rockslide they had triggered would only slow the enemy, not destroy it. They needed something much more massive. He rammed the jug up against the Pommel's throat on its north side, facing the valley. Then he murmured the incantation needed to summon a flame. Lorath didn't have Donan's skill with magic, but he knew a few useful spells, and a moment later, he had lit the fuse. Then he clambered away, getting as much distance as he could before the jug exploded with a thunderous crack, throwing a cloud of smoke and shrapnel outward.

Nothing happened at first. Then the Pommel shifted slowly, grinding and grumbling, and as it leaned, its shifting weight crushed more and more of its own base, until it finally tipped over like a tower falling to an earthquake.

When it slammed into the hillside, it sank into the shale and sundered, scattering monolithic pieces of itself, all of which took the mountainside down with them as they tumbled into the glen. The roar of it was deafening, and Lorath felt the entire ridge trembling beneath his feet as the rockslide swelled into a much greater avalanche than he had expected. He could do nothing but watch, hoping the Amazons had gotten themselves clear.

The Drowned army had not. Through the choking billow of dust, Lorath could see the bulk of the horde had been caught beneath it, smashed into oblivion by a churning tide of rock. When the pieces of the Pommel finally settled in their bed of shale, fixed in the wedge of the valley, they blocked the mouth of the glen like a towering dam.

The moments of quiet that followed felt shocked, throttled into silence. Lorath waved the dust away from his face, coughing and peering at the ridge below. "Keldon!" he shouted. "Are you there?"

"Barely!" the sailor shouted. "Warn me the next time you plan to break a mountain in half!"

Lorath laughed with relief. Then he heard war cries coming from the north. He looked across the valley at the opposing ridge, and through the settling haze he glimpsed the Amazon cavalry racing along the old trackway. In their feigned retreat, they had backtracked to climb up onto the hill, which carried them over and around the landslide now blocking the lower road, then down to the field before the fort. Lorath could see little of their work, but he could hear the enemy shrieking and dying. The few remaining Drowned were in disarray and could hardly mount a defense as the cavalry stampeded through them with spear and bow. The Amazons within the fort had opened the gates and charged out to assist in slaying the last of the horde.

Lorath descended to the lower ridge and found Keldon coated with rock dust like a miller covered in flour. The two of them shared another laugh and then picked their way downward as fast as they could to join the battle, but by the time they reached the field, the Drowned had been annihilated. The fort was saved. The incursion had been defeated.

The Athulua Garrison was a much smaller encampment than Fort Galina, but after their victory, no one objected to the cramped quarters. Keldon found somewhere to rest and celebrate, but Lorath immediately went to help with the horses in the crowded stables, checking them over after their hard ride and the battle. A few of them had gone lame, and others had been mortally injured in the battle, but Lorath was relieved to find that Zerae had come through her ordeal and would hopefully return to Arjak soon.

The sunset that evening appeared crimson through the lingering dust and the thick columns of smoke rising from the bonfires of Drowned corpses. As Lorath was heaving fresh straw bedding into the stalls, Adreona came looking for him. She wore a bandage wrapped around her arm through which had soaked a bit of blood. Dirt had collected in the fine creases of her skin, and by the red evening light, her green eyes seemed illuminated from within.

"I wondered where you had got to," she said.

"You assigned me to the stables. I'm simply performing the duty I was given." He nodded toward her bandage. "Are you okay?"

"It will heal." She took a step closer to him. "Listen, what you did . . . that was quite the landslide."

He quit shoveling straw and propped the pitchfork against the side of the stall. "Wasn't that the plan?"

"Yes. But bringing down the Pommel was not. You—"

"I know," he said. "I don't know when to quit."

She smiled. "No, you don't, but that's not what I was going to say."

"No? Then what were you going to say?"

"I was going to thank you, actually. I don't think the plan would have worked if you hadn't done what you did. You were right, and you keep managing to surprise me."

Lorath had not expected a thank-you, but he accepted it with a bow of his head. "The plan would not have worked without you, either. It was you who baited the Drowned. I watched you from the ridge, and that was an impressive ride."

She looked down at the bandage on her arm. "I did only what any of my war-sisters would have done."

Then they stood in a silence that felt suddenly charged. Until this moment, Lorath's attraction to Adreona had been easy to dismiss, along with Keldon's taunts. In another time and place, he would not have hesitated to pursue her, but she was not a passing flirtation in a tavern, and he was no longer a soldier marching through her village. He was in Skovos as a member of the Horadrim, and he put that responsibility above all else. She was an Amazon captain, subject to her queen and bound by the oath that she had sworn. Drawn as Lorath was to her, he doubted she felt the same way toward him.

"I am holding a council meeting this evening," she said. "You and Keldon have earned a place there. We have important matters to discuss, and I think your perspectives might be useful."

Attraction aside, at least her view of his martial value had shifted. "We would be glad to attend and offer what help we can."

So, later that night, he and Keldon joined Adreona, Tavie, and a few other Amazons of senior rank around a campfire, as the fort's main hall had been given over to the tending of the wounded. They ate a meager meal of field rations and then passed around a bottle of Skovos wine that someone had found in the fort's stores, taking turns swigging from it.

"I wanted to wait until nightfall to be sure," Adreona said, "but it seems clear now that the great watchfire has gone out."

Tavie cast a quick glance at Lorath. Only days before, she had been standing over the map at Fort Galina, talking with him about this very possibility.

"We don't know how," Adreona continued. "The watchfire has

never been extinguished. That's why I plan to take a ship and investigate what happened."

"You want to sail out there?" asked one of the other Amazons. "Now? With the Drowned massing offshore?"

"Yes." Adreona looked into the eyes of everyone sitting around the fire. "I think the Drowned are gathering out there *because* the watchfire has somehow been extinguished. We have dealt them a blow today, but without the watchfire, more of them will come, and they will keep coming. This incursion isn't over. It's just beginning, and the longer we wait, the harder it will be to get out there and determine what happened."

The fire popped and sparked. No one spoke for several moments.

"Who will you send?" asked Tavie.

"I won't ask anyone else to take such a risk," Adreona answered. "I will go."

Tavie looked down suddenly at her boots, shaking her head and bouncing one of her knees.

"Do you have an objection, Shieldmatron?" Adreona asked.

"Yes," Tavie said, looking up. "Yes, I do. This is not a risk you should take—nor anyone else. Not right now." She sat up straight and pointed westward. "We can all see from here the watchfire is out. In this moment, what more do we need to know? I think we should notify Queen Etara and request that Captain Myrina send us a legion of silks to reinforce our position. Once we are secure, *then* we can investigate what happened."

"Thank you for your input," Adreona said. Lorath could see her neck muscles tightening in the firelight. "Does anyone else have something to add?"

No one spoke. Lorath fought with himself over whether he should remain silent, but he decided to trust that Adreona had meant what she said when she invited him to this council. He cleared his throat. "I have something to say."

Everyone around the fire turned to stare at him.

"If I may?" he added.

"You may," said Adreona.

Tavie looked like she wanted to object, but she refrained from doing so.

"I know I'm an outsider," Lorath said, "but I agree with the captain. This incursion only happened because the watchfire went out. To plan your future defense, you need to understand the capabilities of your enemy, which means it is critical to find out if the Drowned somehow managed to extinguish the fire."

A few of the Amazons nodded in agreement with him. Adreona gave him a very subtle bow of her head in thanks.

"Exactly my thinking," she said. "I will sail tomorrow, alone if I must."

Tavie stood. "You know I will follow your command. If you are going, then I will go with you. I know others will volunteer. We'll take one of the warships—"

"No," said Adreona. "All our ships are needed here, to maintain the sea defense of this garrison."

"Well, that answers my question," said Keldon, tipping back the dregs of the wine bottle. "I was wondering why you invited an old sailor like me to this esteemed gathering."

Adreona acknowledged this with a nod. "But I won't force you to allow us the use of your ship."

"You don't have to," Keldon said, and then he turned to Lorath. "Isn't that right?"

"That's right," said Lorath. He would have wanted to offer the *Arabel* even if Adreona had not asked. "We'll leave at first light."

After the fireside council, Keldon went to sleep on the *Arabel,* while Lorath returned to the stables. A bed of hay on land seemed more appealing to him than the tight, rocking confines of a ship's bunk, especially since they would be setting sail the next morning. He had just spread his blanket over the straw when a shadow fell across him, and he looked back to see that Adreona had returned.

"I hope I didn't speak out of turn," he said.

"Not at all. I appreciated what you said."

"Well, I meant it. I think you're right to go investigate—"

"No more talk of that tonight." She stepped closer toward him. "Let me help you with your armor."

"I don't need—"

She looked directly into his eyes as she gently but insistently turned him around. His back to her, she loosened the straps securing his pauldrons to his shoulders, which she removed and set carefully down in the straw. He felt her hands at his sides next, unfastening the buckles connecting his back and breastplates until she pulled both pieces away. She turned him back around, and together they stripped off his mail shirt, which fell to the ground with a heavy clink, followed by his gambeson. Then she knelt, and her hands felt around his cuisses, reaching between his legs to remove the armor from his thighs.

After that, she stood. "Now help me with mine," she said.

He did as she asked, loosening the ties and straps of her leather armor, removing it piece by piece from her body in the same order that she had removed his, revealing the linen tunic she wore beneath. The blue moonlight put the sea in her green eyes, and his earlier reservations fell away. It seemed she was as drawn to him as he was to her.

"Adreona—"

She pulled him into an aggressive kiss, her breath hot against his lips, his face, his neck. He wrapped his arms around her waist and drew her up against him, returning her kiss. His own lips traced a line along her cheek to her ear, then down her neck to her collarbone and out across her bare shoulder as he yanked the collar of her tunic aside. She peeled off her shirt, then pulled him down on top of her into the bed he had made in the straw.

CHAPTER EIGHTEEN

When Donan left the Oracle Queen's cave, he did so by a different route from the path by which he had arrived, emerging near a small mountainous Askari settlement he learned was called Vision's End. The villagers there were very kind, providing Donan with food and drink before directing him to the trail that would bring him back to where he had started his journey on Philios.

Near the Oracle Queen's cave, water flowed more abundantly than it did elsewhere on the island. Streams that began their lives as ice atop Mount Karcheus came winding down through dense forests, gathering here and there in pools that somehow seemed much deeper and murkier than they ought to be. The trees that drank from those meres grew thick and gnarled, with enclosing canopies that stifled the air and blocked much of the light from the sun. With every step along the road through the wood, Donan felt watched, as if the whole of the forest were alert to his presence, observing him with the all-seeing eye of the seers.

He felt some relief when the trees began to thin, the streambeds dried up, and the woodland path became a road that descended from the mountain toward the coast. Lycander could be seen on the horizon, green and wild, and Temis stood across the channel. By the late afternoon, he could see the monumental Bridge of the Eye in the distance.

It was evening by the time he returned to Alenia's inn, and he found her busy serving drink and food to the same patrons he had conversed with the night before last. He took a seat inside, and when she saw him, she brought over an ale and a plate of food, setting both down in front of him with a knowing nod. He ate and drank slowly, waiting for the crowd to disperse, and after the last patron had gone, Alenia came over and sat down at his table.

"Did you learn what you wanted to learn?" she asked.

"Not yet," he said. "But I learned where my journey takes me next."

"And where is that?"

"I was told there is an abandoned Amazon fortress on Philios."

"There is," she said. "Why do you want to go there?"

"I'm following a trail," he said. "According to the Oracle Queen, that is my next destination."

"Ah." Her brow leapt up and down. "I see."

"The Oracle Queen also told me that you could take me to the fortress."

At that, Alenia leaned back in her chair, fixing him with a direct stare. "Did she, now?"

"I don't expect you to," Donan added. "But if you could provide me with directions, that would be appreciated."

"It's not that simple. Prophecy is never that simple." She folded her arms. "Did the queen tell you anything else?"

He hesitated before answering, keeping his eyes cast downward on the table. "She said you are her sister."

A moment passed. "I am," she said. "I was."

Donan thought better of questioning the meaning of that.

"She said I would help you?" Alenia asked.

He nodded. "She did. But again, I have no expectation—"

"Yes, you do. That's what a prophecy is. If she had said nothing about me, would you have even come back here to my inn?" She pressed the tip of her index finger against the table. "You are here because my sister sent you here. And for the same reason that you're here, I will aid you."

"You could refuse," Donan said. "You have the freedom to choose—"

"You were free to walk right on down the road without coming inside. But you didn't. Are you sitting here with me because you want to, or because of fate? Am I going to help you because I want to, or because she said I would?" Alenia had become agitated, but seemingly about more than their discussion, as if she had begun to argue with someone other than him.

"I don't know," he said. "But I do know that I will travel to the Amazon fortress tomorrow, and I would be grateful for directions."

The older woman's shoulders slumped a little as she sighed. "You remember where your room is?"

He nodded.

"I left it as you did. I had a feeling you might return." She stood. "We'll head out in the morning after breakfast. Good night, Donan."

She stepped into a back room. After sitting another moment or two, he made his way up the narrow staircase to the small chamber where he had slept two nights before, but he lay awake in bed for a long time, turning over questions of fate. Then his thoughts wandered back to the vision he had endured on this path up the mountain: the death of his mother, his failure to protect her. The Oracle Queen had been right; his path had indeed shown him the memory that most determined his present. If his mother had lived, he would never have joined the Horadrim. He would never have studied and learned all that he now knew. He would have had no reason to. He would not have come to Skovos and would not be lying awake, beset by the vagaries of destiny.

Grass and thorny bramble had encroached on the road, obscuring the path, but Alenia knew the way. Donan could see that the fortress appearing over the rise had once been a formidable bulwark against pirates and the Drowned. But where those enemies had failed to breach its defenses, the endlessly patient plant life surrounding it had succeeded in its slow, creeping invasion. Grass and scrub had found purchase in the crumbling mortar. The inexorable expansion of their roots and falling rain had cracked stone, opening gaps in the walls and collapsing towers and vaulted roofs. What had once been a beacon of strength and safety had fallen to a symbol of hubris and defeat.

"It's even more overgrown than the last time I saw it," Alenia said. "What did you hope to find here?"

"I'm searching for some associates who came to Skovos several years ago. Your sister said they were given leave to occupy this fortress."

"Well, they're obviously not here now. The only occupants of this place are likely to be beasts or bandits."

Donan agreed with that assessment. An uncanny silence brooded over the ruin, and the dank odor of decomposing plant matter suffused the heavy air. The darkened windows, doorways, and crevices held shadows thick enough to hide all manner of enemies. "Thank you for guiding me here," he said. "You are free to leave."

"Wait, you're not going in there, are you?"

"I need to find out if my comrades left behind any indication of where they went next."

She glanced back and forth between him and the ruin. "Let's be quick about it, then."

"What? No, you should return to your inn. There isn't any need to put yourself in danger—"

"We won't know that unless I go in with you."

"I don't understand."

"And I don't want to take the time to explain. We need to get in and out and be away from here before nightfall." She spoke with matronly authority, and before he could object, she marched toward the ruin.

He hurried after her. "Alenia, please, you don't—"

"Shh," she said. "It's settled. And we should keep our voices down. Make as little noise as possible."

Donan could not understand why she would risk her own safety for him, a stranger she had met only a few days before. In his mind, the Oracle Queen's offer of aid did not obligate her to endanger herself in this way, but for some reason, she insisted. It even seemed that she had come prepared for the possibility of entering the fort, because she stopped before the broken gates and pulled a small torch out of her pack.

"Ready?" she asked.

He wanted to object, but he could see it would have no effect and took the torch from her. "I'll go first."

They entered the fortress yard through the gate. The stables and other outbuildings had buckled some time ago, their wooden spines rotted away by rain, termites, and pale threads of fungus. Vegetation had spread across the paving stones, covering them in a tangled net of leafy vines, and young bushes and trees had sprouted from the gaps, their roots grasping the rock like slender fingers.

"Your associates settled here?" Alenia whispered.

"Apparently," said Donan.

They proceeded slowly, listening and watching for movement as they crossed the courtyard. When they reached the central keep, they paused outside the entrance to light the torch, then crossed the threshold. The interior smelled of damp stone. Swags of cobwebs drifted from the ceiling. Grit and stray leaves littered the floor, carried inward by the wind and rain. A few shafts of determined light entered through arrow slits and cracks, but the flickering torch did more to help them see where they were going.

They pressed forward through a passageway and came into a modest hall with a low ceiling. Signs of previous occupation littered the floor. Donan saw broken crockery, a bundle of kindling left by the blackened fireplace, animal bones, and other refuse, but none of it appeared recent. He knew from a cursory glance that the chamber held nothing of interest.

"Let's keep moving," he said.

"Where to?"

Donan knew that if Sho-Ren and the other Horadrim had intentionally left anything behind, they would have placed it belowground, as secure from the elements as they could manage in a crumbling wreck. But he kept these thoughts to himself and simply answered, "The cellar."

"If you say so," Alenia said.

She had more familiarity than he did with the typical layout of Skovos architecture, so she led the way. They found a spiral stone staircase and followed it downward into the lower level of the fortress, where the only light came from their torch. Sound seemed to tighten around them in the narrower corridors, every scuff and scrape against the stone loud in Donan's ears. Even his own breath seemed to fill the tunnel with noise.

They investigated each chamber and storeroom they came across. The torch cast wide shadows behind the broad, heavy columns supporting the foundations of the fortress, and Donan circled them, shoving the darkness aside, leaving no corner unexamined.

"What are you looking for?" Alenia asked.

"Signs. Symbols."

"Like those?"

She pointed at a section of wall, and upon closer inspection, Donan noticed faint Horadric protection runes scratched into the stone. "Exactly like those," he said, tracing them with his finger. "Hold this." He passed Alenia the torch and stood back to take in the inscription.

He lacked the proper guide, but from what he could translate, the runes created a shroud of illusion. It took him a few tries to speak the proper incantation to dispel the magic, but when he did so, the wall's appearance shifted. The stones seemed to melt and slide away, reshaping themselves until they revealed a simple wooden door where plain wall had been.

Alenia stepped back in shock. "Are you a mage?"

"I know a few spells. Come."

The door was padlocked, but with its magical defenses now down, Donan was able to break the lock using the heel of his staff. The chamber on the other side of the door had been left clean and orderly compared to the rest of the fortress. It held bookshelves, which were empty, a few bed frames, a table, and chairs.

Alenia glanced around the room. "There's nothing here. Why hide this?"

"To leave a message behind," Donan said, except it did not appear the previous Horadrim had left anything behind. He strode past the bookshelf, wondering what tomes it might have held. He crouched down to look under the beds. He sat at the table, and that was when he noticed more symbols carved into the wood, but unlike the runes of illusion outside the chamber, these had no magic associated with them. When translated, they simply spelled a name.

"They went to Celestia," he said.

Alenia strode over to the table and held the torch closer to look at the symbols. "I assume that's where you'll be heading next?"

"It is."

"Then I will go with you."

Donan looked up at her. "Why would you do that?"

"The Oracle Queen said I would aid you."

"And you have. You guided me to this place. You came in with me when you didn't need to. I am very grateful, but you have done enough."

She held herself with firm resolve, but tears glistened suddenly in the corners of her eyes, catching the torchlight. "I don't know if I have."

Donan stood and placed his hand on her shoulder. "Let's be gone from this wretched place. Then perhaps you can explain what you mean."

She nodded, and together they returned the way they had come, back through the cellar passages, up the winding stairs, through the hall, and out into the courtyard. The sultry air outside smelled fresh compared to the subterranean vapors they had been breathing. Moments later, they left the main gates of the ruin and were back on the road. They spoke little for the first league or so, and Donan refrained from asking Alenia any questions, instead allowing her the freedom to fill the silence how she chose.

Eventually, she did speak. "We were children when the seers came, but I still remember that day as if it just happened. They said their visions had guided them to our door and that my sister would one day be their queen. My parents were so proud. But I felt abandoned. And angry. I hated the seers for many years."

"You missed your sister."

"I did."

"Did you ever consider joining the seers yourself? To be with her?"

"Perhaps briefly. Never seriously. Even if I had wanted to, I knew one of us had to stay with my parents to help run the inn."

They walked slowly. Alenia looked down at her feet often, or else up into the trees and the sky, as if struggling with her past.

"My sister came home periodically," she went on. "That is, while our parents were still alive. After they died, she came less."

"When was the last time you saw her?" Donan asked.

"It was just before her coronation three years ago. She said after she became queen, it would be difficult for her to visit me again. So that was our goodbye."

"That must have been difficult."

"You would think so, but it wasn't, not really. By then she was almost a stranger to me. She had already aged, and she had cut off parts of herself. I made her remove her veil, and then I wished I hadn't. I no longer recognized her. But . . . that wasn't the worst part."

Again, Donan waited.

"Before she left, she foresaw a vision of my future. My younger sister laid a terrible fate upon me."

"Do you mind if I ask what fate she pronounced?"

Alenia inhaled deeply. "She said that one day, I would save all of Skovos."

For a moment, Donan was too stunned to speak. "That kind of prophecy would be . . . a very heavy burden."

Her nod was slow and ponderous. "I was obsessed with it for a long time. Did she mean that I would do something heroic? A middle-aged woman like me? Or did she mean something much simpler and more indirect than that? Maybe I would serve someone in my inn, and because of me *that* person would save Skovos. I thought about every decision I made, every action—no matter how small—as if it might be the most important thing I would ever do. Then I started to wonder if I had already done it, and Skovos is still here because of something I did without even realizing it."

"That sounds like a kind of torture."

"It was enough to drive me mad."

"And now?"

"I try not to think about it anymore. I live my life according to the virtues as best I can. I leave fate to fate. But if I'm being honest, the only reason I'm here with you is because of that prophecy. So, I guess I haven't completely stopped thinking about it." She halted in the road and turned to look at him. "I don't believe I am done helping you. And this may be how I save Skovos." Then she turned away with a shrug and started walking again. "Or maybe it's not, and I would be better off returning to my inn. The point is . . . I don't know, and that's why I am coming with you to Celestia."

CHAPTER NINETEEN

From the abandoned fort, Alenia guided Donan up along narrow game trails and then over hilly goat paths toward the northwest shore of the island. A storm the following day caught them out in the open, pouring enough rain to soak them through before they could find shelter beneath an outcrop. They decided to rest there to wait out the worst of it, and Donan settled his back against the earth, watching the water carve sudden channels through the hard soil. Next to him, Alenia pushed her wet hair back and wiped the glistening water from her face. He had not stopped thinking about the weight of the prophecy that she carried on her shoulders, and he decided to risk asking questions that he hoped would not offend her.

"Have you considered the possibility that your sister might be wrong?"

"You mean her prophecy about me?" Alenia laughed. "The Oracle Queen is never wrong."

"Never?"

"Never."

"But . . . forgive me, I heard something from a woman on Temis."

"What did you hear?"

He wondered if it was wise to have started down this road. "This would have been prior to your sister's reign," he added. "But I heard the queen before her failed to see the reapers coming."

She frowned. "They *would* say that on Temis." Then she leaned in closer, as if preparing to share a secret in her crowded tavern. "On Philios, they say the Oracle Queen *did* warn the Amazon Queen, but Etara refused to believe her."

The implications of that settled quickly over Donan's mind. In the wake of the reapers, it would have been natural to look for someone to hold responsible, but the casting of blame on either the Amazons or the seers would have political consequences for all of Skovos. "What do *you* believe?" he asked.

"I suppose I believe the seers, but I'm not sure it matters. Even if Queen Etara did know, what could she have done? The Amazons died along with everyone else."

The storm eventually passed, and they resumed their journey overland until they came down to a rocky coastal inlet with a makeshift pier tucked deep in its folds. Three small boats lay at anchor there. Not Amazon warships, but sailing vessels for fishing or trading. Donan noted that the harbor would not be visible to any ships passing by outside the narrow bay.

"What is this place?" he asked.

"It's a market," Alenia said. "Though not a strictly legal one."

"A smugglers' port?"

"We prefer to think of it as a free port."

"Free from what?"

"The Askarra Guard."

As they made their way toward the pier, Donan could see a few merchants waiting with carts and small wagons for the ships to be unloaded. Suddenly, a man stepped into the path ahead of them, blocking their way with sword and shield. Upon seeing Alenia, he gave her a nod and stepped aside to allow them through.

"The silks take almost everything," she went on. "They claim they're distributing it equally throughout the islands, but what we get back just doesn't add up. It's obvious they're keeping the best for themselves, or they're smuggling it for profit."

Donan thought back to the bounty of the Harbormaster's table and the trident stamp. "I've seen evidence of smuggling in Kingsport."

"I'm sure you have," she said as they reached the pier. "That's why some of us have found independent ways to trade our wares."

On the pier, Donan saw that the goods she referred to included basic commodities like grain and garden produce, as well as some manufactured goods such as bolts of woven fabric, iron, and copperware. Nothing luxurious or decadent, just the common needs and comforts of life that they were otherwise being denied.

Of the three ships moored at the smugglers' pier, one was bound for Celestia, and Alenia used her connections to secure them passage. The small vessel offered little in the way of sleeping quarters, but it would carry them where they needed to go. The voyage took longer than travel aboard the *Arabel* would have, owing to the slow speed of the small boat and the captain's understandable choice to sail wide around Atanos. Donan and Alenia spent that time getting better acquainted, though the lack of privacy from the ship's crew kept their conversations away from more sensitive topics.

When they reached Celestia, they docked in a sheltered harbor on the northeast coast, where another free port operated in secret. From there, Alenia suggested they begin their search by asking the island's astronomers if they had any knowledge of Donan's associates.

"Who are these astronomers?" he asked.

"They're a group of seers," she said. "But instead of disfiguring themselves to gain the gift of foresight, they use the movement of the stars to divine the future."

"How do the stars help them see the future?"

"You would have to ask them." She offered him a wry grin. "But I've heard they guard their secrets from any they deem unworthy, so I wouldn't expect an answer."

"I will try to rein in my disappointment," he said. "Where do we find these astronomers?"

She looked northward. "I've heard they have an observatory not far from here."

Donan accepted this with a nod. "Let's start there."

He soon discovered that Celestia was a far more sparsely inhabited island than either Temis or Philios. Farmsteads they passed appeared abandoned, but longer ago than Malthael's Reaping. In the distance at the center of the island, there stood the remains of a large and empty city. Its broken spires and fallen walls lay on the horizon like the pale bones of a gargantuan beast, and an eerie pall of silence hung over the ruins. Donan wondered if the cause of its abandonment lay on the western horizon, where the volcanic island of Skartara, endlessly threatening to erupt, kept the sky in that direction perpetually darkened with smoke and vapor. But Celestia was not entirely devoid of life. Grass carpeted the hills. Hardy flowering shrubs sprouted in the sheltered crannies, a curious white fungus grew prolifically in the ruins, and tough little songbirds trilled from sinewy trees.

Soon the Observatory appeared above them, crowning an eminence of bare rock. The structure appeared to be a Firstborn creation, built from the same white marble as much of Temis, with a single tower rising from a massive angular pedestal. Concentric metal rings glinted atop the tower, and statues of angels and demons stood guard around its base.

After ascending a winding path to reach it, they found its main doors open to them. An astronomer stood before the entrance, wearing robes much like those Donan had seen the seers wearing back on Philios, except these were decorated with the orbits of stars and constellations sewn in silver thread. The astronomer wore no veil. She had dark skin beneath her hood, with full cheeks and a serene smile.

"Welcome, Horadrim," she said.

Her greeting brought Donan to a halt, and Alenia turned to look at him in surprise.

"Horadrim?" she said.

He nodded without looking at her and addressed his question to the astronomer. "How did you know I am one of the Horadrim?"

She gestured toward the sky, her wrist loose, fingers falling open. "We foresaw your coming in the movement of the stars."

That did not precisely give him an answer. "How do the stars—?"

"Please," the astronomer said, "enter our Observatory, where we will try to answer your questions as best we can." She stepped aside from the door and gestured them inward with her open palm.

Donan glanced at Alenia. She raised her eyebrows in uncertainty, but they moved toward the doorway, past the waiting astronomer, and into the building.

Within the Observatory, he found a serene space devoted to the night sky. A vast mosaic covered the floor with a map of the constellations. Mythical heroes and beasts wheeled their way around the tower beneath his feet, the stars that defined their shapes glinting like jewels. Bookshelves of texts and scrolls drew Donan's eyes immediately, as did the astronomical equipment standing upon worktables that lined the walls. Tall murals depicted the legendary history of Skovos, the founding of the Amazons, and the finding of the Sightless Eye.

"Every happening has its season," said the astronomer as she came up behind Donan. "Just as the apple tree blossoms in the spring, and the ripened wheat stalk bends in the fall, so does everything have a time of occurrence. The stars foretold it was the season for the Horadrim to return."

"Return?" Donan said. "So, we *have* come to you before."

The astronomer inclined her head. "Of course. We have exchanged much knowledge and wisdom with your order through the centuries."

"Did the stars also tell you why I have come?"

She shook her head with a gentle smile. "No, they do not explain why seasons occur. They simply help us to observe their passing, and to predict their next coming. So, perhaps *you* will tell me why you have come?"

"I am looking for a Horadric expedition led by a mage named Sho-Ren."

The astronomer's smile fell. "I am sorry to say they are no longer here. They stayed with us for a time. You may recognize their influence in some of our devices and machinery of celestial measurement. When the reapers came, the Horadrim fought valiantly to defend us, and three of their number died. They departed not long after that."

Donan was dismayed to hear of the company's losses. "Do you know where they went?"

"Again, I am sorry, but I do not."

Donan bowed his head in disappointment and defeat. None of the clues thus far had brought him any closer to discovering the fate of the expedition.

Alenia then spoke, asking, "Where did they live when they were here on Celestia?"

"They made use of a residence to the south," answered the astronomer.

Donan looked up. "May we go see it?"

"Of course."

She then gave them directions, and they learned that the residence lay a day's journey away from the Observatory, on the island's western shore. As they made to leave, the astronomer addressed Alenia directly.

"We know who you are, sister of our queen."

Alenia leaned away with sudden wariness. "How do you know that?"

"The season of your destiny is upon you," the astronomer said.

Alenia paled. "My destiny?"

"Yes. But I see that you are prepared for what is to come."

"Prepared?" Alenia's apparent suspicion turned to open hostility and anger. "How could I possibly be prepared? I don't even know what—"

Donan took her hand. He did so without thinking. He knew only that despite Alenia's outward anger, he could sense her fear, and he wanted to reassure her. She looked down at his hand, but he held on to hers with a gentle grip. Her weathered and calloused fingers reminded him of his mother's. "Come," he said. "She has no answers for you."

She allowed him to lead her from the tower, back outside and away from the Observatory. As they departed, he let go of her hand and glanced back. The astronomer stood in the doorway, her face etched with confusion and worry.

"I hate them," Alenia said. "Seers. Astronomers. I hate them all."

Donan said nothing, thinking it better to give her space as they traveled southward across the island's forlorn landscape. Eventually, they passed through the outskirts of the empty city, down streets lined with fallen buildings. In that place the echoes of their footsteps somehow sounded louder, and though all signs suggested they were alone, Donan feared their presence would draw the attention of . . . something. They hurried through as quickly as they could, and Donan kept an eye on the road behind them to make sure they had not been followed.

They made no fire that evening, huddling close together for warmth in the crook of a rock cleft, far off the trackway and out of sight. Donan fell asleep easily, but he was awakened later in the night by Alenia trembling next to him. At first, he thought she was shivering from the cold, but then he realized she was awake, and she was crying.

Later the next morning, they arrived at the location where the astronomer had directed them, but they discovered it was little more than a whitewashed stone hut squatting on a grassy bluff overlooking the sea. Skartara raged to the west like a winged demon sitting on the horizon, the faint glow of its inner fire now visible near the crater at its summit, while ribbons of molten rock curled down across its livid face. It made sense the Horadrim would dwell here, in sight of the island where their vault lay hidden.

Donan knew the hut would be empty, just as the fortress on Philios had been, but he also suspected it held more secrets. He went searching around its foundations until he found an inconspicuous door to a root cellar. It had no lock, and he lifted it open, releasing the smell of loam and decaying potatoes.

"Do you still have your torch?" he asked.

Alenia pulled it from her pack and struck a flint to light it. They descended a steep set of steps more ladder than staircase and found a single chamber at the bottom. The shelves still held a few jars of preserved fruit and pickled vegetables and a few sacks of rancid barley. Shriveled and blackened potatoes lay in a corner heap. Donan walked slowly around the room, studying every inch of all four walls with methodical care until he found the hidden latch he was searching for. When he pulled it, a secret door popped out with a hiss and a squeal of rusted hinges as a section of shelving opened, revealing a passageway.

Donan took the torch to go through the door first, and they followed the tunnel, which seemed to have lain undisturbed since Sho-Ren and her expedition had been there years before. The narrow corridor eventually led them to the entrance of a ritual chamber, where a pair of mammoth stone doors barred the way forward. Sigils and symbols covered the portal in a complex pattern of interlocking circles, producing layers of magical protection. No one without the proper Horadric spell-keys would be able to gain entrance, and they would likely find the experience of failure extremely unpleasant.

"This may require some time," he said, taking a seat on the floor before the doors. Then he began working through the proper sequence, unlocking each layer in turn, attaining an almost trancelike state before the final seal broke and the doors yawned open.

"I almost feel as if I don't belong here," Alenia said.

"I suspect the Horadrim who built this place would probably agree with you." Donan gave her a smile. "But I don't. Come."

When they entered the chamber, glass orb lanterns ignited, glowing with a gaseous light, suspended from chains like fishing floats in netting. The first room held tables and workbenches against its walls bearing alembics, other alchemical equipment, and tools for occult craftsmanship. Subsequent chambers contained cabinets, reliquaries, and shelves, all of which held a small quantity of curious objects, but nothing that struck Donan as being particularly unique or powerful. He also saw nothing to indicate what had happened to Sho-Ren and the expedition.

"This is incredible," Alenia said. "I've never seen anything like it."

"Hmm," Donan replied.

"You seem disappointed."

He sighed. "I still have unanswered questions."

"Such as?"

"What happened to them?"

"Let's keep looking," she said. "Maybe you'll find another sign or clue."

One of the bookshelves did contain a decent collection of volumes, and Donan decided to examine them more closely. Some were chronicle texts, including a brief account of the Mage Clan Wars and others on the history of Skovos. There were books of magic spells and rituals, a copy of Gerhard's herbal compendium, and a few collections of potion recipes, none of which were especially rare. Altogether, a lackluster library for a Horadric workshop. But then Donan noticed a book of Xiansai lore, and he pulled it off the shelf, thinking perhaps it had been put there by Sho-Ren. As he flipped through its pages, a sheaf of paper fell out, and when he bent to pick it up, he saw that it contained a cipher, apparently based on an ancient Xian language unfamiliar to him. A thrill raced up the back of his neck, and in the next moment, he pulled out the journal he had bought in Kingsport and hurried to one of the desks.

"Did you find something?" Alenia asked as she eased into one of the chairs.

Donan noticed she winced, and once she was settled, she began rubbing her knees. "Are you okay?" he asked.

She shrugged. "I'm not a young woman anymore. All this island hopping is catching up to me, I think."

Donan scanned the nearby shelves for anything that might be of help to her, and he found an amulet of healing. A common but effective magical relic that should work as well on swollen joints as it did on battle injuries. "Here, put this on."

She looked at it skeptically as she accepted it, but she put it on, and Donan watched her for a few moments.

"Better?" he asked.

She cocked her head, then gave a nod with a spreading grin. "Yes, I do believe that helped. Thank you, lad."

"You're welcome," he said, and then returned his attention to the journal.

It was not a complicated code in the end, merely a highly obscure one, but with the proper key to its decryption, he was soon translating passages of the journal.

The record belonged to Sho-Ren herself and began at the inception of her expedition to Skovos, detailing the assignment Tyrael had given to her, just as he had described it. There would be time later to make a study of their journey's beginning, but in this moment, Donan felt a more urgent curiosity about the end of their mission and how the book had quite improbably come to wash up on the southern shore of Westmarch. He skipped to the last few entries and began to translate them.

Anders has returned. He was unsuccessful in retrieving the scepter. That is most disappointing, but I'm more troubled by his suspicion that he was being followed. He can't say who it was, but he was worried enough to spend a few days in the wilds on Lycander just to lose his pursuers, so as not to lead them back here. I'm very grateful for his precaution. I'm glad I followed my instincts when we first arrived and the Amazons remain unaware of who we truly are. The astronomers know we are Horadrim, but I'm confident they can be trusted. Still, we must be more careful going forward.

A titan—created by the Firstborn—has been released. I can't believe I am writing these words. I can't believe anyone would be foolish or desperate enough to do such a thing, but Anders saw the empty cell with his own eyes during another attempt to recover the scepter. I had deep reservations letting him go, but our desperation outweighed the risks—unfortunately, he returned empty-handed. I can only hope he's wrong about the titan, but I have a hard time doubting it. He's levelheaded, not given to panic. The situation here is becoming untenable. I wish I had Tyrael's counsel to guide me.

We are being watched. We still don't know who is spying on us, but I suspect someone in the palace may be involved. I doubt our adversaries are simple bandits or smugglers. That's why I have made the decision to depart from Skovos. I fear our continued presence will only draw attention to the vault, and the relics contained within it are simply too powerful to risk them falling into the hands of someone like Captain Myrina. It grieves me to leave Skovos, but I cannot see another way.

The titan is pursuing us. We hear it everywhere. It shakes the timbers of our ship. We're close to Kingsport, but I'm not sure we can make it. I only hope that if the monster sinks us, the few relics we carry will be safe at the bottom of the sea. I don't know if anyone will ever read this account, or if they'll be able to decipher it. I've placed a charm on it to guide it toward friendly hands. That is all I can do. So, if you are reading this, I trust in your good intentions and would ask that if you should ever encounter a man wearing angelic armor, give him this book. Beyond that, I will say only this: Avoid Skovos. A Firstborn monster swims in its waters. Danger and corruption fester in its courts. Stay away from those islands until the Askari have recovered their virtues.

Donan closed the journal and sat back in the chair, saddened and bewildered. It seemed clear to him that Sho-Ren and the remaining Horadrim had drowned at sea, shipwrecked by a beast she referred to as a titan, likely the same beast he and the others had encountered during their own crossing. He could now guess why Horadric relics had been washing up at Kingsport for the Harbormaster to acquire. But the journal had also posed many questions that it left unanswered. Donan thought perhaps the earlier entries would provide more information, but they would take time to translate. For now, he thought it best to return to Tyrael on Temis and convey this information.

When he looked up from the book, he found he was alone in the chamber. He called out to Alenia but received no reply. Assuming she must have left the workshop to get some fresh air, he made his way back down the passage and out of the cellar.

A company of Askarra Guard waited for him in the blinding daylight. As soon as his head emerged from the ground, a dozen of them drew their bows, aimed at him. Two of the warriors held Alenia. Bound and gagged, she looked at him with bulging eyes, her face flushed with desperate fear. The leader of the Amazon troop stepped forward, sword drawn.

"You are under arrest, Horadrim."

CHAPTER TWENTY

When Lorath awoke, it was before dawn, and Adreona had left sometime during the night. That did not surprise him. Later that morning, when they came back together on the deck of the *Arabel,* she greeted him with grim intent. He sensed no regret from her, no embarrassment, no denial of what had happened, and no need to justify it or explain herself, but she had put her armor back on, and her focus had returned entirely to the purpose before them. Lorath understood. Whatever existed between them now had no bearing on their present mission into Drowned territory.

He stood with Keldon at the stern, watching as Adreona, Tavie, and a small company of Amazons got situated at the bow. The lingering smoke and dust in the air turned the sunrise murky and thin, despite a gentle breeze that would make the going easier on their journey west. The old sailor held the tiller with a half smile of amusement as he watched the warriors.

"I wonder how Eshella would've felt about this."

"About what?" Lorath asked.

"Me with a boatful of beautiful women. Probably would've laughed. She wasn't the jealous type, my Esh." He shook his head in wonder. "Who'd have guessed that one day my *Arabel* would have a crew of Amazons?"

Lorath felt he knew the sailor well enough now to ask something he had been wondering since boarding the sloop. "Where does the name come from? *Arabel?*"

Keldon's smile subsided. "That were my daughter's name."

Lorath wondered why the sailor had never mentioned having a daughter. "Did she leave with her mother?"

"Leave?"

Lorath thought back to what the sailor had already told him. "Forgive me, I thought you said your wife left you."

Keldon shook his head. "I said my wife had been gone for several years now, and that she ain't coming back."

"But—"

"Esh and Arabel were murdered."

Lorath's breath caught in his throat. "Murdered?"

"Aye."

"By the reapers?"

Keldon shook his head. "After that. Kingsport never was a proper place for a wife and child, but after the reapers . . . I should have got them out of there. I just didn't know where to go. You remember how it was. All that chaos. Nowhere was safe. But anywhere would have been better if it meant they could still be with me. It's my fault, you see."

Lorath's rage stirred on the sailor's behalf for a woman and child he could do nothing to help or avenge. "It is not your fault, Keldon. It is the fault of the one who murdered them. Do you know who it was?"

"I do."

Before he could elaborate, Adreona came back to the helm from the bow. "Are we ready to sail?"

"We are, indeed, Captain," Keldon said. "Just give the word."

"The word is given."

Lorath and Adreona then hoisted the sails, and the *Arabel* got underway. As they eased past the line of safety behind the warships and out into the sluggish waters of Atanos, the mood on the deck shifted. The Amazons fell silent, alert, weapons drawn and ready, with all eyes on the surface of the sea. They had won a decisive victory against the Drowned but had no way of knowing how strong the opposition remained, lurking in the mist.

Adreona guided Keldon through the snarl of channels and shallows that lay between them and the place where the watchfire should have been burning. They had only a league or so to cover, but given the tortuous nature of their course and the feebleness of the wind, it took them longer than any of them would have liked. Each moment they spent out there gave the Drowned more opportunity to gather and attack, and every carrion bird they disturbed, every aquatic creature they startled into the water only increased their dread.

At last, the Amazons watching at the prow shouted that they had sighted the watchfire—or, rather, what remained of it. As the structure took shape in the fog, Lorath saw that its foundation remained intact, a plinth of stone twenty paces to a side, tall as a two-story building, rooted to a jagged islet not much larger than the edifice it supported. Only the stump of the former tower remained on that footing, felled like a tree. Its great trunk lay broken along the marshy ground and sumps, a ruin that stretched away to such a length, it seemed clear the watchfire could not have simply collapsed or fallen on its own. Rather, it appeared as if it had been thrown down.

"It didn't just burn out," Tavie whispered. "Something destroyed it."

"Bring us in closer," Adreona said.

They lowered the sails, then Lorath used the sculling oar to creep up alongside the island. Then he, Adreona, and the other Amazons leapt ashore to see what clues might be found there, hoping to glean some indication of how the tower had been demolished.

"The Drowned didn't do this," Adreona said, staring up at the wreck. "This surpasses any cunning they have ever shown."

Lorath looked down at the islet's craggy terrain. He saw no bracken, no seaweed, no crustaceans or other marine life. It appeared the pools and crevices had been scoured clean, as if a giant tidal wave had washed over the entire rock. "A storm?" he suggested.

"What storm?" Adreona said, then shook her head. "A tempest capable of this would have wreaked havoc across the isles. Besides, this tower has stood for a thousand years of gales and waves."

Tavie pointed at the stubborn remnant of the tower still attached to the plinth. "It's like something just . . . chopped it down. What in all of Sanctuary could do that?"

"I don't know," said Adreona. "For now, let's—"

A bell rang out in the mist. Even on land, its dire tone would never be mistaken for a church bell. In Atanos, it filled Lorath with instant dread.

"Drowned!" One of the Amazons shot an arrow at the waterline, where an undead wretch squealed, flailing, and went under.

"Back to the ship!" Adreona shouted as more Drowned lurched out of the sea, dozens of them clambering upward like a swarm of crabs. Lorath pulled his polearm free and leapt at the enemy, carving a path of escape toward the *Arabel.* Keldon had taken the sculling oar in hand and heaved his ship up against the rocks so the Amazons could jump onto the deck, but the Drowned had begun to claw their way over the gunwale.

Lorath waited on the islet until Adreona and the Amazons had made it safely aboard. Then he vaulted onto the ship and joined the fight to free them. Keldon let out a roar behind him, and when Lorath spun around, he saw a Drowned wretch had come over the stern and sunk its teeth into the sailor's forearm. Before Lorath could attack it, Adreona skewered it with her spear and flung it over the side. The old sailor clutched his arm, and blood seeped between his fingers.

Lorath rushed to help him at the oar. "How bad is it?"

"I won't bleed out," he replied through gritted teeth.

Tavie lobbed a flaming jug into the air behind them, which another Amazon shattered with a shot from her bow, raining fiery oil onto the fiends below. Elsewhere along the deck, the Amazons had ignited other incendiary weapons, driving the Drowned back into the water.

"Head north!" Adreona shouted.

"Why north?" Keldon asked. "Why not east, back to the fort?"

"Do what she says," Lorath replied. "I trust her judgment."

As soon as they had cleared the enemy, they raised the *Arabel*'s sails and left the fallen tower behind them. Keldon insisted on staying at the tiller, but he allowed Lorath to wrap his injured arm in the shredded tatters of his own sleeve. It was an evil-looking wound and would need a thorough cleaning and tending soon. They moved northward, even more vigilant now, with torches and blades at the ready, listening to distant shrieks and the baleful ringing of bells off in the fog, but they came under no further attack. Eventually, the Amazons let down their guard somewhat, though they remained alert. As they sailed for Temis, Adreona came over to Keldon, frowning at his arm. "We should tend to your injury."

"I'm well enough," he said. "I'll see to it once we're out of these cursed waters."

Adreona ignored him and reached for his forearm, but he yanked it away from her. "Leave it be, woman. I've had worse."

She gave Lorath a look of grave concern and appeared reluctant to accept Keldon's answer, but she eventually let him be. The sailor remained at the tiller as they pressed onward, with Lorath occasionally sculling when they lost the wind. The day waned, and Keldon looked weaker and more haggard with each passing league, sweat glistening across his pallid brow, but he seemed determined to get them all to safety. They encountered no more Drowned, but as they reached the edges of the Atanos mist, they heard a rumbling moan from the deep of the Great Ocean to the northwest. It was a sound Lorath recognized.

"What is that?" asked Tavie.

"A leviathan," Lorath answered. "We encountered it during our crossing from Kingsport."

"You saw it?" asked Adreona.

"Only its wake," Lorath answered. "It was . . . quite large."

"Large enough to tear down the watchfire?" Adreona asked.

"Possibly," he said. To imagine such a beast challenged his faculties of reason, but he had traveled with Tyrael long enough to know that Sanctuary contained a multitude of abominations that defied the mortal mind's ability to comprehend.

At last, the *Arabel* reached untainted blue waters and turned eastward. That was when Keldon finally collapsed to the deck. Tavie took hold of the tiller, and Adreona helped Lorath carry him down into the forward cabin.

"I should have checked," she said below her breath. "I should have insisted."

"He is stubborn," Lorath said.

"So am I," she answered, which Lorath had come to know very well.

They laid Keldon into one of the bunks, and he groaned, cradling his arm. When Adreona unwrapped the bandage, Lorath was shocked by how quickly the wound had festered. The bite seemed to have opened his arm in a grotesque blossom of flesh. Tendrils of discoloration snaked under his skin from his hand to his shoulder, and a livid algal growth had taken root in the deepest recesses of the injury. Adreona pulled back his clothing, revealing the extent of the contamination. "What is that?" Lorath asked in horror.

She bowed her head, appearing more defeated than he had ever seen her. "The Drowned can spread a necrosis through their violence," she said. "There are times when the injuries they give turn their victim into one of them. *That* is the true curse of Atanos."

"What can be done?"

"Nothing. If we had amputated his arm when he was first wounded, we might have saved him."

"Can we not amputate now?"

"No." She pointed at the veins that almost seemed to be wriggling beneath his skin. "The corruption has reached his chest. There is nothing to be done. We have seen this many times before. Too many times. We have an elixir to ease his passing, but . . . I am sorry, Lorath. I blame myself."

"It isn't your fault," said Lorath.

"He was my responsibility—"

"He would not see it that way, I promise you. He knew the risks when he agreed to take you on his ship. His *Arabel.*"

A shiver took hold of Keldon that racked his whole body and rattled his teeth. A grimace of pain contorted his pale face.

"Give him your elixir," Lorath said.

Adreona nodded and was gone for only a few moments. When she returned, she carried a vial of a clear syrup, which she poured into Keldon's mouth. He sputtered and coughed as it passed his lips.

"Shh, shh," she said. "Just drink it down. I know it burns, but it will help."

The sailor smacked his mouth, eyes clenched shut, and his throat bobbed as he swallowed.

Adreona leaned down and whispered in his ear, "I am sorry, Keldon. Be at peace." Then she rose, and as she passed Lorath on her way out of the cabin, she took his hand and squeezed it. "He may come back to himself for a few moments."

Lorath nodded, and after she was gone, he crouched down next to the bunk and watched as the tension in Keldon's face and body slowly eased. A few moments later, his eyes fluttered open.

"Where am I?"

"The forward cabin."

That seemed to please him. He closed his eyes again, but in rest, rather than distress. "Am I dying?"

"You are."

"I wish I were at her tiller," he said, "but I suppose a bunk is good enough. At least I'm at sea."

"You are," Lorath said. "You got us to safety."

He nodded. "Before I die, I need you to know something."

"What, Keldon?"

"It's about my debt to the Harbormaster."

"Surely that doesn't matter now—"

"It matters." He opened his eyes and looked directly at Lorath. "I need someone to know the truth."

Lorath felt his urgency and nodded.

"You asked if I knew who killed my wife and child. Well, I do. I tried to find the ones that did it, but I was drunken and clumsy and full of rage. I was useless. Then, one night, the Harbormaster pulls me up out of the gutter and brings me to one of her warehouses. She says she can give me the ones responsible. She takes me inside, and there they are. Three men, gagged and bound. The Harbormaster shows me a necklace they tried to fence. My wife's necklace that belonged to her mother. That's when . . ." He shut his mouth, and for a moment, he blocked his lips with the fist of his good hand. "The Harbormaster puts a knife in my hand. And I use it. I take that knife, and I go to work on those three unarmed men." He stared up at the ceiling of the cabin, tears running down his temples. "I lost myself to the rage. I carved them up 'til there weren't much left."

Lorath had no words, nothing of comfort to say to his friend, and that shamed him.

"But here's the thing," Keldon went on. "Afterward, I was *still* full of rage. I wish I could tell you that killing those men gave me peace. But it didn't. Maybe there was some justice in their deaths, I don't know. All I know is, my wife and daughter are still dead."

"I'm sorry, Keldon—"

"I've seen that same rage in you." He turned to face Lorath, rolling as far onto his side as he could manage. "I saw it the moment I met you. That's why I need you to hear me now. You see, I realized something, in time. I realized that giving blood and violence to my rage only fed it. If I wanted peace, I had to let it go . . . *You* need to let it go, lad."

"How?" Lorath felt out of breath; there were tears in his own eyes without him knowing why. "How do I let it go?"

"You let yourself feel whatever the rage is guarding. You let yourself see whatever is hiding behind it. For me, that was my grief." He relaxed and rolled onto his back, out of breath, closing his eyes. "But there's a beauty in grief. It's akin to love, you see? I'll take grief over rage. There's no beauty in rage. None at all."

"Keldon, I—"

"But now I'm ready to put down my grief too. I'm . . . I'm ready to put it all down. Bury me at sea . . . and when you see Donan, you tell him I'm glad he sat down at my table. You all gave me back my ship. You gave me back my *Arabel* . . ."

The old sailor trailed off and let out a sigh so deep his chest seemed to collapse. Then he was gone.

They wrapped Keldon's body in a spare jib Lorath found stowed belowdecks, and they weighed it down with a small but heavy chest they found among the sailor's personal belongings. The chest was locked, and Lorath had no desire to open it. Whatever it contained belonged to Keldon, and it would go down to the bottom of the sea with him. Lorath had worried about his body becoming one of the undead Drowned, given the corruption that had taken hold, but Adreona assured him that the elixir prevented that. The old sailor would become part of the sea where he settled.

No one spoke as they eased the body over the gunwale beneath the light of the moon. It landed with a splash, floating for a moment before the chest pulled it down by the feet, and then the waves closed over the head, and he was gone. Adreona stood close at Lorath's side. Their shoulders touched, and she took his hand.

"I will remember him," she said. "I saw the virtues in him. He showed great courage. He defended life. He possessed wisdom."

"I think he possessed more wisdom than I realized," Lorath said. "You know, when I first met him, I doubted him. I insulted him. I wish I'd apologized for that."

He stood a moment longer, watching the dancing reflections of the stars and moon as the place of Keldon's burial fell behind them. Then he turned from loss toward the task ahead of them. He released Adreona's hand and faced their eastward course. Tavie stood at the tiller, steering the ship around Athulua, while the other Amazons worked the lines to trim the sails.

"What is the plan when we reach Temis?" he asked.

"I go to the palace and report to Queen Etara," Adreona said.

"What about Myrina?"

"What about her?"

"I've inferred there is some . . . discord between you. Do you expect opposition from her?"

"It's true that she and I don't always have the same priorities, but I trust that our differences can be put aside for the good of Skovos."

"I will support you however I can, but I think we both know I won't be much help when it comes to palace politics. I'm still a mainlander."

"You've done more than enough," she said. "Leave the rest to me."

She stood there in the moonlight, and he wanted to pull her into an embrace, a kiss. If they had been alone on the deck, he would have, and he hoped that she would have welcomed it. But they were not alone. A small company of her subordinates surrounded them, so he treated her as the captain she was.

It was dawn when they reached Temis. The colossal statues guarding the entrance to the Great Harbor seemed to shine with golden light as they passed beneath them. Lorath prepared to lower the sculling oar into the water but noticed the same cutter that had towed them in upon their first arrival speeding toward them. Adreona waved, but as the vessel drew up alongside them, Lorath saw a crew of Askarra Guard, and an Amazon at the helm instead of Parmo.

"In the name of Queen Etara," she said, "I hereby impound this ship."

"On what grounds?" Adreona demanded.

"I do not have that information," she answered. "I only have my orders. Please, throw down a towing line, and we will row this ship to its berth."

None of Adreona's Amazons moved, waiting for her to command them. Tavie strode up beside her and asked, "What is this?"

"I don't know." Adreona glanced at Lorath. "Perhaps one of your comrades got into some trouble?"

"Unlikely," Lorath said. "Out of the three of us, I am the one most likely to cause trouble. The other two have a much easier time avoiding it."

"I can believe that," said Tavie.

Lorath had spoken the truth about his comrades, but he nevertheless worried that Tyrael or Donan might have been exposed as Horadrim, or that the true nature of their mission had been discovered, either of which could lead to diplomatic complications. He leaned in closer to Adreona and said, "Whatever this is, don't risk anything on my account."

"I won't," she said, arms folded. "I just don't like being kept in the dark."

"Let them take the ship," Lorath said. "We'll find out what's going on soon enough."

Another moment or two went by before Adreona finally agreed with a nod, and one of her warriors tossed a line down to the cutter. Not long after that, the *Arabel* lay secured to a dock among warships. As Lorath disembarked with Adreona, a company of Askarra Guard thumped down the pier toward them, armed and resolute. They halted a few paces away, at which time their leader stepped forward.

"Captain, we're here to take this man into custody. If you would please step aside—"

"Is he under arrest?" Adreona asked, stepping between Lorath and the silks.

"I'm afraid he is."

"What crime is he charged with committing?"

"That is not your concern—"

"It is most definitely my concern. This man has risked his life and proven himself an ally of Skovos. Moreover, he has been in my custody, and I would know if he had broken our laws."

"Captain, please, we are under orders—"

"Whose orders?"

"The queen's."

From behind, Lorath could see Adreona's posture lose some of its strength. The Askarra Guard held their weapons in a stance that suggested a willingness toward violence, if that became necessary. He knew Adreona's warriors would fight if she commanded it, especially given the disdain they held for the silks, but Lorath refused to let Amazons fight Amazons on the Temis docks over him. "I accept the queen's judgment," he said, stepping out from behind Adreona. "I will go peacefully. I don't want any conflict on my account."

"You flatter yourself," Tavie said, glowering at the Askarra Guards. "This conflict has been brewing for a long time."

"All the same," Lorath said, turning to Adreona, "I'll go with them. For now." He took his polearm from his back and gave it to her. "Hang on to this for me."

She took it with a nod. "I'll find out what's going on."

"I know you will."

He turned away from her and marched forward. At his approach, the leader of the silks stepped around him and bound his hands behind his back. Then the Askarra Guard escorted him from the pier into the city, where Lorath ignored the stares of suspicion he drew along the way. He did not know Temis well, but the silks did not seem to be leading him back to the garrison where the Horadrim had been held captive the first time. Instead, they moved up the tiers of the metropolis, but not in the direction of the palace—or, at least, not toward a part of the palace Lorath had seen before. They stopped a few levels short of the city's crest, just below the royal complex, facing a heavy gate in a massive retaining wall. Askarra Guards stood watch on both sides of the entrance.

"I know a dungeon when I see one," Lorath said.

His escort said nothing, and a moment later, they handed him off to the two guards waiting outside. Then the gates opened, admitting the three of them into a subterranean complex of Firstborn passageways, chambers, and cages, all lit by wavering torches. It was a prison, and quite a few of the cells held captives—many of them bandits and pirates, if Lorath had to guess based on the rags that had once been their clothing, but some of the prisoners appeared to be farmers and other common folk. The fetid air smelled of sweat and the buckets they all used as chamber pots.

Lorath's escorts prodded him along, eventually pushing him through a doorway into a private block, where he passed a row of empty cells before coming upon a cage holding Donan.

"Lorath!" the younger Horadrim stepped up to grip the bars.

"They got you too, eh?" Lorath said as one of the guards unlocked the cell opposite Donan's. The other removed his bindings, freeing his hands, and then heaved him into the small chamber. The bars closed behind him with a clang, and then they were alone.

"Where is Tyrael?" Lorath asked.

"I don't know," said Donan. "They arrested me on Celestia days ago. Put me on a ship and brought me straight here."

A gray-haired Askari woman stepped forward into the torchlight in the cell next to Donan's.

"Who's this?" Lorath asked.

"Alenia," she answered. "And you must be Lorath. Donan has told me about you."

"I'm sure he has."

"Alenia was helping me as a guide," Donan said. "When the Askarra Guard arrested me, they grabbed her too."

"Why did they arrest you?" Lorath asked. "Did you break any of their laws?"

"Of course not," Donan said. Then he lowered his voice. "But I know why they took me. I think they've been following me since I left Temis." He glanced around, looking up at the ceiling and into the shadowy corners as if someone might be spying on their conversation through a peephole. "They know we're Horadrim, and they want the vault."

CHAPTER TWENTY-ONE

Tyrael sat at a desk in the Askari archive, surrounded by stacks of books, ledgers, and scrolls. A tremendous rainstorm lashed the tower, pelting the roof and slapping the windows with heavy droplets, but the library within remained dry and warm. He had been poring through the official court records for nearly a week, searching for evidence of the first Horadrim and their activities in the Skovos Isles, but he had found no sign nor clue, not even indirect. Neither could he find any mention of the lost expedition. He wondered if he should even bother continuing, but he could think of no other way to be useful while confined to Temis. He hoped only that Donan had been more successful.

Hours passed, as they had every day he had spent in the archive, and as the rain eased, Maziel came down from his work on one of the floors above.

"Are you hungry?" he asked. "They'll be serving the midday meal."

Tyrael looked at the stack of parchment in front of him and rubbed his eyes, realizing that his body did need some nourishment. "Yes, I think I should probably eat something."

He rose and followed the librarian out into the cloister, where runoff from the rainstorm dripped down from the roof tiles and splashed against the cobblestones. The cloister had become Tyrael's world these past several days, containing both his sleeping quarters and the refectory where he took his meals. Maziel also lived there, alone but for Tyrael. In the past, that wing of the palace had apparently housed many scholars, but most of them had died during Malthael's Reaping, and now only Maziel lived there, the last librarian remaining.

The two of them entered the refectory and sat down at a dining table large enough to host a dozen or more. They ate well in the palace, better than the commoners Tyrael had seen receiving rations in the city below. Today, they dined on grilled fish and root vegetables, all drizzled with lemon juice and olive oil.

"Do you ever get lonely here?" Tyrael asked.

"Lonely?" Maziel cocked his head, eyes turned upward as if he were trying to remember the definition of the word. "I suppose I do enjoy the camaraderie of fellow scholars—it has been a pleasure to have you here. But if I am being honest, no, I do not miss the company of more common folk. Too few of them care about history and other subjects that matter."

"Do you ever leave the cloister?"

"I can, if I wish. There is a passage." He leaned closer. "This whole island is an anthill of tunnels and chambers." Then he shrugged. "Did you find anything of interest in your studies this morning?"

Tyrael sighed. "I read a transcript of a meeting between the Oracle Queen and yet another Zakarum missionary from Travincal."

"The followers of Akarat were quite persistent in their proselytizing. Was this transcript from before or after their corruption by Mephisto?"

"Before," Tyrael said, although that was a more difficult question to answer than the librarian assumed. The downfall of the Zakarum church had in some ways begun the moment the Horadrim first entrusted its priests with Mephisto's Soulstone prison, even though the demon's influence took many years to manifest.

"I'm still not exactly clear on what it is you're looking for." Maziel put a bite of fish into his mouth.

Until now, Tyrael had resisted disclosing anything specific to the librarian, but his patience with the confines of the library had reached its limit. "I suppose I am a bit surprised that I haven't encountered any mention of the Horadrim. They were active during the period I have been studying."

"Hmm." Maziel put his fork down. "The Horadrim are a slippery topic to research, aren't they? Much of what we have is rumor and hearsay. Perhaps that is because they kept their own repositories. If you believe the legends."

Tyrael moved the conversation away from the idea of repositories. "According to those same legends, the Horadrim traveled widely. I thought perhaps there would be records of their visits to Skovos in the court chronicles. But perhaps they did not always make their presence known."

Maziel nodded, stroking his chin. "It may be time to move up one floor, to the unofficial records."

"Do you think I would find something up there?"

"Oh, certainly." He resumed eating, munching on a charred carrot. "The Horadrim are not a common topic of interest to the Askari, but a few historians have written about them."

After they had finished their meal, they returned to the library and climbed to the third floor, where Maziel pointed out the volumes that he knew mentioned the Horadrim. Tyrael began to read them, and they did indeed describe the activities of the order, though not with great accuracy, according to Tyrael's memories—although, in fairness, he had not been with the Horadrim at all times and in all places, and the gaps in his memory caused him further doubt.

It now felt odd to contemplate that era of his existence, back when he was still an archangel. He had founded the Horadrim nearly three hundred years ago, and to the mortal he had since become, such a span exceeded several lifetimes and generations. But he still retained a glimmer of his former eternal sense of time, back when he counted years as hours, and centuries as mere seasons. There were moments when it seemed he had just recruited Tal Rasha and Jered Cain, and there were other moments when he had trouble recalling their faces and the timbre of their voices.

He spent the next several days combing through the books on the library's third floor until he eventually stumbled upon a history that mentioned a group of visiting mages. It did not name them as Horadrim, but the way they were described put Tyrael in mind of the order. These travelers had apparently assisted an Askari scholar named Ambrose with the excavation of a Firstborn tomb, and the text referenced a field journal as its source.

Tyrael remembered Maziel saying the fourth level of the library contained journals and other such materials, so he went looking there for the text in question, but he was unable to locate it. He considered asking for the librarian's help but decided against it, having already revealed more than he would have preferred by mentioning the Horadrim at all. Instead, Tyrael spent several more days conducting his own search.

Eventually, he located the field journal of Ambrose. It had been shelved in the wrong place at some point in the past, and its binding was rather plain and inconspicuous, allowing the error to go unnoticed. He scanned through its pages until he came to an entry mentioning the Horadrim by name. It seemed that members of the order had been assisting with the study of a Firstborn location the writer referred to as the Crypts. The field journal mentioned beasts called titans and described a theory that the Firstborn had created these monsters for blood sport in their arenas. The journal also recorded the discovery of a magical scepter, which was believed to have once offered a method of control over the titans.

After that, the Horadrim vanished from the pages of the journal, but their mention in association with the Crypts gave Tyrael the desire to seek out the ruin. He remembered that the archive's fifth floor contained more formal, scholarly studies of Firstborn history, so he went up the staircase.

On the next floor, he encountered Maziel replacing books on a shelf, having dusted and polished the wood behind them.

"Is there something with which I can assist you?" the librarian asked.

"Perhaps," said Tyrael, thinking an interest in Firstborn history might serve to disguise his true purpose. "Have you ever read about titans?"

The librarian's mouth opened in a miniscule gasp that he immediately hid by looking away. "Hmm. Titans, you say?"

"Yes. I came across a reference to Firstborn Crypts that once housed titans, and now I am curious to read more."

"I see." Maziel worked hard to appear disinterested, but it was a poor charade. "Where did you come across this reference?"

Tyrael did not understand why the subject had so agitated the librarian, but he decided that circumspection would be wise. "I don't remember, exactly. I've been reading so many books, and it was only a passing comment. If you are busy, I'm happy to explore on my own—"

"No, no. I'm happy to help. Let's go up together." Maziel left what he had been doing, and they went up the stairs to the next floor. "Now, let me think," he said. "Titans."

"I recall the name of a scholar. Ambrose?"

"Ambrose, you say? I do know of an Ambrose from a few centuries ago." He lumbered over to a section of shelves and ran a finger along the spines of the books; Tyrael noticed his hand trembling. "I don't see any of his work at the moment, however."

Tyrael stepped toward the librarian. "Maziel, is everything all right?"

"Yes, of course, why do you ask?"

"The mention of titans seems to have . . . upset you."

"You think so?" He laughed; sweat had formed on his forehead. "I can't imagine why—"

"Maziel. You can speak freely. I would do nothing to betray your trust."

The librarian paled, and he bit his lip for a moment. "I don't know what I would do if I lost my position here," he whispered, almost breathless. "I am not suited for any other work."

"Has someone threatened your position?"

"Captain Myrina." He let out a long sigh, as if releasing a pressure he had held inside himself for a great while. "Some years ago, she came to me and asked about titans. I had never heard of them before, but I conducted a search of the library for her, and after that, she confiscated all the volumes that mentioned them. I haven't thought about it much until today."

"Not all of the volumes," Tyrael said.

"If she knew that, I think she might have me arrested."

"I will say nothing. You have my word." Tyrael stepped away from the librarian and paced with his hands steepled in front of his chest, head down, fingertips pressed against his chin. He had no idea why the subject of titans would be of such interest to Myrina, but he felt alarmed by her secrecy, especially given the journal's mention of the Horadrim. The volumes she had confiscated from the library may have revealed much more. Finding the Crypts had become an even greater imperative, for reasons he hoped would become clear along the way.

"Maziel, days ago you mentioned a passage by which you could leave the cloister."

The librarian nodded. "That's true. Why?"

"I need you to show me this passage."

"But—"

"If you are asked later, you may say I coerced you, or whatever you feel you need to say. I don't wish any harm to come to you, but I must leave the palace undetected. Can you help me?"

Tyrael knew he was taking a risk—the librarian had already demonstrated a limited resolve in the face of confrontation—but he had few options.

Finally, Maziel nodded, and then he led Tyrael down the tower stairs to the first level. He moved aside a wooden screen standing in the gap between two bookshelves, revealing a trapdoor in the floor.

"This leads to the tower's cellar," the librarian said.

"And from there?"

"I will show you."

He took down a lantern hanging from a hook in the wall nearby and lit it. Then he lifted the trapdoor, and Tyrael followed him down a narrow flight of steps into a storage room so packed with rows of bookshelves, they had to turn sideways to move between them. Against one of the walls, a locked grate blocked access to what appeared to be an old drainage tunnel. Maziel produced a key and opened the squealing grate. Then he handed the lantern to Tyrael.

"Take this," he said. "Follow the tunnel. Turn right twice, left once, then right again. You will come to an exit into the city. Have a care before you leave the tunnel. Be sure no one is there to see you."

"Thank you," Tyrael said.

"I won't say anything unless I am asked." He bowed his head a little, as if in shame. "But if I *am* asked, I must reveal what I know."

Tyrael clasped his shoulder in parting. "I meant what I said. I would not want you to suffer on my account. You do what you must."

With that, he bade farewell to the librarian and entered the tunnels. The low ceilings forced him to walk in a crouch, almost sideways, like a crab, bent low at the waist. He followed the turns Maziel had given him. Though the passageways were dry, he was surrounded by the sound of trickling water. A short while later, he came to the promised exit, where another grate blocked his path, with a catch that allowed him to open it from inside the tunnel. He waited until he saw no pedestrians passing, then he went through, closing and latching the grate behind him.

He stood next to a dry fountain in a small square, the palace walls above and behind him. He extinguished the lantern and brought it with him, making his way downward toward the Great Harbor while keeping to the alleys and back ways as much as he could. He even wrapped himself in a filthy cloak that he found discarded in a gutter. He would hopefully have some time yet before anyone noticed his absence in the library cloister, but he took no chances and ducked out of sight whenever he glimpsed the Askarra Guards.

The journal had not been highly specific in describing the location of the titan Crypts, but he knew the surface entrance to the underground complex lay somewhere near the foundation of Temis's eastern seawall. It was evening by the time he reached that towering landmark and began his search, and night had fallen by the time he found what he hoped to be the correct ingress. He had a difficult time imagining this entrance could lead to anything else.

Its exterior resembled a natural sea cave, sculpted and hollowed by the forces of wave and wind, but a short distance inward, the walls took on a hewn appearance, carved with intention and design. Ornamental features gilding the worked surfaces resembled the Firstborn architecture that Tyrael had observed throughout the island.

He relit the lantern Maziel had given him and pressed on, following the cave ever deeper. The sounds of the sea behind him faded, and he became surrounded by an ill-defined chthonic susurration, as if he were suspended in the slow, almost imperceptible inhalation and exhalation of the earth. He began to encounter piles of rubble and slag, evidence of the excavation that had taken place to open the cave centuries before, and after picking his way over and around them, he came to a door of stone set into the rock wall. The symbols carved into its face represented an admixture of angelic sigils and demonic scrawl. With only a little difficulty, Tyrael was able to decipher the message and speak the proper incantation to open the door, though he wondered how the Askari historians had managed it.

On the other side, he entered a subterranean complex that seemed subtly familiar, reminding him of somewhere he couldn't quite place. In its ancient sculptural and decorative elements, he saw the influences of humanity's parentage, demon and angel, the Heavens and Hells. It was clear now that Maziel had not exaggerated, and the interior of Temis was indeed a warren of grand corridors, soaring staircases, mammoth pillars, and vaulted galleries. The willing light of his little lantern lacked the strength to reach the distant ceilings and walls of the chambers through which he passed. It would be easy to get lost in such a place, so Tyrael used El'druin to carve markings into the black stone as he traversed the cave, leaving a trail with his blade by which he could find his way back out.

The Askari historians had left a wake of their own in the form of abandoned equipment, campsites, and other signs of their exploration, all moldering and covered in dust. Tyrael followed these clues downward, led by instinct and the few details contained in the journal, making his way toward the Crypts and whatever they contained. It seemed he walked for hours, surrounded by the echoes of his own passage and the ambient presence of the living rock, until at last he reached a space like a cathedral built for giants, and he smelled the sea.

Down each side of the central nave stood doors the height of the tallest trees he had ever beheld in Sanctuary, each of which opened onto a vast, lifeless chamber. Tyrael entered one, trying to imagine a beast large enough to require such a stable. There were eight of them, all opened, all empty, but the last of them struck him differently. The smell still lingering within was that of something living, an ancient musk like ambergris. Also, behind the ponderous doors were fresh scrapes along the floor, as if they had only recently been opened—he could not say when, but certainly within the last months or years. The intuition he formed was that a titan had slumbered for eons within that cell, outliving its creators, and had now escaped or been intentionally set free.

At the end of the nave, a black lake the size of a harbor lapped the edges of the carved stone. The lantern could reveal nothing of its depths, but phosphorescent creatures drifted far below the surface, flickering as distantly as stars. Tyrael assumed the inlet would eventually grant access to the open sea by way of a submerged channel.

He had found no sign of the Horadrim in the caves, but his disappointment over that was of little importance compared to his fear over what else he had discovered. It could not be coincidence that Myrina had taken possession of all the books on titans from the archive at a time when it seemed just such a creature had been freed, although her motives for doing so remained unknown to him.

Tyrael left the Crypts to return to the surface, following the marks he had carved with his sword. By the time he reached the boundary of the sea cave, he could tell by the glow at the end of the tunnel that he had passed the night underground, and he now emerged into the slantwise golden light of dawn.

After exiting the cave, he extinguished his lantern and sat among the shadows beneath the high seawall, contemplating what he had learned and what he must do about it. He had no direct evidence of a living titan, only a very strong suspicion, and he certainly had no evidence that Myrina had been involved in the release of the beast. What report could he make to Queen Etara, or to the Oracle Queen, assuming they knew nothing about the Crypts to begin with? He recalled the leviathan he had witnessed in the crossing from Kingsport and wondered whether he had already seen the titan without knowing it, as well as what should or could be done about such a beast.

As he considered all of this, he watched the Great Harbor coming to life with the morning tide, the passage of ships and the bustle on the docks. The sun had risen above the horizon by the time he glimpsed the familiar silhouette of the *Arabel* sailing into the port. Tyrael considered the timing of its arrival to be a rare event of good fortune but felt the need to intercept it before Lorath and anyone else aboard the sloop went up to the palace.

He rose to his feet, and he watched as a cutter met the *Arabel* and towed it toward one of the piers. Tyrael moved toward its anchorage as quickly as he could while attempting to remain inconspicuous. He came close enough to witness Lorath disembark, only to then observe as a company of Askarra Guards bound him and took him into custody.

Confused and dismayed, Tyrael feared for a moment that he was to blame and the palace had already been alerted to his activities, but if that were the case, he thought it unlikely they would have acted this quickly.

Adreona stood on the dock with some of her Amazons, watching as the Askarra Guards took Lorath away, and she did not appear at all pleased. It was possible she was angry with Lorath, but Tyrael believed it more likely that her ire was directed at the warriors who had taken him.

He needed to know what had happened, so he decided to take a risk and make himself known to the captain. He waited until she and her warriors had left the *Arabel* and its pier and approached her in the midst of the throng on the docks, the hood of his cloak raised.

"Adreona," he said.

She looked up at him, at first appearing surprised to hear her name spoken in the crowd, but then she recognized him. "Faysal?"

"We need to talk."

CHAPTER TWENTY-TWO

Donan gave Lorath a brief account of his explorations on Philios and Celestia, and he described what he had succeeded in deciphering of the journal before it was confiscated by the Askarra Guard. Despite present circumstances, he felt a bit of pride in reporting his success.

Lorath listened, leaning against the door of his cage, gripping the bars. "I guess your insatiable curiosity paid off," he said.

"Aided by the charm Sho-Ren placed on the book."

"So, the Horadrim tried to flee Skovos."

"And they almost made it," Donan added. "I think we narrowly avoided the same titan that sank their ship."

Lorath let go of the bars and paced within the narrow confines of his cell. "It's possible that same beast tore down the watchfire that has protected Skovos from the Drowned."

Thinking about their crossing from Kingsport reminded Donan of the *Arabel.* "Where is Keldon?" he asked. "Was he not arrested with you?"

Lorath stopped pacing. "Keldon is gone. He died fighting the Drowned."

"What?" Donan's chest went cold. "Keldon is dead?"

"I am very sorry to say he is."

Donan slumped against the wall of his cell. He had liked the old sailor. He was the reason they had found Keldon and brought him along, and Donan could not help feeling responsible for his death.

"Hey," Lorath said. "None of that. Before he died, Keldon gave me a message for you."

"What message?" Donan asked, barely above a whisper.

"He said to tell you he was glad you sat down at his table."

Donan rolled his eyes. "You don't need to lie for my sake—"

"I swear it's true," Lorath said. "And he meant it. He was grateful to you for restoring his ship to him. There's more, but . . . I'll save it for a better time and place."

Donan nodded, accepting the message with reluctant gratitude. He saw Alenia's hand reaching as far through the bars of her cell as she could, and he reached out his own hand to take hers. She had never met Keldon, but he appreciated her compassion. He would miss the old sailor, but Lorath was right: any remorse or grief he might feel needed to be set aside.

"What now?" he asked.

"We wait," Lorath said. "We're still alive, which means someone wants something from us."

"We've been here for days." Alenia gave Donan's hand a final squeeze before letting it go. "The only people we've seen are the guards who bring us our meals."

"But now I'm here," Lorath said.

Donan wasn't sure why that should make a difference, but apparently it did, because a few hours later, the door to their cell block opened, and Captain Myrina marched in, wielding a spear. He was not surprised to see her, given that he had been arrested by her Askarra Guards, but he was somewhat discomfited when she dismissed her escort and closed the door behind them so that she was alone with her prisoners.

"I don't suppose you know where Faysal is," she said.

Donan had no idea. If Lorath knew, he said nothing. At least her question suggested that she had not yet uncovered his true nature and that Tyrael had somehow eluded her.

"Fine." Myrina rubbed her hands together. "Here is what we will do. I will tell you what I know so we don't waste any precious time on denials." She did not wait for their agreement before continuing. "I know you are Horadrim. I have known that from the moment I had your ship searched and found your hidden emblems. I encouraged the queen to permit your presence in Skovos only because I wanted to have you followed. You see, I guessed that you came here searching for an Askari relic hoard, just like that Xian mage before you."

"I guess you don't know as much as you think you do," said Lorath. "We have no interest in Askari relics—"

Myrina whipped her spear around and lunged, thrusting its blade between the bars of Lorath's cell so fast, she seemed to blur. In the next moment, she had returned her weapon to its previous stance at her side, and Lorath had a trickle of blood across his cheek where she had sliced him. He had not even had time to flinch.

"That was a warning," she said. "I will tolerate no lies. If you attempt any further deception, my spear will find your throat."

"What makes you think the Horadrim are interested in Askari relics?" Donan asked.

She swung the head of the spear around and pointed it at him. "Because a group of Horadrim stole our relics and hid them in their vault long ago. Now you come here thinking our heritage belongs to you, but the passage of time does not erase their theft. I want only what belongs to us." She stepped closer to Donan. "Tell me, where is the vault?"

"Do you mean the workshop where you had me arrested?"

"No. That cellar is empty. I want the real vault. I want the relics."

She brought her spear up to her shoulder and adjusted her stance, poised to run him through. Donan looked into her eyes and saw no hesitancy, only confident, murderous determination, and his heart-beat quickened. He held up his hands and kept his voice calm.

"I am afraid the ship carrying the Horadrim went down off Kingsport. A titan pursued and sank them."

Myrina showed no surprise at the mention of the titan, nor at the revelation that the Horadrim's ship had been wrecked. "A tragedy for your order," she said.

Donan went on, "No, what I mean is, they carried powerful relics on that ship, which are now at the bottom of the sea."

Myrina's eyes narrowed, and her voice went cold. "I do not believe you."

"Some of the artifacts do wash up on occasion," Lorath said. "But the Harbormaster of Kingsport claims them. Perhaps you ought to speak with her and come to another arrangement."

Myrina spun to glare at him for a moment. Then she turned her gaze on Alenia and strode toward her cell. "What about you? A shame to see an Askari woman fall in with men such as these. But it's not too late for you. Do you have anything useful to tell me?"

"You have made a mistake," said Alenia.

"I have? Do tell me, what mistake have I made?"

"You have arrested the older sister of the Oracle Queen."

Myrina froze, and for the first time since entering the cell block, she appeared uncertain and troubled. But the moment passed quickly, after which she recovered her composure. "Listen to me, Horadrim. If you wish to leave Skovos alive, you will give me what I want. You have until tomorrow. If you have not revealed the true location of your vault by then, we have methods to extract the truth from you. I do not want it to come to that, but these are desperate times."

With that, she marched from the cell block and left them alone.

Lorath leaned his shoulder against the bars, arms folded, and looked at Alenia. "I think you rattled her."

"Perhaps," she said. "But only temporarily. Whatever she accuses you of doing, she can easily accuse me of conspiring with you and brand me a traitor. My sister wouldn't be able to stop her, even if she wanted to. The seers wield a different kind of power than the Amazons."

"All the same," Lorath said, "it was a pleasure to watch her squirm, if only for a moment."

Alenia regarded him slightly askance. "You don't seem worried about her threat of torture."

Lorath shrugged. "I doubt it will come to that." Then he pushed off from the bars and began to pace his cell again. "I'm much more troubled by what we're missing here. The titan, Myrina, and the vault . . . these are all related. But how?"

"Demonic influence?" Donan asked.

Lorath shook his head. "We would have sensed it."

They persisted in fruitless speculation for a while, but that conversation eventually dwindled. Hours passed, though without a window to the world outside the prison, their meals offered the only means of marking the passage of time. Eventually, Donan's fatigue and the silence of the prison told him it had grown late. His mind and his thoughts drifted, but he found no true sleep.

Sometime in the middle of the night, distant shouts and the clash of weapons roused him to alertness. He went to the door of his cell, where he saw the commotion had stirred Lorath as well. They looked at each other across the corridor, and he saw Lorath was smiling. Moments later, the door to their cell block burst open, and Tyrael strode in wielding El'druin, ready for a fight. Several warriors accompanied him, obviously Amazons, though they had their faces hidden beneath hoods and cowls. Upon realizing there were no more foes in the cell block, one of the warriors produced a ring of keys, which she used to unlock Lorath's cell.

"Are you all right?" she asked, and Donan recognized Adreona's voice.

"We are unharmed," Lorath answered.

Adreona then used the key to free Donan, but she paused at Alenia's cell.

"She's with us," Lorath said, at which Adreona opened her door.

"We have much to discuss," said Tyrael. "But not here. Let's move."

He then led them back the way they had come through the dungeon, and along their route they passed numerous Askarra Guards lying unconscious and bound. None of them looked too gravely injured, but it appeared that Adreona's Amazons had nevertheless dealt roughly with their silken rivals.

At last, they came to the main gates and exited the prison. Night lay on Temis, casting a blue haze over the white stone buildings, blooms of yellow candlelight still glowing in some of the windows.

"Follow me," Adreona whispered.

She led them for some distance, skulking through winding lanes and silent courtyards, down narrow stairs and alleys. Crickets chirped, and bats darted silently after moths overhead. Eventually, Adreona halted them in front of one of the many abandoned villas. They crept along its walls to a boarded-up window at the rear of the building, and after wrenching the slats of wood free as quietly as they could, they climbed through it one at a time. Still not content with the secrecy and safety of their position, Adreona held a finger to her lips. She left her warriors behind to keep watch and ushered the rest of them deeper into the house until they reached a small, open courtyard at its heart.

Beneath the stars, an empty fountain stood dry amidst withered plants and dead trees. A layer of dirt and grit covered the mosaic floor, thick enough to hide the pattern in the tile. The neglect and the painful emptiness of it struck Donan, who could easily imagine the Askari family who had once enjoyed spending time together in this private sanctuary.

Only here did Adreona remove her cowl and reveal her face. "I believe we will be safe here," she whispered. "But only for a short time. When Myrina discovers your escape, she will scour the city to find you."

"She threatened to torture us," Alenia said.

Lorath nudged her. "I told you it wouldn't come to that."

Tyrael sat on the edge of the fountain. "I recognize that our time is limited, but as I said inside the prison, we have much to discuss."

He then explained what he had discovered, first in the palace archive, then deep below the city. His description of the ruin filled Donan with awe, and he almost wished he had been there to explore the Firstborn city himself. Lorath and Adreona then recounted their experiences on Athulua, including the Drowned incursion, the fallen watchfire tower, and the sound of the leviathan, which all now agreed must be the same titan that sank Sho-Ren's vessel.

After Donan shared what he had discovered in the vault and in the pages of the journal, Tyrael fell silent for several moments.

"It grieves me to learn what happened to Keldon," he finally said, "and to the other Horadrim, for I am the one who sent them here." Then he stood. "We know this much: A titan has been released. We know that Sho-Ren was aware of this, and she sought a scepter with the power to control the titan. We know that she and the surviving Horadrim fled Skovos without this scepter, and it seems likely the titan sank their ship. It appears the titan also destroyed the watchfire, allowing the Drowned to assault Athulua."

"And let's not forget that Myrina knew about all of this," Adreona added. Even in the dim light of the courtyard, Donan could see her face redden with anger. "She has known it for some time, and she has kept it all her secret."

"But why?" Alenia asked. "Does she *want* to destroy Skovos?"

Adreona seemed to give that possibility some thought. "I don't believe so. I have known Myrina for a very long time. She is ambitious, and she can be cruel, but I don't believe she is a traitor."

"What about Etara?" Lorath asked. "Do you think she's aware?"

"No," Adreona said. "I cannot allow myself to believe that any of this was done on the orders of the queen. This was Myrina, whatever her true purpose might be, and that means the queen must be told. I doubt she will listen to me over her own daughter, but I must try."

"*We* must try," said Lorath.

Adreona turned toward him and took his hands in hers, a gesture of affection that was more surprising to Donan than it perhaps should have been.

"Lorath, listen to me," she said. "I have learned there is corruption in the palace of my people. Corruption among the Amazons. I *will* find it and root it out. But you must go."

"Go?" Tyrael said.

"Yes." She let go of Lorath's hands. "Skovos is no longer safe for you. Tavie and I will help you free the *Arabel,* and then you must flee."

"I think you're forgetting something," Lorath said.

"What?"

"I don't know when to quit. And I'm not starting now."

The mention of the *Arabel* had caused a pang in Donan's chest, a reminder of what they had already lost. "You're forgetting something else," he said. "Someone else. Keldon died for Skovos. If we leave now, his sacrifice will have been for nothing, because the Drowned threat is still out there—emboldened by the extinguished watchfire—and if we don't stop it, all of Skovos could be lost."

His mention of Keldon turned the mood in the courtyard solemn, and Adreona said nothing to argue with him.

"I am no seer," Tyrael said, "but if Skovos falls to the Drowned, I believe that all of Sanctuary will suffer greatly. We Horadrim have a duty to stay and defend these islands."

Adreona looked back and forth among them, overruled and without any recourse but to surrender with a shake of her head. "I think you're all fools."

"I'm inclined to agree," said Alenia. "But they are brave fools."

"Fools or not," Adreona added, with a glance at Lorath, "I am grateful to you. Though I'm still not sure how we'll convince the queen. We need evidence if we're going to openly accuse Myrina of treachery."

Tyrael asked, "How certain are you the queen knows nothing of this?"

"Certain?" Adreona puffed out her cheeks and sighed. "I'm not *certain* of anything anymore. But I have to believe she is ignorant of it. Perhaps willfully so, but not directly involved. Why?"

"Is there anyone left in the palace you trust?" Tyrael asked.

She nodded. "Myrina may own the silks, but I still have a friend or two."

"If they can get a message to the queen," Tyrael said, "I believe Etara would agree to meet with me."

"Why would she meet with you?" Lorath asked.

"Because I will agree to answer her questions," he said. "And if I do, it is my hope she will trust me enough to believe what we tell her about Myrina."

"You're taking a risk," Donan said. "You don't know what Myrina may have already told her about you. And the queen could still be part of this whole thing."

"That is true," Tyrael said. "But I trust Adreona."

"I appreciate that," she said. "I only hope your trust is not misplaced in either direction."

After a brief search of the villa, Tyrael found a scrap of parchment and a bit of charcoal in one of its fireplaces, which he used to write a letter to the queen. He expressed regret at not having been more forthcoming with her considering the hospitality she had shown him, and he requested an audience with her the following day at midday, in the garden where she had returned El'druin. He had no seal nor wax, but he folded the parchment, and Adreona took the letter with her when she and her Amazons left.

After that, the Horadrim and Alenia settled in to wait, doing what they could to make themselves comfortable for the night. The villa had long ago been looted of most furniture and valuables, but they managed to scrounge up a few rugs and tapestries to use as bedding. Donan made Alenia a spot of her own, set away from the men for her privacy. She thanked him as she laid down on the woven rug he had brought her, and once again he was reminded of his mother.

They spent the rest of that night and the next morning resting, which Donan found he needed after his sleepless nights in the prison. When Adreona returned, she brought them food, and as they ate, she reported that the message had been delivered and the queen had agreed to meet with Tyrael.

"So now we just have to get you inside the palace before midday," she said.

"That will not be an issue." Tyrael smiled. "We will simply enter the palace the same way I left."

CHAPTER TWENTY-THREE

Tyrael guided them up along the tunnels below the city, emerging into the palace grounds through the cellar of a library that Donan wished he had more time to explore. Their party startled the librarian at his work as they came up through a trapdoor in the floor, but Tyrael seemed to be on friendly, even conspiratorial terms with the man. He said little as they made their way from the library and across a small cloister where the warm midday sun looked directly down on them.

Tyrael paused at a doorway on the other side of the enclosure. "We may encounter opposition in the courtyard beyond."

Adreona offered to go first, and a moment later, she motioned for them to hurry through. They skirted the edge of the broad courtyard until they reached an archway, and after passing beneath it, they entered a garden.

Donan had no time to admire the lushness of the greenery; he followed Tyrael as he led the way along a gravel path through trees and hedges until they arrived at a fountain of leaping dolphins.

Queen Etara sat at a small table near the splashing water, and she stood at the sight of Tyrael's retinue, seeming startled.

"Faysal," she said. "I did not expect— Captain Adreona, why are you here? Shouldn't you and Lorath be on Athulua?"

That settled the question of the queen's involvement in their arrest, at least to Donan's satisfaction. It also seemed to put the others at ease. The Askarra Guard who stood nearby guarding the queen did not look at all pleased to see the Horadrim in the garden. They closed in from their positions, weapons and shields raised.

Tyrael stepped forward, eyeing the enemy. "May we speak in private, your majesty?"

"Of course," the queen said. She turned toward the advancing warriors. "Leave us."

The nearest of the silks balked. "But my queen, you mustn't—"

"Captain Adreona may remain," Tyrael offered. "Surely Queen Etara will be safe in her presence."

It seemed the Askarra Guard could think of no argument to counter that, nor justification for disobeying their queen, so they removed themselves. Their backward glances suggested that they would rush straight to Myrina to warn her of what was happening, which meant the Horadrim now had little time to accomplish their purpose.

"Now we are alone." The queen gestured Tyrael toward the chair opposite hers at the table, and they both sat.

Donan and the rest of those present took up positions a few paces away, listening to the conversation but ready for the arrival of Myrina and her Askarra Guard.

"Your message said you wanted to share some truths with me," Etara said.

"And so I do," Tyrael said. "I fear we are short on time, so I hope you will forgive the lack of preamble as I come right to the point: we are Horadrim, Lorath, Donan, and myself."

The queen merely nodded. "I suspected you might be something of the sort."

"You did?"

"I am no fool, Faysal. I have seldom encountered scholars who dress and conduct themselves as you do. Why did you not declare yourselves from the beginning?"

"These are perilous times, as you well know," Tyrael said. "We feared we would not be welcome."

"Some may have objected to your presence," the queen acknowledged.

"That is not all, your majesty." Tyrael lifted his head a little as he spoke, looking directly into Etara's eyes. "My name is not Faysal. It is Tyrael."

The queen's eyes widened in recognition of the name, and her mouth opened slightly with a subtle gasp. "Tyrael? But— You can't be . . . ?"

"Yes," he said. "I am he. I wear this armor and carry this sword because I was once an archangel. Some time ago, I renounced my nature and sacrificed much of my power to become a mortal man."

Next to Donan, Alenia inhaled sharply. Adreona turned to Lorath, who gave her a nod of confirmation. None of them interrupted Tyrael's audience with Etara by speaking.

The queen closed her mouth and straightened her back. "Why would an archangel do such a thing, if I may ask?"

"I have long made it my life's purpose to defend humanity against the tyranny of the Burning Hells. There were times when this put me at odds with others in the High Heavens, those who do not always share my regard for humanity. I had to make a choice, and I chose to align myself with you."

The queen said nothing for a moment, perhaps too stunned to speak. She took a deep breath and recovered. "Why are you here?"

"We came to learn what happened to an expedition of Horadrim that I sent to Skovos some years past, before the Reaping."

"I'm afraid I don't know anything about that." The queen touched her lips, frowning, and once again, it seemed to Donan that she spoke the truth. "Have you been able to find them?"

"We have, your majesty. Sadly, they all perished."

"I'm very sorry to hear it, but . . . why do you tell me all of this?"

Tyrael leaned toward her. "Because I want you to know that I am being completely honest in what else I am about to say."

The queen almost laughed. "You mean there's more?"

"There is," Tyrael said. "And I am afraid this news will be less welcome to you." He then explained all they had witnessed and learned, with help from Adreona, Lorath, and Donan, including the smuggling activity, the loosing of the titan, and the destruction of the watchfire. The queen listened throughout, growing more agitated with each revelation, more restless in her chair, and at the conclusion of it all, she stood, looking much smaller and more frail than she had when Donan first saw her upon her driftwood throne.

"This is unwelcome news, indeed," she said, pacing away from Tyrael. "If what you say is true, then why have I not heard of it before now? Have you informed Myrina?"

It was Adreona who stepped forward to answer her. "My queen, it gives me no pleasure to say this, but I swear to you on my life as an Amazon that Myrina knows all that we have just told you."

The queen shot her a glare. "That is not possible."

"It is true, your majesty," Tyrael said. "Not only is Myrina aware of these events, but we believe she has been instrumental in bringing them about."

"Now you go too far," she said. "I don't care who you are. You expect me to believe that my own daughter has betrayed our people? That she has betrayed *me*?"

"I wish we were wrong," Adreona said. "But everything we have told you is true. Each of the warriors with me will swear to the destruction of the watchfire and the existence of the titan. Many more will testify to the Drowned incursion that we defeated only with Lorath's aid."

"I do not doubt the truth of *those* things," the queen said. "It is your accusation against Myrina that I cannot abide—"

"My queen?" Alenia said, surprising Donan as she stepped forward from her place at his side. "May I speak?"

Etara seemed to regard her with some annoyance. "Who are you?"

"I am Alenia, elder sister to Queen Amira."

"Amira?" Etara's demeanor changed from anger to guarded curiosity. "You are her sister, you say?"

"I am."

"And how are you involved in this affair? Did my sister queen send you?"

"In a manner of speaking, she did. She foretold that I would help Donan, which I have done. I stand before you now because I accompanied him."

"I see." Alenia's connection to the Oracle Queen and the mention of prophecy seemed to have broken through some of the queen's opposition. "And what do you wish to say, Alenia?"

"Only that everyone standing before you in this garden is here to protect and preserve Skovos. These Horadrim have demonstrated that they are willing to die for these isles, but that did not stop Captain Myrina from imprisoning them—"

"Imprisoning them?" The queen looked back and forth between Donan and Lorath. "Is this true?"

Adreona answered, "I'm afraid it is, my queen. And it was done, supposedly, on your authority."

"But I gave no such order—"

In that moment, a large force of Askarra Guards streamed into the garden from multiple directions. Dozens of warriors armed with bows and spears surrounded the Horadrim, outnumbering Adreona's Amazons three to one. Captain Myrina led them, rushing to her mother's side as if preparing to defend her from an attack.

"My queen!" she said. "You are not safe with these traitors!"

"*Traitors?*" the queen said. Donan could see by the shock and sadness in Etara's eyes that with a one-word accusation, Myrina had just broken some of her mother's faith in her. "That is a serious charge, Captain, and I have seen no evidence of it. Tell me, how has Adreona betrayed our people? I am informed that only days ago, she destroyed a Drowned incursion with the help of this man."

Myrina's eyes narrowed, darting as if surveying a shifting terrain, but she stood her ground. "These mainlanders have lied to you, my queen. They are not who they pretend to be. They are *Horadrim.*"

"Yes, I am aware," the queen said. "They have just told me as much themselves. But I wonder, Captain, if you already knew that, why had you not informed me?"

Myrina paled. "Your majesty, I did not want to trouble you with—"

"That is not for you to decide," the queen replied. "I have many questions for you, Captain Myrina. It seems you have been taking a great number of . . . liberties and done much in my name. I fear you have forgotten your place."

"My place?" Myrina's voice cracked with anger. She relaxed her stance, turning from the Horadrim toward her mother. "My place has been at your side for all these years. Through all manner of turmoil. I have defended you when others claimed you were no longer fit to rule. I have supported your crown, even when you weren't aware of it. And now you speak to me about my place?"

Donan noticed that the Askarra Guards remained poised for a fight, their weapons aimed at the Horadrim and Adreona's warriors. He wondered if they would stand down on the order of their queen or if Myrina had so consolidated her power and influence that the silks now answered only to her.

"Who have you defended me against?" demanded the queen. "Who has claimed that I am unfit?"

Myrina shook her head, looking at her mother now with unvarnished contempt. "Why could you not have stepped down?"

"Stepped down?" The queen spoke the words as if they were incomprehensible to her.

Myrina went on as if she and her mother were alone in that garden. "When the reapers attacked, you did nothing. You hid here in your palace. I came to you, do you remember? I begged you to lead us in defending our city, our people. But you refused. Instead, you ordered us to defend *you.*"

That indictment silenced Etara.

Myrina continued. "That was when I knew you were no longer fit to rule. But I couldn't depose you. I couldn't act against my own mother."

"So instead, you acted against your own people?" Adreona asked, sounding bewildered.

Myrina snapped a glare in her direction. "I wanted the queen to see that she isn't strong enough to face the challenges confronting our islands. I hoped she would realize that her time is over." She turned back toward Etara. "I hoped you would recognize all that I have already done in defense of our people, and you would see that my time has come. But you have forced my hand, Mother."

"*You* are the traitor," Queen Etara said, breathless. "To think that I—"

A deafening roar shook the city, causing the ground and the walls of the palace to tremble. Donan knew that sound, but it took a moment for him to realize how it differed from the last time they had heard it. Instead of rising from the depths, the monster's voice echoed with terrifying clarity, free of the water. Then the sounds of screaming and the booming demolition of stone and masonry rose up from the metropolis below.

"The titan," Tyrael said. "It has come."

They all raced from the garden, silk and Amazon alike, their differences momentarily forgotten. Adreona led the way, charging from the courtyard through the palace and the great basilica and out onto the portico. Donan kept track of Alenia in the rushing throng, wanting to make sure she was safe, and together they looked down on the harbor.

The titan had climbed out of the water, as long as three of the largest warships destroyed in its wake. Donan struggled to make sense of its shape and anatomy. It moved with the lithe and lethal speed of an eel, rows of fangs lining its gaping mouth, eyes as red as liver. Thick plates of armor covered it like a crustacean, and massive claws and legs ran down the length of its monstrous form. Donan had never faced such an enemy.

"How can we fight that?" he said to no one in particular.

As the titan whipped and scrambled over the city, it crushed the buildings beneath it, tearing through the stone walls as if they were made of paper and straw.

"It's coming this way," Adreona said.

She was right. The beast seemed to be climbing upward toward the palace, even as the city had begun to defend itself. Amazons and Askarra Guards around its limbs and belly hurled spears and shot arrows, but nothing seemed able to penetrate the titan's shell. Even the heavy missiles from catapults and ballista appeared to bounce off without causing any damage or even slowing it down. Its roar and its smell overwhelmed the senses, but Donan finally collected himself.

He took Alenia by the shoulders and pushed her away from the portico. "You must hide!" he said, thinking of that night long ago in his mother's shop. "Go! Quickly! I will protect you!"

"But—"

"Go!" he shouted, and she did as he asked, scurrying away into the city. Then, without forethought, he rushed from the palace portico toward the beast, ignoring Lorath's shouts behind him, and descended the streets to get within range of the titan.

In the chaos of the attack, with frantic townsfolk rushing to escape, the labyrinth of alleyways disoriented him, but he followed the sounds of destruction, catching darting glimpses of the monster above the rooftops and down arched passages. Eventually, he found a terrace street overlooking the titan, where he decided to make a stand. He used his staff and shouted the most powerful spells he knew, assailing the beast with violet flames. His magic found its mark, striking the pocked and barnacle-encrusted armor, but no flame could take hold of it. The titan continued to climb, seemingly unaffected.

But Donan refused to give up. He pursued the creature upward, striking it again and again until he had utterly exhausted his font of will and energy. His limbs had little strength left in them, and it felt like he couldn't suck in enough air. Though reeling and forced to pull back his attack, he staggered up the mountain, dodging the debris sent tumbling downward by the titan's ascent.

A cloud of smoke and dust lay over the city by the time the thing reached the uppermost tier, where Adreona, her Amazons, and the Askarra Guard had mustered an impressive fusillade of missiles and Askari fire. Donan witnessed the barrage, which at first seemed to finally halt the titan's advance, but not for long. The enraged beast charged straight at the palace, where it scattered warriors, ripped through the main gates, and crashed into the basilica.

Donan stood in mute horror, legs wobbling, hands shaking so badly it was difficult to hold on to his staff. He could do nothing, and he believed Skovos had come to its end, but then he witnessed the titan burst from the basilica in retreat. At first, he doubted what he was seeing, but it soon became apparent that something had cowed the creature and driven it backward. Then Captain Myrina emerged from the splintered palace gates wielding her mother's spear. Inexplicably, the titan acted as if it were afraid of her.

She led a large force of Amazons and Askarra Guards, and they appeared to follow her with the same terror and befuddlement that Donan felt.

"Go back to the abyss!" Myrina shouted at the titan. Then she threw the spear at its face, where it lodged in the softer flesh of the beast's cheek. Not a deep wound, and certainly not a lethal injury, but the titan nevertheless turned back on itself, roaring, and then slid down the mountain along the path of wreckage it had just carved through the city. When it reached the harbor, it slunk into the water and vanished.

In those first moments after the attack, the city of Temis seemed to hold its breath. That was how it felt to Donan. Nothing moved. No one spoke or made a sound. The screaming had stopped. Then, one by one, the Amazons and Askarra Guards standing behind Myrina all dropped to one knee, heads bowed toward her. She turned to face them and spoke in a loud, commanding voice that carried in the silence.

"Hear me, Askari! My people! Queen Etara is dead! She was slain in her throne room by the beast! Though we mourn her passing, I am ready to sit in her place upon the throne! I swear upon my mother's memory that I will defend our islands from all threats and dangers, just as I fought that beast of the deep! Together, we will restore Skovos to greatness!"

The crowd before the basilica had only continued to grow, and when Myrina had finished her speech, the mob applauded and cheered her, including the warriors who had witnessed her supposed defeat of the titan. Donan lumbered through the throng, searching the faces until he found Alenia, who shuffled toward him covered in dust. In relief, he took her by the shoulder, supporting her, and together they located Lorath and Tyrael, standing at the edge of the gathering with Adreona and Tavie.

"I guess it was your turn to go looking for a fight," Lorath said as they approached.

Donan could only shrug, still exhausted.

"I am relieved to see you unharmed," Tyrael said, clasping his shoulder.

Lorath turned back to watch Myrina. "None of us are buying this, right?"

"Of course not," Donan replied. The attack and Myrina's victory had obviously been staged. He was reminded of a line from the prophecy given to him by the Oracle. "*One queen shall call the beast,*" he said. "Myrina has the scepter. She used the titan to kill her own mother—"

"That thing didn't kill Etara." Adreona limped forward a few steps, leaning on her spear and favoring her left ankle, which had apparently been wounded in the attack. "Myrina is responsible, and she must be stopped."

"How?" Alenia asked. "With that monster at her command . . ."

"We need to get the scepter from her," Lorath said.

"No." Adreona's lip almost curled into a snarl. "I just need to kill her."

"I have no objection," Lorath said. "But just how do you propose to do that?"

Adreona looked at Tavie in a knowing way, and something wordless passed between the two.

"But you are wounded—"

"There is no other way," Adreona said. "I am a captain of the Amazons. I have sworn to protect my people against all threats, and today the enemy is one of our own. This is my duty, in service to the virtues we uphold. It must be me, and it must be now, before she fully seizes power."

"What are you going to do?" Donan asked.

"I will challenge her," Adreona said. "By ancient custom, I will fight her for the right to rule Skovos."

CHAPTER TWENTY-FOUR

Myrina had begun to move among the crowd before the palace portico, thanking her Askarra Guards and greeting the common Askari folk who had gathered in the aftermath of the titan's attack. While Etara had isolated herself in the palace, Myrina had a way with the people—Lorath could give her that much—and she obviously understood the value of theatrics. He also knew that she wouldn't have forgotten about the Horadrim or their vault and would soon turn her attention toward them; this time, there would be no higher authority to stop her. Whatever they planned to do, they had to do it quickly.

With Adreona's injury, she was in no condition to fight, but that didn't stop her from pushing her way through the crowd, a look of such intense hatred on her face that Lorath feared she might skip the honor duel and simply execute her opponent on the spot.

"Are you certain about this?" Lorath asked as he jostled his way to her side.

"I am," she said.

"But your leg—"

"I can still kill her."

"What if you name me your champion?" he said. "Let me fight her for you." But even as he said it, he knew what an absurd suggestion it was. The Amazon sense of honor would never allow a mainlander like him to do such a thing. "What about Tavie? Can she fight in your place?"

"I guess you still don't know when to quit," she said. "It must be *me,* Lorath. This is the only way."

The throng thickened the nearer they got to Myrina. Everyone wanted to get closer to the woman who had defeated the beast. Few had directly witnessed the event, which meant the story had already begun to spread, and the people would believe it. At last, Adreona lost her patience.

"*Captain* Myrina!" she shouted, emphasizing her opponent's rank.

The ferocity in her voice parted the crowd before her, opening an avenue to the would-be queen. A hush fell over the square as Myrina turned toward Adreona, and Lorath watched her quickly consider her response, weighing the relative risks of the options before her. He knew she couldn't arrest or kill Adreona then and there, even though she probably wanted to. That would cause shock and confusion, undermining her moment of triumph, and her rival remained too trusted and popular.

Myrina's mouth broke into a forced smile. "Captain Adreona! I am pleased to see you are unharmed."

"Are you?" Adreona limped toward her, the heel of her spear clicking against the paving stones. "Captain Myrina, in the name of life, in the name of courage, and in the name of wisdom, I declare you unfit to rule, and I challenge you by ancient right to single combat for the crown!"

She had raised her voice so that all in the square could hear her. Again, Lorath watched Myrina quickly work through her possible courses of action. She held herself high, her demeanor regal as her eyes flicked across the crowd, perhaps trying to assess the mood of the people. Then she seemed to appraise Adreona, and her gaze locked on to her enemy's limp.

"I seek no quarrel with you, Captain," she said, sounding both confident and calm. "I see no reason to engage in a petty fight. I have proven myself worthy of the crown—"

"How worthy can you be if you defy our laws and traditions?" Adreona demanded.

A murmur swept through the crowd, which Myrina seemed to notice, and her expression hardened. "I have no intention of defying tradition. If you are committed to this course, I cannot ignore your challenge, and I will abide by the ancient laws of our people. I only ask that we settle the matter now to avoid prolonging this conflict. Our people need certainty and peace."

Lorath had hoped Adreona might have some time to recover before the actual duel, but Myrina had shrewdly cut off that possibly.

"I agree," Adreona said. "And I accept. Let us finish this."

The Amazons and Askarra Guards then cleared a path for both women to make their way toward the basilica. Lorath fell in behind them with Tyrael, Donan, Alenia, and Tavie, and together they moved with the tide of warriors through the shattered gates and into the palace. Adreona and Myrina marched to the center of the vast floor and stood facing each other within the borders of a circular mosaic. The other Amazons all seemed to know exactly what must happen to satisfy the traditional demands of the ritual. They enclosed the combat space in a ring, holding up their shields to form a wall.

Outside that enclosure, some of the common folk had followed the procession into the basilica and now stood among the columns gape-mouthed, staring up at the monumental reliefs and the vaulted ceiling. Others stood on the portico outside the open gates, peering in. Lorath assumed that under normal circumstances, they might not have been allowed to witness the fight about to take place, but the titan had broken open the basilica to their view.

Tavie brought Adreona a shield to use with her spear, and one of the silks brought Myrina both a shield and a spear to replace the weapon she had thrown at the titan. No one spoke. No one cheered or jeered, even among the Askarra Guard. A kind of reverence had taken hold of the assembly, transcending political allegiances, more valuable than the flimsy loyalty Myrina had bought with bribery. Every step and scrape on the floor echoed loudly as all within the basilica waited for the fight to unfold.

When both combatants stood armed, they saluted each other.

"I fight for the virtues unto my death," Adreona pronounced.

"I fight for the virtues unto my death," Myrina repeated. "May fate determine the victor."

With that, their combat began.

Myrina lunged first, pressing what she obviously believed to be her advantage against an injured adversary. She leapt high and thrust downward with her spear at Adreona's right side, but Adreona raised her shield and deflected the blow, forcing her to leap away onto her bad ankle. She winced and stumbled, and Myrina attacked again and again, spear ringing against shield, driving Adreona backward on her unsteady feet. Lorath feared she might fall, and if she did, he knew that would mean her death. He felt his own rage rising, roaring in his ears, tunneling his vision, but he could do nothing to defend her.

But gradually, Adreona seemed to find her footing, adjusting her stance to compensate for her weak side, and she soon began countering with attacks of her own. The two warriors circled each other, thrusting and ducking, pressing and falling back with lethal grace, as if engaged in a kind of deadly dance.

"Admit it," Myrina said. "You've been wanting to do this for a long time."

"We've had our differences," Adreona said, breathing hard through her clenched teeth. "But I have never wished you harm, Myrina. I thought Skovos needed you." She darted forward, but her ankle slowed her attack.

Myrina easily dodged her strike. "Skovos *does* need me. I am the only one who can—"

Adreona charged again, only this time, Myrina managed to shoulder her attack aside with such force that she knocked Adreona to the ground. Her spear broke in half beneath her as she fell, and in the next breath, Myrina pounced, aiming her own spearpoint at the middle of her enemy's chest. Adreona managed to deflect the blow high enough that the blade penetrated her shoulder instead. She let out a howl of anger and pain. At the sound of her anguish, Lorath almost leapt into the circle, but Tyrael extended an arm across his chest to hold him back.

"You cannot enter that ring," he said. "There is nothing you can do."

And that was the source of Lorath's torment. That was the fear that hid behind his rage: the feeling of utter powerlessness and helplessness as the people around him suffered and died. The night of Malthael's Reaping had broken something in him. He could do nothing to stop the attack, and the ensuing carnage had left him full of hatred and anger toward those who would hurt the innocent. Toward evil like Myrina.

He felt his body shaking and feared he would not be able to control what he did next. But he thought back to what Keldon had said, and he let himself feel what his rage was guarding. He let in his fear, and he let in his grief, and he let go of his drive to intervene.

Adreona had seized Myrina's spear with her hands, while Myrina threw aside her shield and leaned on the shaft, driving it downward. Adreona let out a primal roar, her face contorted in pain, then released the spear shaft. Its head drove deeper, and she screamed again, but with her freed hand, she felt for the broken point of her spear, grabbed it in her fist, and jabbed it upward into Myrina's side, through the gap in her armor.

Myrina flinched, released the grip on her own weapon, and leapt back, looking down at herself as if trying to understand what had just happened. She felt her side and touched the broken spear shaft protruding from her ribs. She gasped but couldn't breathe. She coughed, and blood spurted from her lips onto her chin, her eyes widening with the realization of her own death. She looked around at her Askarra Guards, searching for help that could not and would not come. She took one step, and then she collapsed.

Lorath could restrain himself no longer. He broke through the shield wall and raced to Adreona's side. She looked up at him with a grim smile, and she opened her mouth to say something, but before she could, her eyes rolled back and closed.

He leaned over her, cradling her neck. "No, no, stay with me," he said. "Adreona, stay with me."

"Lorath," Alenia said. "Would this help?"

She had brought an amulet to his side, which Lorath recognized as a healing talisman. He had no idea where she had found it, but he took it from her gratefully and placed it around Adreona's neck. It wasn't powerful enough to heal her instantly, but it might just tip the scale between life and death.

Lorath stayed by Adreona's bedside. He took his meals there, and he slept in the chair next to her, waiting for the amulet, medicines, poultices, and potions to work their effects. For the first couple of days, she was in and out of consciousness, and when she spoke, it made little sense. But then one afternoon, she opened her eyes and looked at Lorath with recognition, and he knew she had come through her ordeal.

"Hello, your majesty," he said. "Welcome back to the world of the living."

She tried to sit up, but Lorath placed his hand gently against her uninjured shoulder.

"You need rest."

"I do not need to rest," she said. "Not when there is a titan on the loose and the watchfire has fallen—"

"Tavie has returned to Athulua," he said. "She took a large cohort of Askarra Guards to reinforce your troops there. They can hold the line against the Drowned. As for the titan, we have seen no sign of it."

Adreona closed her eyes, clearly still exhausted but seemingly reassured.

"While you have been recovering," Lorath said, "your people have embraced you as their queen."

Her eyes shot open again.

Lorath chuckled. "I'm afraid you won't be returning to Fort Galina anytime soon. There is a throne waiting for you here."

"I never wanted the throne."

"Nevertheless, it is yours."

She stared up at the ceiling of the chamber, shaking her head. "What am I going to do?"

"That's easy," he said. "You are going to rule Skovos according to the virtues to which you aspire." She looked beautiful to him, lying in bed bruised and wrapped in bandages. She was the kind of woman he thought he could love, were the circumstances of their lives other than what they were. "All hail Queen Adreona," he said.

She laughed, then winced. "Quit that."

"Quit what?"

"You know what."

"Fine. I'll quit, if only to show you that I do know how."

They sat in silence for a few moments. Adreona seemed lost in thought until she suddenly asked, "The scepter?"

Lorath brought it out and laid it on the bed beside her. It was a golden wand nearly the length of her forearm, adorned with gems and precious stones and engraved with Firstborn sigils that Tyrael and Donan had spent some time studying. "It was found on Myrina's body," he said. "It belongs to you."

She took it in her hand and raised it up as if testing its weight. "Having control over a titan would not be without its benefits."

"I would trust *you* to use the scepter wisely," Lorath said. "I wouldn't trust those who come after you, or those who might try to steal it from you. What's to stop someone from challenging you to single combat, just as you challenged Myrina?"

She lowered her arm, as if the weight of the scepter had exhausted her, and she set it down on the bed next to her. "What do you think I should do with it?"

"That isn't for me to say."

"It isn't your decision to make," Adreona corrected, "but I do want to hear what you think."

Lorath looked at the wand, rubbing his beard, which by that point was in need of a thorough trimming. "I'm reminded of something Keldon said to me before he died."

"What's that?"

"He was talking about the beast that some of us keep imprisoned within us. He said the only thing to do is to let it go."

A short time later, the Horadrim escorted Adreona to the island of Lycander, where they now stood on its southern coast. The island's seemingly endless canopy of trees teemed with birds and insects and offered deep shade. The air smelled thick and heavy with the perfume of blossoms Lorath had never encountered before. A firm wind buffeted the shore, sending gray clouds scudding across the sky. Adreona strode down to where the waves lapped the sugary sand, held up the scepter, and summoned the titan.

Then they waited, and before long, a swell appeared on the flat eastern horizon. Even knowing that Adreona had control over the beast, Lorath still felt an involuntary apprehension as it churned toward them, and he fought the urge to retreat from the waterline into the safety of the trees.

When the titan finally reached them, it lumbered up out of the sea, curtains of water raining down from the plates and joints of its gnarled carapace, its heavy claws striking the ground with a deep thudding that Lorath felt in the core of his chest. Its breath reeked of dredged muck. Its crimson eyes stared down at them, large as wagon wheels, the memories and thoughts behind them inscrutable.

Adreona strode closer to it, appearing unafraid, her arm still held in a sling. At a silent command, the beast bent its head down toward her, and she took the spear still jutting from its cheek in her good hand. With a sharp wrench, she pulled the weapon free, after which the titan raised its head and roared into the sky. It was so loud that Lorath had to cover his ears, and he was unable to tell whether it was expressing pain, joy, anger, or an entirely unique emotion unknown to any creature but itself.

"Go now!" Adreona commanded. "But hear my command and obey: Never again will you leave the water. Never again will you approach these islands or the continents beyond. You are free to swim the deepest depths of the most distant seas, and they shall forever be your home!"

The titan roared again, and this time, Lorath thought he could detect a clear exuberance beneath its deafening rumbles. Then it turned and slid back under the water, sending waves crashing all the way up to the knees of those who stood watching its departure. Within moments, it was gone.

Adreona then turned to Tyrael. "I wonder if I might ask a favor of you."

"Of course, your majesty."

"Lorath tells me your blade is angelic."

"It is . . . a powerful blade," Tyrael said.

She showed him the scepter. "Can it cut through this?"

Tyrael pulled El'druin from its scabbard. "I believe it can, if that is what you wish."

"It is," she replied.

Then she held the scepter before him, and with one mighty swing, Tyrael severed the wand in half. Upon its sundering, the rod emitted a sharp light, discharging its energies as it ceased to be a relic of power and became nothing more than an artifact of historical curiosity. Adreona collected the piece that had fallen to the ground. "Thank you," she said. "Lorath, may I have a word with you?"

"Of course, your majesty," Lorath said.

They strolled away from the others along the beach. Cormorants flew overhead, diving for fish in the sparkling waves. Crabs and other crawling things ducked into the crevices of rocks at their passing.

Adreona said nothing for a long time, and Lorath waited. He thought he knew some of the thoughts that were going through her mind because they were thoughts he had considered during his vigil at her bedside. As much as he might wish for more between them, the circumstances of their lives made that impossible.

"You are Horadrim," she finally said, as if she had seen into his mind.

"And you are the Amazon Queen of the Askari," he answered.

"We have responsibilities that come before any personal desires. No matter how much we might want something."

"That is true, your majesty."

"Please," she said, "you may continue to call me Adreona."

"But I like to think of you as a queen."

"I would prefer you think of me as a friend," she said. "And I want you to know that you will always be welcome in Skovos. The palace doors will never be shut to you."

"I appreciate the invitation, your majesty." Lorath walked with his hands clasped behind his back, eyes cast downward. "Perhaps I may return one day."

EPILOGUE

The *Arabel* had been destroyed by the titan's rise through the harbor, along with many other ships. All the Horadrim found of it were a few large pieces of wreckage, still bearing the paint of midnight blue with yellow trim. The three men mourned its loss, just as they mourned Keldon's death, but they were also aware that it somehow would not have felt right to sail the *Arabel* without her captain. Tyrael did wonder how they would leave Skovos and return to the continents, but Adreona solved that problem by giving them a small ship, another single-masted sloop to speed them on their way. After bidding farewell to the new queen, they departed the Great Harbor of Temis. The three Horadrim stood at the helm, with Lorath at the tiller.

"Where to?" he asked.

"North, for a time," Tyrael said. "But then, turn west. We sail for Skartara."

Lorath and Donan looked at each other. Tyrael had kept his plan to himself until that moment. Though he trusted Adreona and believed she would be a good queen, it would take time for her to disband the Askarra Guard, end the smuggling, and root out the corruption within the Amazon ranks. The location of the vault had to remain a secret, which meant they had to disguise their course.

Lorath did as Tyrael asked, and the three of them sailed in silence for some time. Tyrael knew they were each of them lost in private thoughts about everything they had just experienced. Lorath had obviously formed an attachment to Adreona and would no doubt miss her for a time. Their relationship seemed to have helped Lorath to heal, at least a little, from the pain and fear that fueled his rage. Donan had likewise bonded in some way with Alenia, whom Tyrael secretly noted was about the age of the younger man's mother; it seemed perhaps Donan had also experienced some healing from past guilt and loss.

As for Tyrael, he had not found in Skovos what he had hoped to find. Sho-Ren and the other Horadrim in her expedition had perished, which meant that he, Lorath, and Donan truly were the last of its members. They still had much work to do in strengthening the order.

Eventually, Lorath steered them west. They sailed until the roiling smoke of Skartara reached over them, as if it were trying to pull them into its fiery domain. They observed no permanent Askari settlements on its jagged shores, which allowed them to land unobserved. From there, they made their way across a torn and lifeless landscape. The black basalt beneath their feet never seemed to cease trembling. Rivers of molten lava tumbled down fissures and channels like feverish gashes that could not heal. Other cracks in the island's surface vented noxious gases, which burned their lungs and caused the three of them to cough and gag when Mount Hefaetrus enveloped them in its volcanic breath.

As they ascended the island's treacherous slopes, they began to see signs of Firstborn construction: fallen pillars and plazas half covered by flows of lava, cooled and hardened like stone tumors. Eventually, they came to a tunnel that led them into the mountain, to the entrance of the vault, and at last, Tyrael felt waves of memory crash over him. He recalled the last time he had stood in that same place, the first Horadrim at his side. He remembered each of them vividly—Tal Rasha's leadership and optimism, Jered Cain's humble solemnity, Iben Fahd's insatiable curiosity, and Zoltun Kulle's ambitious genius—as if they were there with him now.

He held up his hands and unlocked the magical seals upon the vault entrance with ease, and then he entered, with Lorath and Donan behind him.

Tyrael found the vault within as he had left it. It seemed Sho-Ren had done little to disturb its contents. A cold pale light shimmered over its library of ancient texts, its reliquaries and relics of power.

Donan hurried straight to one of the bookshelves, where he scanned the volumes. "This is more like it," he said.

Lorath chuckled. "Don't get too comfortable. I doubt we'll be here long." He turned to Tyrael. "Right?"

Tyrael nodded. "We should not linger. The longer we stay, the more chance there is of being observed. This vault must remain hidden." He glanced around. "I am satisfied that no one else has found it."

A short while later, they left the vault, and Tyrael again raised his hands to restore the magical seals upon its doors. Only someone with knowledge of Horadric spell-keys would be able to open them. Then they descended the mountain, returned to their ship, and were soon back on the open water, sailing away from Skovos.

"It all came true," Donan said.

"What did?" Lorath asked.

"The prophecy given to me by the Oracle Queen. *One queen shall fall, and two shall rise. One queen shall throw the spear, and another queen shall retrieve it. One queen shall call the beast, and another queen shall free it. Thus, shall Skovos be saved.*"

"It is said the Oracle Queen is never wrong," Tyrael said.

"But how can that be?" Donan asked. "Then do any of us have free will? Could our mission to Skovos have ended another way?"

"I don't know," said Lorath. "But thinking about it hurts my head, and I'd rather believe that I am in control of my fate, just as I am controlling this tiller. Speaking of which, where to? If we three are the last Horadrim, I think we should turn our efforts to recruitment."

"I agree." Tyrael turned toward the northern horizon. "Let us travel to Aranoch. I have heard rumors of a very promising mage in Lut Gholein."

"What's their name?" Lorath asked.

Tyrael answered, "Elias."

ACKNOWLEDGMENTS

I have been a *Diablo* fan since the first game released in '97, so it is always a privilege and a pleasure when I am invited to tell a story set in Sanctuary. I am grateful to many people who accompanied me on this journey to Skovos. My thanks to the Blizzard team, including Chloe Fraboni, Megan Walker, Ian Landa-Beavers, Sean Copeland, Matt Burns, and Brie Messina. I would also like to express my appreciation to Tom Hoeler and Erum Khan at Penguin Random House, as well as to Nachie Marsham. I remain deeply grateful to my agent, Michael Bourret, who continues to champion and encourage me in the varied projects I pursue. As always, I am thankful to Jaime, who makes all of my books possible with her love and support.

ABOUT THE AUTHOR

Matthew J. Kirby is the critically acclaimed and award-winning author of many novels, including *The Clockwork Three, Icefall, The Lost Kingdom, A Taste for Monsters,* and *Star Splitter.* He has written for the Assassin's Creed game franchise, including the Last Descendants series and *Geirmund's Saga,* and he is the author of *Book of Lorath* and *Book of Prava,* set in the *Diablo* game universe. His work has received numerous honors, including the Edgar Award for Best Juvenile Mystery and the PEN Center USA award for Children's Literature. He and his family live in Idaho.

ABOUT THE TYPE

This book was set in Caslon, a typeface first designed in 1722 by William Caslon (1692–1766). Its widespread use by most English printers in the early eighteenth century soon supplanted the Dutch typefaces that had formerly prevailed. The roman is considered a "workhorse" typeface due to its pleasant, open appearance, while the italic is exceedingly decorative.